SCANDALS, SECRETS, AND MURDER

THE WIDOW AND THE ROGUE MYSTERIES

Maggie Sefton

ISBN: 1499267959
ISBN 13: 9781499267952
Library of Congress Control Number: 2014908407
LCCN Imprint Name: CreateSpace Independent Publishing Platform
North Charleston, South Carolina

Cover design by Scarlett Rugers Design
www.scarlettrugers.com

SCANDALS, SECRETS, AND MURDER

THE WIDOW AND THE ROGUE MYSTERIES

PROLOGUE

1890, Washington, D.C.

"C'mon, Lizzie, move that fat ass of yours," Joey Quinn growled. "I told His Highness you'd be there half an hour ago." He yanked the arm of the woman beside him and moved faster along the narrow hallway, brushing against a broken gas light that dangled along the grimy clapboard wall. A raucous clamor of drunken shouts and laughter rose up from the floor below.

Lizzie screwed up her painted face and tugged at his grip. "Fer Crissakes, what's he in such a hurry for? He's already got Polly in there with him. I ain't had time to catch m' breath yet. You know how long ol' Benjy takes. A girl's gotta rest, ya know." She reached up to brush a frizzy wisp of coppery hair out of her face with one hand while she tried to hold the faded dressing gown together with the other. The royal blue satin did an inadequate job of concealing her charms.

"'Cuz he ain't got Polly, that's why. She's coughing so bad I couldn't send her, so I gave him Francie. And she ain't never been with him before."

"Jeez, you sent that little chit in with the Senator?" Lizzie's smudged black eyebrows shot up. "You've gotta be crazy. He'll scare her to death."

"That's why I want ya to hurry up, ya stupid cow! Now, get in there before I swat ya!" He pulled her along the hall. No fixtures, broken or otherwise, threw light into this darkened stretch. A woman's high-pitched laugh shrieked from below, followed by a man's angry curse.

"Leggo my arm. I'm comin' as fast as I can, dammit!" Lizzie half-tripped on her dressing gown in her attempt to keep up with Quinn.

He gave her arm a final yank before he stopped at the far end of the hallway. Finally releasing his grip, he knocked a quick rat-a-tat-tat on the door, then fumbled in the pocket of his soiled brown wool trousers and withdrew a key.

Lizzie rearranged herself, straightening her dressing gown and smoothing her hair, then lifted her chin and fixed Quinn with a glare. "He better not get rough like he did last time or I'm not doing him again. You can find yerself another. I had bruises for a month."

Quinn paused, the key already in the lock. His black eyes narrowed to slits as he leaned his unshaven face menacingly close to Lizzie's. "You'll do as yer told unless you want to be on the street again. You remember the street, don'cha Lizzie? You give me any more of yer lip, and I'll send you back. Only this time, ya won't be as pretty." He ran a finger slowly across Lizzie's cheek, which had paled beneath the paint. "Ya know what I mean?"

Lizzie held her defiant pose a second longer, then fear darted through her eyes. She swallowed and looked away, muttering, "Okay, okay."

"Now, that's better," Quinn said, lips twisting with a sneer. He turned the key in the lock and pushed the door open. "Now, go in and get to work," he warned, gesturing inside the room.

Lizzie pulled back her shoulders, lifted her chin and sailed through the doorway without another word. Quinn started to walk away when he heard a bloodcurdling scream from inside the room. Lizzie.

"Jesus H. Christ! I'm gonna beat ya within an inch of yer life, Lizzie, I swear I am!" He charged through the doorway.

Lizzie was kneeling on the floor, her hands clasped to her face, making little whimpering sounds and staring wild-eyed at the bed.

"What the hell do you think you're doing?" Joey snarled at her.

She pointed toward the bed, her arm shaking.

Senator Horace Chester's large, pale, naked body lay absolutely still atop the slight young girl who was his evening's entertainment. His left arm hung limp over the side of the bed. The dark eyes in his grey-bearded face stared at the wall, not blinking.

"What the...!" Quinn drew closer, then abruptly stopped. Blood. Lots of it. Running down Senator Chester's back from the jagged gashes between his shoulder blades, pooling on the bed, crimson beside his white, white skin. Quinn took in his breath with a loud gasp. "Sweet Jesus!" He cringed away, then reached out and touched the Senator's shoulder. Still warm.

Quinn quickly scanned the bedroom, but there was no one hiding in the corners. Only the door to the outside stairway was ajar. "Quick, Lizzie, run to the door and see if you spy anybody! This must've just happened."

But Lizzie didn't answer. She continued to stare, making little sounds, her hands folded as if in prayer.

Quinn shoved Chester's shoulder over to reach the girl beneath. Judging from the blood drenching the bed sheets, she couldn't be alive either. On the Senator's chest was a nasty gaping wound, right over the heart. Quinn screwed up his face. "Call Sammy up here. Tell him I need him now. I've got a dead Senator and a dead whore and I'm not gonna take the..."

Just then, the young girl gave a low moan. Quinn jumped, obviously startled, and nearly let the Senator's dead weight drop on top of her again.

"Jesus, she's alive! Francie's alive!" he cried.

At that, Lizzie snapped out of her trance. She scrambled to her feet and rushed to the bed. "Oh, Holy Mother, she's still alive! Praise God. I'll go get a doctor." She dashed out the doorway.

"Dammit, Lizzie! Come back here!" Quinn shouted as he finally pushed the Senator's lifeless form off the girl. Her face and hair were smeared with blood, and there was an ugly gash on her slender neck. Blood ran from the wound. Quinn stared at the injured girl. "Jesus, Francie, who did this to ya? Who was it?"

Francie moaned a low, soft sound, her trembling hands reaching for her neck. Blood spilled over her fingertips and down her frail arms. Suddenly, her eyelids opened. Francie gazed up at Quinn and clutched at her throat, while her low moan turned to a scream.

CHAPTER ONE

That same night

Amanda Duncan leaned out her carriage window and looked down at the elderly nun standing in the darkened street. "Don't worry, Sister Bernice. It's only a few blocks to my home, and Mathias keeps a lively pace."

"I feel dreadful keeping you out so late," Sister Bernice said, her wimple-framed face illuminated by the pale glow from the corner streetlamp. "Bridget will rail at me for sure on Sunday."

"I was happy to help. And don't worry about Bridget. I'll tell her you begged me to leave earlier, but I refused."

Loud male voices sounded nearby. Hoots of raucous drunken laughter. Amanda glimpsed three men staggering around the corner of Twenty-First Street and onto Pennsylvania Avenue directly ahead of her carriage.

Mathias leaned down from the driver's seat. "We best be goin', Miz Duncan."

"Oh, dear, I was afraid this would happen," Sister Bernice said, watching the drunken men approach. "The taverns are starting to throw out the rowdier ones. Amanda, I'm so sorry to expose you to this."

Amanda smiled at the worried nun. "Sister, I assure you this is not the first time I have seen drunken citizens on the streets of Washington. In fact, there are as many stumbling from the salons as there are from the saloons. Now you'd best get inside the convent right now. Good night." She made a shooing motion.

Mathias cracked his whip and Amanda's carriage jerked away from the sidewalk and into the street. Clearly startled by the carriage's abrupt movement, the three drunks lurched toward the street, cursing. Then their shouts became more personal.

"What's yer hurry, sweetheart?"

"Staying late fer church?"

"Come 'ere, and I'll *church* ya!" All were accompanied by hoots of laughter and lewd movements.

Amanda let their taunts drift past her as she leaned her face into the chilled spring breeze coming from the other window. She'd heard far worse. Every time she accompanied Sister Bernice into the tenement alleys, all sorts of obscene comments were muttered in her direction. Amanda ignored them just as she ignored the filth on the narrow streets that wound through those dense warrens hiding inside Washington's tidy city blocks of brick row houses.

The chill of the breeze caused her to shiver, but Amanda forced herself to stay beside the window. If she sat back, the rhythmic swaying of the coach and the sound of the horse's hooves clip clopping on the avenue would surely lull her to sleep. Bridget could spy fatigue on Amanda's face the moment she set foot in the house. Then, Bridget would scold. Again. Worse, she would scold Sister Bernice for keeping Amanda out so late. Amanda couldn't risk Sister Bernice refusing her help. It was too important.

Another carriage approached on the other side of the wide avenue, traveling the opposite direction. Amanda heard the sounds of gay laughter floating on the night air, and she spotted a man and woman inside the coach, clearly enjoying each other's company. She caught a brief glimpse of the woman's fashionable evening gown with deep décolletage. So like the gowns still hanging in the back of her closet. The man was wearing an evening cape. Lined with white silk, no doubt. Those no longer hung in her closet.

Amanda felt the deep pang of memory and averted her eyes from the happy couple. She glanced out the other window and saw the President's House come into view. Only a few lights shone through the mansion's wide windows. There was no doubt that the President was already in bed. The good Midwesterner and Presbyterian that he was, Benjamin Harrison didn't hold with late night partying. Not like some of his predecessors. Amanda had noticed Washington Society paid no heed and partied without him.

The faint scent of apple blossoms drifted into the coach, telling Amanda that they were turning onto Lafayette Square. Home at last. Mathias steered the horse around the corner of Jackson Place and slowed his pace until he drew to a stop in front of Amanda's row house on H Street. Nestled cheek-by-jowl between other Federal brick homes nearly identical to each other, neat, and ordered and safe.

"We're home, Miz Duncan," Mathias announced as he stepped down to the pavement. Opening the door, he helped Amanda to the bridge between carriage and sidewalk.

"Thank you, Mathias. I confess I am a bit tired this evening." She smiled at her coachman, his ebony face reflecting the streetlamp's gleam. "Don't let on to Bridget."

"No, ma'am, I won't," he said with a nod.

Amanda ascended the front steps as swiftly as her full skirts and cloak would allow. The door opened before she reached the top step. A tiny silver-haired woman in a black dress stood in the entryway.

"Well, it's high time you're home, Amanda Duncan. I'll have to have a word or two with Sister Bernice this Sunday. She can't be keepin' you out so late." Bridget O'Farrell stood stiff as a flagpole, fist on her hip.

"It was entirely my doing, Bridget," Amanda lied to her housekeeper as she walked inside the foyer. "Sister Bernice urged me to leave earlier, but I refused."

The gaslights along the walnut-paneled hallway flickered low, but the warm yellow glow coming from the parlor beckoned her. Bridget had all the etched crystal globe lamps turned on. Home. Amanda slipped off her gloves and walked into the parlor's welcoming embrace. She felt the fatigue ooze out of her muscles and stifled a yarn.

"I saw that, Amanda Duncan," she heard Bridget's voice behind her.

Amanda loosened the clasp on her cloak. "I always knew you had eyes in the back of your head, Bridget, but I had no idea you could see right through me. How could you tell I yawned when I had my back turned?"

"You're forgettin' about the mirror, my girl," Bridget replied, as she took Amanda's cloak and gloves.

Amanda unpinned her stylish hat as she glanced toward the gilt-edged, oval mirror mounted on the opposite wall, directly above a sapphire blue settee. She watched Bridget's reflected glance catch hers in the glass and smiled.

"You're always one step ahead of me, Bridget," Amanda said, placing the hat on an end table. Giving in to fatigue at last, she massaged her temples with her fingertips.

"You really should be gettin' to bed, dearie," Bridget advised, peering at Amanda's face. "I won't have ya exhaustin' yourself. 'Twill do you no good at all. You need your rest."

"I'll go up in a few moments, I promise. Let me collect my thoughts first. It took us over three hours to move that poor woman from an alley hovel into another tenement."

Bridget clucked her tongue and shook her head. "Poor wretched souls. Let me bring you a cup of my chamomile tea. It'll soothe your nerves." She quietly slipped from the room.

Amanda walked over to one of the two tall windows looking out on Lafayette Square. Tall oak trees rimmed the park-like setting. The President's House sat solid and stately across the avenue. And in the center of the square, mounted on his horse, General Andrew Jackson kept watch over all. Past midnight, and all was well.

Just then, an eerily familiar tingle rippled across her skin. Amanda stared out into the darkened square, unseeing this time. Suddenly, she was somewhere else. She saw a grim, bare room. A bed. Two people. A knife ripping through flesh. Blood. Amanda went cold. She saw the knife slashing down. Again and again. A young girl crying out in terror, her screams choked off by the slashing blade. Blood. Blood. The man's large body collapsed. The girl silenced. Blood pooling on the bed. The shadowy assailant dropping the knife. Was it a knife?

Amanda closed her eyes, hoping the vision would stop. The horror of it sickened her. So much blood. The young girl's silenced screams.

Was she dead? The huge man sprawled lifeless on top of her. Blood everywhere, drenching the bed, blood, blood...

"Oh, sweet Mother Mary! You've had a vision. I knew you should have gone to bed. Now, you've exhausted yourself, you poor lamb." Bridget patted her shoulder, chamomile tea sloshing in its flowered china cup.

Amanda blinked, saw Bridget, then closed her eyes in relief. The terrifying scene was gone. She shivered.

"That's it. I'll not have any more argument. You'll be getting' up to bed this minute. Now drink this tea while I fetch a warmer for your bed." Bridget set the teacup on the writing desk with a loud clank.

The vision's urgency tugged at Amanda inside. The horrifying sights were no longer flashing before her eyes, but the young girl's face still radiated in her mind. "Bridget, please tell Mathias to fetch my carriage."

"What! You can't be serious?" Bridget cried. "Go out after midnight? 'Tis not proper. Not at all, at all. Whatever it is you saw, dearie, can wait for the morrow."

"No, it cannot, Bridget," Amanda insisted, lifting her moss green taffeta skirt as she sped across the jewel-toned Persian carpet. "I must alert the authorities about what I've seen. A young girl's life may be at stake. Now go and alert Mathias right away while I fetch my cloak."

Bridget shoved both fists onto her skinny hips and held her ground. "I'll be doin' no such thing! Racin' out to the chief inspector's office in the middle of the day is one thing. But traipsin' out in the middle of the night is another. Do you have any idea the sort of undesirables that roam the streets this time of night?"

Amanda suppressed her smile as she paused before the gilt-edged beveled mirror and rearranged her chestnut curls into their proper upswept fashion beneath her hat. "I am well aware of the sort of people who inhabit the city at night, Bridget, and I promise I will not consort with them. I'll go straight to the chief inspector's office then back again. Now, either you have Mathias fetch the carriage, or I'll be forced to go out onto Pennsylvania Avenue and hire a hansom."

With that, she hastened from the parlor, Bridget sputtering after her.

CHAPTER TWO

Devlin Burke scanned the front page of the *Washington POST* until he found the article he sought. Folding the paper, he absentmindedly stirred his cup of tea while he read, oblivious to the muted rustle of servants around him in the octagonal-shaped, sun drenched breakfast room. He aimed a silver spoon at the egg perched in its porcelain cup before him. Two sharp strokes were needed before the shell gave way. Only when his sister, Winnie, burst through the doors of the breakfast room did he look up.

"Dev, darling, do put that newspaper away quickly. Jonathan's grandmother is about to descend upon us, and she cannot abide the press. Thinks they're all scandal sheets." Winnie hastened to her place at the polished walnut table, straightening the skirt of her yellow silk gown while patting her honey-gold hair, piled into curls at her crown.

Glancing at his flustered sister, Devlin obediently re-folded the newspaper and held it up. He pretended a scowl when the butler whisked it away. "Don't throw it out, Jameson. I've not finished the article."

Winnie sent her brother a sympathetic glance as she poured tea into an alabaster china cup. "Don't be cross, Dev. I know you want to read about Dr. Gustafson's lecture, but you'll simply have to wait 'till after breakfast. And promise me you'll be on your very best behavior while Grandmother Carrington is visiting. None of those sly remarks of yours. She has absolutely *no* sense of humor."

Devlin grinned devilishly. "I'll have you know I'm always on my best behavior, dear Winnie. Now what has stirred you up so? Surely Jonathan's grandmother cannot be that objectionable."

At that moment, the doors swung open again and Devlin had the opportunity to judge for himself. An enormous woman, body encased in acres of black taffeta, swept into the room. Her pewter grey hair was pulled back into a severe coil atop her head, which accentuated her sharp features even more.

Devlin sprang to his feet, his chair making a sharp sound as it scraped against the parquet floors.

"A very good morning, Grandmother Carrington. How delightful of you to join us for breakfast." Devlin gave a polite smile as well as a deep bow, granting age its proper deference.

"There is absolutely *nothing* good about this morning, young man," Grandmother Carrington decreed as she settled her bulk into the chair Jameson offered. "There is a draught in my bedroom which has aggravated my rheumatism severely. I was awake half the night with it."

Winnie shot Jameson a quick glance, and he hastened to the door. Before he left, he gave a curt nod to the two young serving girls who stood in mute attendance on either side of the walnut buffet, their hands clasped still against their crisp white aprons. At Jameson's nod, each girl took a large sterling silver serving dish and approached the table.

"I'm dreadfully sorry, Grandmother," Winnie soothed, pouring another cup of tea. "Jameson will see to it first thing." She sent a sidelong glance to Devlin, and he obediently wiped away his smile. The youngest serving girl took the teacup from Winnie's hand and delivered it safely to Grandmother Carrington.

The older woman proceeded to spoon copious amounts of sugar into the amber liquid. Then she cast a sharp eye in Devlin's direction. "You must be Winifred's black-sheep-of-a-brother, Devlin. I've heard about you, young man. Especially your misguided, misspent past. Scandalous, simply scandalous. What a disgrace to your family. I'm shocked that the Earl still receives you. Winifred, whatever possessed you to invite this rakehell to Washington when I am visiting? Washington has enough rogues already. There is no need for more." A shudder worked its way down her considerable bosom, causing seismic tremors of black taffeta along the way.

Devlin knew enough to hold his tongue after an upbraiding like that. It reminded him of his late father's tirades. However, his sister did not. Winnie flushed from her forehead down to the modest décolletage of her canary-yellow gown.

"Grandmother Carrington, really," she sputtered. "That is quite unfair to Devlin. He is most certainly not a disgrace to our family. Why... why he has become absolutely invaluable to my brother and...and whatever youthful misadventures he engaged in are all in the past. He's really quite respectable now."

Devlin winced inwardly at that. He rather preferred Grandmother Carrington's version.

"A leopard cannot change his spots, Winifred," Grandmother decreed, scrutinizing the egg perched in its cup before her. She shattered the eggshell with one sharp crack of her spoon. The severed shell fairly leapt from the egg and slid obligingly into her plate. Devlin watched in admiration.

Winnie screwed up her attractive features in patent exasperation. "Well, Devlin has changed. He is the very cleverest advisor my brother, Bertie, has ever had. Why, Bertie says that Devlin has trebled the estate's investments in these last three years alone."

"He who serves Mammon cannot serve God," Grandmother intoned as she chose several hot biscuits from the proffered tray.

Winnie glanced heavenward, while Devlin simply looked on in amusement. He accepted the hot bread when the serving girl paused beside him and smeared a flaky biscuit with strawberry jam.

"Scripture aside, Grandmother, I'm sure even the Almighty admires a shrewd investor," Jonathan Carrington announced on entering. He sent a mischievous wink to his brother-in-law then bestowed a polite kiss on his grandmother's cheek. Glancing sympathetically to his wife, he took his place at the head of the table. "Winifred's absolutely right. Devlin's expertise and financial acumen have enriched their family estate immensely. And that, dearest Grandmother, is why he's here in Washington. In addition to providing you with an attractive target," Jonathan added with a laugh before he helped himself to a hearty serving of ham and sausages.

Devlin strove to appear properly contrite. "I pledge to you, Grandmother Carrington, that I will do my best to remain scandal-free while in Washington."

"Time will tell," quoth she, arching a supercilious brow. "And it's Mrs. Carrington to you, young man." She served herself several sausages.

Devlin kept his smile hidden, while Winnie sighed audibly behind her teacup. Jonathan, meanwhile, continued to eat with enthusiasm, apparently unconcerned about Grandmother's fulminations. Devlin decided he should make his escape before the old harridan let loose with another tiresome truism. He dropped his white linen napery beside his plate and stood. "If you ladies would be so good as to excuse me, I shall be off. My brother's investments need my constant attention," he lied.

Nodding first to Mrs. Carrington, then to Winnie, he turned to leave. Jonathan scraped back his own chair and hastened to join him. "Ladies, I shall rejoin you shortly. I must confer with Devlin for a moment."

"Jonathan, you really should not leap about in the midst of a meal. It is ruinous to one's digestion," warned Grandmother Carrington, with the look of one whose digestion was hardly ever perturbed.

Jonathan closed the double doors of the breakfast room behind them and motioned Devlin into the parlor across the hall. "I take it that was a ruse simply to escape." He steered Devlin toward a burgundy velvet wing chair beside the hearth and seated himself in its mate.

"Most assuredly," Devlin confessed. "I plan to seek out Freddie first thing this morning. I hope to catch him before he has left his hotel. He's staying at the Willard?"

Jonathan nodded and breathed a sigh. "I'm sorry we did not have a chance to talk privately last night, Dev, what with the Senate subcommittee meeting keeping me away until nearly midnight. Bertie had already wired that he had given you an additional charge on this visit. Freddie and his eminent rescue."

"Exactly what has our wayward nephew been up to this time?" Devlin leaned back into the wing chair's velvet embrace. "Bertie and I last heard he had made unwise investments. That sounds like an understatement, knowing Freddie's predilection for risky schemes."

"It seems he's bankrupted himself again." Jonathan sighed wearily.

"Then I cannot rescue him, Jonathan. This is the third position I have found for Freddie. If he has repeated his last mistakes, no brokerage in the East will have him. I had to use all my persuasive powers to convince the senior partner of Hastings and Sons to take him on last year. That and a considerable investment in the brokerage itself." He scowled. "I'm not sure Freddie is worth the money we lost."

"I'm afraid it's worse than that, Dev. This time, he's not only lost his own funds, but his client's and the brokerage's funds as well. Foolish boy! He allowed himself to be ensnared in one of Senator Horace Chester's nefarious schemes. Chester could see him coming. I warned Freddie to beware of that viper. He's entirely without scruples, that Chester." Jonathan's face darkened with a scowl. "But, no, Freddie wouldn't listen. He believed all of Chester's lies. Even though I told him of others who had been cheated by that vulture."

"Exactly what did this paragon of Senatorial virtue do? To Freddie, that is?"

"The same ruse which he has so successfully used on other greedy investors. He convinces them he will consider legislation particular to their cause for a price. As chairman of the Senate Commerce committee, his support is crucial. Then later, after he's extracted all the money he can from them, he informs the trusting souls that he has changed his mind. He will not recommend their bill in committee after all. Meanwhile, he pockets their bribes."

"Sterling individual."

Jonathan scowled. "The man and his ilk are a cancer on the Senate. I have no sympathy for the greedy fools who think he will make them rich. It's the other honest businessmen he has cheated over the years. The list is endless."

"Well, let me see if I can shake some sense into one greedy young fool. Then I shall arrange to reimburse the brokerage and their clients for the losses. But this will be the last time." Devlin pulled his long slender frame from the comfortable chair. "I am exceedingly glad that Freddie is related by marriage rather than blood. It would be unsettling to think such lack of mental acuity ran in the family."

Jonathan rose and placed his hand on Devlin's shoulder, his face still clouded with obvious concern. "I'm afraid the situation has worsened, Dev. Freddie's temper led him into a rash and foolish act. When Chester rebuffed him the other day, Freddie flew into a rage. He accosted Chester, right outside his office. In the very halls of the Senate. Apparently, there were several witnesses. I fully expect Chester to file charges. He's a vindictive wretch."

"Good God, has Freddie lost his senses? Accost a United States Senator in the Capitol?" Devlin grimaced. "I'm not sure he's even worth saving."

"I know, I know, but you will try, won't you?"

Devlin released a long aggrieved sigh of exasperation, then turned toward the foyer. Jameson appeared as if by magic and handed him his hat and walking cane. "I'll do more than try, Jonathan. I plan to take Freddie by the scruff of the neck and shake some sense into the young fool before I ship him back to Devonshire where he can no longer cause the family any embarrassment." With a flourish of his hat, Devlin was out the door and into the warm sunshine bathing Connecticut Avenue.

Joey Quinn stared hard at the bandaged-wrapped young girl who lay on the cot in the dingy, closet-sized room. Lizzie and another woman, as drab as Lizzie was painted, hovered in the cramped space beside the cot. Quinn squinted his bloodshot eyes as if pondering something, then scratched his dirty thumbnail along the two-day old stubble of beard. He caught Lizzie's eye, beckoning her out into the dimly lit hall.

"We gotta get rid of Francie," he growled in a low voice.

Lizzie stared in obvious horror. "Whaddya talkin' about? The doc just saved her life!"

"Keep yer voice down," he rasped, yanking Lizzie by the arm until they stood farther down the hall.

"Leggo, ya bastard," Lizzie swore, pulling away from him.

"All I mean is we gotta get her outta here, that's all. We ain't a hospital. We got her patched up, now she'll havta go somewheres else."

Quinn peered over his shoulder into the unusually quiet foyer below. "Besides, it's bad fer business having her here. Keeps customers away."

Lizzie fixed Quinn with a withering stare. "You're all heart, Joey. You know how weak Francie is. Why, she barely survived that monster's attack, and now you're gonna throw her out."

"I ain't throwin' her out, Lizzie. I just want ya to find her another place to stay. Send her back to her father, why don'cha?"

"Him? Ya gotta be kidding! He's a drunken bum and nearly beat her to death when she was there, and you want to send her back?" She snorted in disgust, crossing her arms below her ample bosom, faded dressing gown gaping wide.

Quinn took a deep breath and shoved his thumbs beneath his suspenders, then narrowed his bloodshot gaze on Lizzie. "Look, I ain't arguin' with ya no more, Lizzie. You find someplace else for Francie. I don't care where, but she leaves tomorrow morning, ya got that?" With one last disgusted look toward the recuperating girl, he stomped down the hall.

CHAPTER THREE

For the third time in twenty minutes, Devlin pulled out his gold pocket watch and checked the hour. Ten o'clock. Shifting his position in the damask covered armchair, he shut the case with an aggravated snap. Seated in a richly decorated parlor adjacent to the Willard Hotel's lobby, he drummed his fingers and waited.

If this was the way Freddie conducted his business, no wonder he was such a failure. Devlin could scarcely believe his eyes when a sleepy Freddie finally opened his hotel room door this morning after Devlin had knocked loudly for several minutes. Still in bed at nine-thirty.

No matter how many dawns Devlin had witnessed after a night's youthful carousing, he always managed to rise and be ready for another day's adventures by eight o'clock in the morning at the very latest. He never could understand the sluggards who lay in bed for hours. Wenching he could understand. But asleep?

He remembered an oft-repeated quote of Napoleon's: "Four hours of sleep for a man, six for a woman, and eight for a fool." Devlin snorted. If that were the case, Freddie was a blithering idiot by the Little Emperor's standards.

Devlin distracted himself by observing the two couples seated in the parlor with him. An elderly pair sat sipping tea and dissecting last evening's dinner party. Devlin guessed the gentleman to be a retired judge of some rank, considering his frequent mention of various courts. Then, there was the young couple who sat beside the sunny window looking out on Pennsylvania Avenue. They gazed at each other, their hands clasped across the table. Newlyweds, without a doubt.

At last, Freddie hastened through the parlor doorway, his cravat slightly askew, his face flushed. Devlin hoped the flush was from embarrassment.

"Devlin ..."Freddie threw himself awkwardly into the wing chair opposite, breathless. "You must ... forgive my tardiness. I do not know what came ... over me. I seldom oversleep. Most unusual." He brushed a lock of reddish brown hair from his forehead and stared sheepishly at his uncle.

"Yes, I was rather amazed that you could sleep so soundly you didn't even hear my knocking. Considering all that has occurred in your life recently, I wonder you can sleep at all." He fixed Freddie with a critical gaze.

Freddie flushed from his smooth unlined forehead to his sloppily tied silk cravat. "I suppose you've heard about my ... my difficulties."

"Difficulties is rather an understatement, wouldn't you say, Freddie? Three financial disasters in as many years. Squandering your uncle's bequest, not once, but thrice. Why... Bertie's gamekeeper could support his entire family of eight for a decade on what you frittered in your first loss alone."

Devlin watched Freddie's flush turn crimson. Even though Devlin had kept his voice modulated so that it would not carry to the other couples in the parlor, the tone he used was calculated to leave Freddie no quarter. If Devlin was going to have to clean up after Freddie, he'd bloody well make sure the young fool was properly shamed.

"You realize, of course, that your future here is finished, don't you? This was your third position. No investment house or brokerage will touch you now. If what I've heard is true, you've gambled the brokerage's money on this scheme. Gambled and lost. And then you were foolish enough to assault a United States Senator in the very Capitol." Devlin let his disgust show in his face as well as his voice now. "I swear, Freddie, if I didn't know it would cause our family immense pain, I would let you stew in your own juice. Let the brokerage press charges. Oh ... and speaking of charges, you'd best pray the Senator doesn't."

At that, Freddie exploded. "Damn his bloody soul to hell!" He clenched his fists and pounded the chair. "I trusted him. And he *deliberately* cheated me!"

Devlin noticed the elderly couple across the room turn their heads at Freddie's outburst. The older man frowned in disapproval. The newlyweds, however, barely noticed. Devlin let his voice drop to the cellar. "Whether he cheated you or simply played you for a fool, it doesn't matter. The money is lost. Yours and your clients. I will clean up this mess for you, Freddie, but it is the last time. Your career in the world of *haute finance* is over. You will be shipped back to Devonshire where you can be put to some harmless task and stay out of trouble. I will remain here and pay off the debts. Although I don't mind saying so, I told Bertie you're not worth another shilling."

Freddie's belligerent expression of a moment ago crumpled. His boyish face pinched together as if he were trying to hold back unwelcome tears. For one split second, Devlin was almost sorry he had upbraided him so severely.

"It's all Chester's fault!" Freddie bit out the words. His tone revealed it wasn't sorrow that pinched his features. It was suppressed rage. "He played me for a fool, all right. A bloody fool. He was the one who suggested that coastal shipping line as an investment. Said he liked to see bright young lads get ahead. Hinted that there was a bill in his committee that would restrict harbor access to local shippers only in some ports. Said he could be persuaded to consider the bill ... under certain circumstances."

Freddie's face had darkened to a thundercloud. "I drained my own accounts first. And then he said there were others who needed persuasion. I was so certain! He swore the bill would be brought to the floor in a matter of days. I bought all the shares I could lay my hands on. Invested my clients' accounts, convinced they would reward me handsomely for my shrewd insight. And then ... then he pulled the carpet from beneath my feet."

Devlin stared, fascinated by the change in his nephew's countenance. Raw hatred replaced the rage. Freddie was barely recognizable. No longer the foolish spendthrift. He seethed with menace now.

"He called me to his office to inform me he could not support the bill after all. Other interests had convinced him to reconsider. Apparently, the shipper was insolvent and about to sell off the line. Every share was worthless. The harbor bill would have to wait. Then he got up and left. Said he had to rush off to a quorum call." Freddie's hands clenched around the upholstered chair arms, fingers bled white.

"And that's when you attacked him?" Devlin spoke gently, hoping a calm tone would diffuse the cloud of anger that hung between them.

"Yes, I chased him down the hallway." Freddie said, his eyes narrowing as if picturing it. "That bastard ruined everything I had planned. Ruined my whole life, and he stood there and smirked. I wanted to break his bloody neck."

Devlin was about to say he was extremely glad Freddie had not accomplished his goal, when a short man in an ill-fitting brown and black checked suit suddenly strode up to them.

Irritated they had been interrupted, Devlin inspected the man in one swift glance, then inquired in a polite tone, "May we help you?"

Broad and solidly built, the man eyed first Devlin then Freddie. "I certainly hope so, gentlemen," he responded, then placed his derby hat on a nearby table. He dug into his coat pocket, which made the suit ride up even more in the back, and withdrew a leather wallet with a metal badge attached. He held it up with one hand while he pulled out a small notebook and pencil with the other. "Permit me to introduce myself. I am Inspector Donnelly, of the District of Columbia Police Department." He pocketed the badge, then turned a page in his notebook. "And I am here to speak with one Freddie Livermore, currently residing at the Willard Hotel." He glanced at Devlin, then Freddie. "Which one of you gentlemen is Mr. Livermore? The hotel clerk wasn't sure."

Devlin held his breath and did not respond, watching Freddie instead. Freddie's angry cloud had evaporated at the man's introduction and the sight of the police badge. He swallowed and spoke. "I ... I am Freddie Livermore, Inspector. Why do you ask?"

"Ohhhhhh, we'd just like to ask you some questions, if you don't mind, sir? Concerning your acquaintances and such matters." Inspector

Donnelly's thick drooping mustache twitched a bit at the ends, and he poised, pencil over his notebook, staring at Freddie.

Noticing the use of the imperial "we", Devlin's sixth sense started to tingle. "Excuse me, Inspector. I am Devlin Burke, Mr. Livermore's uncle and financial advisor. If I may be so bold as to ask exactly what kinds of questions you intend asking my nephew? Are you investigating some criminal activity amongst his many acquaintances, perchance?" Devlin kept his expression deliberately pleasant.

Donnelly turned to Devlin, his gaze neither hostile nor friendly. Businesslike. "Well, you might say that, Mr. Burke." He rocked back on his heels a bit, as if about to relate a story. "It seems that a very important member of Congress met an untimely demise last night and we're contacting every one of his acquaintances to find out when they last spoke with him."

"W-w-who died?" Freddie stammered.

Watching him carefully, the inspector replied in a calm tone, "Senator Horace Chester, the senior senator from New Jersey. Very important man, I'm told. Very important, indeed. And since his demise was not, uh, how should I say—accidental—we have to investigate."

Freddie blanched, but said nothing. Donnelly stood calmly observing Freddie's reaction, while Devlin swore inwardly. What had been a distressing family situation was swiftly steering into far more treacherous waters.

"How did the Senator die, Inspector? Or aren't you allowed to divulge that information?" Devlin inquired in a conversational tone.

"He was murdered, Mr. Burke. Stabbed to death."

Freddie took in a sharp breath and gripped the chair arms. It was all Devlin could do to keep from reaching out and shaking him. Hadn't he noticed Donnelly scrutinizing his every move? Obviously, the Washington constabulary had heard of Freddie's recent altercation with Chester.

"That's appalling," Devlin declared. "Was he accosted on the streets? Who would do such a thing?"

"That's what we're sworn to find out, Mr. Burke," the inspector declared with a regal nod, his notebook tapping his chest. "Now, if you don't mind, Mr. Livermore, could you please tell me about the last time you saw Senator Chester? Where and when would that be, if I may ask?"

Devlin fixed Freddie with a stern warning eye and hoped the young fool wouldn't be idiotic enough to think he could neglect to mention his public argument with Chester. It was obvious to Devlin that Donnelly was well aware of what had passed between the two. That's why he was here. He wanted to hear—and see—Freddie describe the incident.

Freddie blinked at Devlin and swallowed. Glancing up at Donnelly, who was poised pen over pad, he began, "I ... I last saw the Senator on Friday. Yesterday. I, uh ... I went to see him about an investment. And we, uh, we, uh had an argument."

"And what was the argument about, Mr. Livermore, if you don't mind my asking?" Donnelly scribbled in his notebook, not looking up.

Freddie cleared his throat and straightened. "We disagreed about an investment which I ... I had made at the Senator's suggestion." Devlin was glad to see Freddie had composed himself.

"I see. A disagreement. Was the investment for the Senator or yourself, sir?"

"For myself. And my clients. I'm with the brokerage house of Hastings and Sons. Naturally, I handle several clients and their investments. I was ... consulting Senator Chester on some pending legislation."

"How did it turn out, Mr. Livermore? The investment, I mean. Did it make money or lose money?" Donnelly kept scribbling.

A muscle in Freddie's jaw twitched with his obvious effort. "It lost money."

"A great deal, sir?"

"Enough." Freddie lifted his chin.

Donnelly glanced up from his notepad. "Any hard feelings on your part, sir? You just said the investment was Senator Chester's suggestion."

Freddie held Donnelly's probing gaze for a second, then averted his eyes. He examined his trouser leg instead, brushing away invisible lint from the grey striped wool. "Yes. I was a bit put out," he said softly.

Donnelly scribbled away, while Devlin exchanged another warning glance with Freddie. Devlin's sixth sense was no longer tingling. It was raging. Alarm bells rang in his head. This inspector was circuitously leading Freddie to admit that he had a grudge against the Senator. He had lost a great deal of money. Strong motive, indeed, to do violence.

It was all Devlin could do to keep his mouth shut. But he could not interfere. It would only look as if he were trying to shield Freddie from questioning, which would make him appear even more suspicious to the police. Reluctantly, Devlin held his tongue.

"And tell me, Mr. Livermore, where were you last night? From supper time on, I mean."

Devlin sprang at the tiny opening. Feigning an expression of shocked outrage, he declared, "What are you suggesting, Inspector? That my nephew knew of this crime?"

Donnelly turned to Devlin with an exaggerated calm, as if he had to explain brutal murders to outraged citizens every day. "Just a routine question, Mr. Burke. We're contacting everyone who saw the Senator Friday and inquiring as to their whereabouts that night. Just routine, sir. Nothing to get excited about."

Devlin had to give Donnelly credit. His bearing and voice exuded quiet efficiency, but his gaze belied that. There was hawk-like intensity in those pale blue eyes, and they didn't miss a thing.

Remarkably, Freddie replied just as calmly, "I dined with Senator Edmund Remington. We went to his club on New York Avenue. Afterwards, he drove me to this hotel."

Donnelly scribbled. "And what time was that, sir?"

"I believe it was approximately eleven o'clock. I cannot recall precisely."

"Did you leave your hotel after that, sir? Go anywhere else?"

"No, I did not. I retired and went to sleep. I was quite fatigued."

Donnelly's pencil moved rapidly. "Did you go anywhere early this morning when you arose?"

Devlin jumped in again. "He most certainly did not, Inspector. I arrived here an hour ago and found him still asleep upstairs. I must have knocked for several minutes before he awoke. He has been with me ever since."

"I see." The pencil moved for a moment more, then halted. Donnelly flipped his notebook closed and gave Freddie a friendly smile. "Well, thank you very much for your cooperation, sir. You've been most helpful. I'll bid a good day to you both." He nodded to Devlin then Freddie and turned to leave.

Devlin was about to breathe a sigh of relief when the stocky little man wheeled about and fixed Freddie with another of his sociable smiles. "Oh, just one more question, if you don't mind, Mr. Livermore. It seems Senator Chester was killed in a rough area of the city. In a brothel, to be exact. Stabbed in the midst of the act, apparently." He shook his head with a weary expression, while Freddie paled. "It seems that Chester often took friends and business acquaintances to the same sorry place for amusement. This particular little nest of evil was in the midst of Murder Bay, right next to The Devil's Eye tavern. Can't miss the tavern. It has a flaming red pitchfork painted on the door. You wouldn't happen to know anyone who accompanied the Senator on any of these forays, would you, Mr. Livermore?"

To Devlin's dismay, Freddie flushed quickly. A thin sheen of perspiration shone on his forehead. "Uh, no ... no, I would not."

"Now, you yourself, sir. I see that you're a robust young lad. Did you happen to accompany the Senator on any of these nighttime carousing's of his?" Donnelly's smile was in place, but his eyes were scrutinizing the obviously uncomfortable young man before him.

"Uh, no ... no, I did not," Freddie said, examining his trousers again.

"Well, I didn't think so. Much too fine a lad to be mixed up with the Senator's evil doings. I trust you didn't take offense at my questions. Part of my job, you understand."

"Yes, yes, I understand, Inspector. No offense taken," Freddie said in a soft voice.

For the second time, Donnelly gave a slight nod to both gentlemen. "Well, I'll be bidding you good day. And thank you again for your cooperation. Oh, and I hope you plan to remain in the city for a while, Mr. Livermore. Just in case we have any more questions. You understand, I'm sure. Just routine." And with a big smile that caused his droopy mustache to jiggle, Donnelly picked up his hat and strode from the room as forcefully as he had strode in moments ago.

Devlin watched Freddie lean his head back against the chair in obvious relief that the questioning was over. But Devlin's gut twisted in anxiety. He knew the questions had only begun. The oh-so-friendly Inspector Donnelly had caught Freddie in a lie. Devlin knew it, and Inspector Donnelly knew it. The only one blissfully unaware was Freddie.

CHAPTER FOUR

Jonathan Carrington closed his parlor's French doors and leaned against them, a worried expression on his face. Winnie and Devlin were already seated upon the crimson settee across the room. Paintings of Eighteenth century masters filled the walls, gilded frames competing for space above the wainscoting. Velvet draperies the color of aged claret framed lace-covered windows.

Winnie gestured anxiously to her husband. "Do sit down, Jonathan. We must talk before the dinner guests arrive. We have to decide what to do. This is dreadful. Simply dreadful." She fidgeted with the white lace that trailed from the bodice of her peach crepe de chine evening gown.

"Do not fret yourself, Winnie. I will handle this unpleasantness," Devlin announced. "I want none of Freddie's predicament to touch the two of you. Jonathan's position in the Senate is far too important to be jeopardized by foolish Freddie." He pulled a face.

Jonathan seated himself in a mahogany captain's chair directly across from them. "How bad is it, Dev? Winnie only had time to whisper a sentence or two before Grandmother interrupted us."

"I will not deceive you," Devlin eyed them both. "The situation is quite serious. Freddie has no alibi. No one can confirm he spent the entire night at the hotel. What's worse, the police obviously know that Freddie and Chester argued about an investment turned sour, and there were several witnesses to the attack in the Senate. Excellent motive in the officer's mind, I would say. I could tell from Donnelly's questioning that he was already aware of the details of the altercation; he simply wanted to watch Freddie's reaction. Unfortunately, Freddie did not hold up well under the good inspector's scrutiny."

"Poor dear," sympathized Winnie.

"Poor dear, nothing. He's a bloody damn *fool!*" snapped Devlin, allowing his temper to flare at last. "On top of all the other damning evidence, he allows himself to be caught in a lie. To think he could deceive a police inspector ... how could he be so stupid?"

"What can you do, Dev?" Jonathan probed.

Devlin let out an exasperated sigh. "I will undertake my own investigation. If we can agree on one thing, it is that Freddie may be foolish, reckless, and abysmally stupid—"

"Now, Dev," chided Winnie.

"—but he is not a murderer. Freddie does not have the calculating mind of a killer. If he did, he wouldn't have been such a poor investor." Devlin smiled grimly.

"Really, Dev. You make it sound as if a calculating mind is to be admired," Winnie scoffed.

"In the right head, it is," Devlin contested. "Shrewdness doesn't have to lend itself to murder, my dear. Otherwise, Wall Street would be stacked with bodies."

"How will you proceed? If you need more information from the police I can arrange for you to see someone in authority at the District Department," Jonathan offered. "The Commissioner and I are friends. I'm sure he will agree to allow you access to any information that is available."

"Thank you, Jonathan. I plan to start there first thing tomorrow morning. I need to learn more about the murder. Donnelly said the crime took place in one of the seedier sections of your fair city. Surely, there were people about who may have seen something."

"Murder Bay," Winnie murmured with a shiver. "Even the name is dreadful. How could Freddie have been attracted to such a place?"

Devlin exchanged a knowing glance with Jonathan and did not reply. No need to regale his respectable sister with debauchery's universal allure. Personally, Devlin preferred to debauch in less grimy surroundings and with more discriminating playmates than the ones Senator Chester had chosen. No doubt Freddie would rue his decision to accompany the senator on his "nighttime carousing's," as Donnelly put it.

"I wish we could help," Winnie said, her brow knotted in concern. "I feel so useless sitting here entertaining a pompous Supreme Court Justice and an overbearing congressman and his wife."

"Actually, you and Jonathan can help a great deal. If I am to prove Freddie's innocence, then I need to learn more about the Senator's colleagues and acquaintances. One of them may be the murderer."

"Perhaps the scandal sheets are right, Dev. Perhaps the killer really was some crazed maniac," Winnie volunteered in a hopeful tone.

"The press are the only ones who believe so, and they print it because it sells papers. Like the police, I'm inclined to look to the Senator's companions. Who would have wanted him dead?"

Jonathan snorted. "Scores of men. Chester had been abusing his power for years. He and the others who're in the pockets of greedy bankers and railroaders. Corrupt through and through. Chester had his fingers in more pies than I have fingers and toes. It would take you forever to track down all of Chester's enemies."

"Not all of them. Just the ones he had harmed sufficiently so they would hold a lasting grudge. And the ones who would have benefitted from his death, as well." Devlin stared, unseeing, at the Italian marble mantelpiece, pondering.

"Well, in that case, you can start with his arch rival in the Senate. Sherwood Steele. He has inherited Chester's place, you know. With Chester's death, Steele now becomes ranking Republican and head of the Commerce Committee." Jonathan nodded as if to himself. "Yes, he and Chester have been at odds for as long as I've been in the Senate. Steele is every bit as corrupt as Chester was, but he's much more clever at concealing his thefts and patronage. Chester almost flaunted his abuses. Steele is more careful. Ruthless, though. Clever and utterly ruthless."

Devlin listened with rapt attention. "Hmmmm, well, we'll just have to plan an opportunity for me to meet some of these charming government servants. Winnie, could you arrange something on short notice? A soiree for instance? Something where I can wander about and engage unsuspecting souls in conversation." He grinned conspiratorially at his sister.

"Of course, Dev. I'll be delighted to provide you with an opportunity for your sleuthing," she teased. "I imagine it will feel almost like you were back in London. Investigating and all that."

Devlin gave a deprecating wave of his hand, even though his sister's comment had already sent his pulse racing. He felt the familiar anticipation start to course through him. Dark deeds and the people who did them. Dangerous people—and fascinating. Nevertheless, he demurred, "Oh, no, nothing like that at all, my dear. I'll simply make a few polite inquiries. After all, I do not have the connections in Washington that I did in London."

Winnie glanced to her husband as if on cue. "Well, let us see what we can do about that."

"Follow me," Sister Beatrice whispered to Amanda as she closed the bedroom door.

Amanda followed the diminutive, black-garbed figure away from the darkened sickroom, down the familiar convent hallway lined with portraits of the saints, and finally, into a cheerful parlor. The warm glow of oil lamps spread their yellow light into every corner of the small but inviting room, which was stuffed with old furniture. In fact, Amanda noticed with satisfaction that her own donations had been put to good use. The Sisters of St. Anne's were known for their thrift.

"Please, sit down, Amanda," Sister Beatrice waved toward the assortment of furniture. "Rest assured we'll do everything in our power to help the poor child heal. Thank the Lord a doctor saw her in time, otherwise her wounds would have been fatal." Sister Beatrice settled into a tiny rocker, which appeared to have been made especially for her. "God has brought her to us now, and we will take care of her. Father Tom already spoke with the authorities." Her hands reached for the crucifix that lay on her chest and slowly fingered the carved ivory.

Amanda sank into what used to be her own settee, running her gloved hand across the worn blue velvet cushion. "I know you'll do your best, Sister. You always do. I cannot tell you how relieved I was to learn she was brought here."

"It breaks my heart to think what has happened to that poor girl." Sister Beatrice wagged her head, her small face, encircled by the white wimple, pinched with concern. "I remember when Francie used to bring her mother here. Whenever the beatings were too bad. Sometimes Bill Kelly beat Anna so badly she couldn't walk. Ah, me ... no wonder the poor girl ran away after her mother died. I'm sure he turned his hand to her."

Amanda let out a long sigh. "There are too many Francie's and Anna's, aren't there, Sister? No matter how many we reach, there are so many, many more ..." her voice trailed off.

"All we can do is to help the ones we find, Amanda. God will guide us."

Amanda stared at the amber glow the oil lamp cast on her white gloves and her face darkened. "Did God guide Francie? Out of one hell and into a far more wretched one? Forgive me, Sister, but I do not have your faith. I cannot see the Almighty's hand in this at all."

"Do not despair, Amanda. Good will come of this, somehow. We must have trust and faith in God." Sister Beatrice ran her fingers along her rosary and lifted it to her lips, murmuring a silent prayer.

Amanda watched in envy. Such supreme trust and faith in a loving Deity was denied her. Her experience had taught her that God could be curiously untrustworthy—and uninvolved. Good did not always come out of tragedy. Not at all.

She gathered her lavender silk skirts and rose. "I must be going, Sister. Bridget will never let me hear the end of it if I miss her corned beef two weeks in a row. I'll return tomorrow to see how Francie is doing."

Sister Beatrice sprang from the chair surprisingly fast for her age. "Tell Bridget I'll see her at Sunday Mass. Nine o'clock sharp." She patted Amanda's arm as she accompanied her into the foyer. Black and white tiles, once new, now cracked with age beneath their feet. Pausing at the door, Sister Beatrice beamed up at Amanda with a twinkle in her eye. "There's plenty of room in the pew if you would like to join us, my dear. Bridget and I don't take much room, you know. Two old sticks like us. We'd love to hear your clear soprano singing prayers."

Amanda smiled at the scheming little nun and skirted the unspoken issue, teasing instead. "Now, Sister, you know High Church Episcopalians don't sing any more than Catholics. At least they didn't four years ago. Besides, the Methodists do it so well, why bother?"

"I'm sure Father Tom would sing the entire Mass if he saw you beside us," Sister Beatrice promised, her moon-shaped face looking much younger than its sixty years.

Amanda laughed out loud. "It might be worth converting just to hear that gravelly baritone," she said as she strode out the door, escaping. Quickly crossing the handkerchief-sized courtyard, she headed for the rectory.

If she hurried, she could catch Father Tom before six o'clock evening Mass. Amanda had already decided what to do. She'd increase her donation yet again for the parish's work in the tenements. Whatever it took to reach more forgotten souls. There was so much misery and suffering in those wretched slums. As far as Amanda was concerned, the only ones she saw saving lives and easing the misery were Father Tom and the Sisters. Once again, the Almighty was decidedly absent.

CHAPTER FIVE

Devlin crossed one leg over the other and settled as comfortably as possible into the straight-back wooden chair. Seated directly across from him in the cluttered white-walled office behind a scarred walnut desk, sat the head of Washington's Police Department, Chief Inspector William Callahan. Devlin smiled his most unassuming smile as he met the chief inspector's hostile glare, but he sensed Callahan had taken an instant dislike to him the moment he opened his mouth and his British accent fell out.

"I've been instructed to answer any questions you might have about Senator Chester's vicious murder, and answer them I will, Mr. Burke, but I'll be quite frank. I don't like it one bit. This is police business. Private citizens have absolutely no excuse to go poking about. No matter <u>how</u> well-connected they are." Callahan's bushy grey eyebrows drew together in a straight line across his face, while his matching mustache fairly trembled with apparent indignation.

Deciding this was going to be more difficult than he had imagined, Devlin plunged ahead resolutely. "Yes, Chief Inspector, I understand your position completely. I only have a few questions, and I promise I'll be brief. I—"

"You'd best not reveal any of what I say to the press, do you understand? We've had enough trouble with their speculation as it is. Crazed maniac, indeed!" He snorted. "Got half the poor souls in that quarter nearly scared out of their wits. They think some knife-wielding assassin will come looming at them around every corner. Ridiculous."

"Speaking of knives, Chief Inspector. Was the weapon used a knife or another sort of blade?"

Callahan screwed up his face and stared at Devlin for a full minute before he spoke. When he did, it sounded as if he was biting off the words. "The murder weapon was not a knife. It was a letter opener. Gold. With the Willard Hotel's inscription. We found it on the floor beside the bed. Discarded as the culprit fled the scene, no doubt."

A chill ran through Devlin's body, but he made certain he revealed no visible surprise. It was obvious Callahan knew who he was and why he was there. Only intense pressure from the Commissioner above had forced him to reveal this information to the uncle of a possible suspect. Considering the weapon used, Freddie was very likely the prime suspect. "And what time of night was the Senator attacked?" Devlin continued.

"Joey Quinn, the scum who owns the bordello, said he entered the room sometime after midnight that evening. He and another of his girls. Apparently, one girl wasn't enough for the Senator. Quinn was supposed to bring another one to the room about eleven-thirty, but he was running late. He unlocked the door and found the senator dead and the young girl just barely alive. No sign of anyone else, but another door leading to a back stairway was open. Only the senator and he had a key to that door to the street. The senator's private entrance, we're told."

Callahan related all this in a harsh voice, his tone and expression leaving no doubt as to his opinion of Senator Chester's private pastimes. "The poor girl had passed out from loss of blood. If Quinn hadn't come when he had, she would have died too. We think the villain must have been frightened away when he heard knocking at the door. That's why he didn't finish off the girl."

Devlin could barely contain his glee at the discovery of a witness. One of the victims had survived. "What has the girl told you about their attacker?"

Callahan fixed Devlin with a penetrating gaze and paused for another moment before continuing. "Her wounds are so severe she can only talk for a minutes at a time. She didn't recognize the man. He came out of nowhere, it seems. Suddenly there he was, knife in hand. He stabbed Chester in the back, then when the senator pulled away in shock, the killer stabbed him in the heart. Then, he went after her."

For the first time, Devlin saw a softening of Callahan's face. "Poor little thing. She couldn't be more than sixteen or seventeen. Probably tried to escape from some tenement alley, like Snow's Court. Pits of despair, they are. To think she was driven to that life to feed herself. Or, kidnapped, which is more likely. And now, she's brutalized and nearly killed. It's a disgrace."

Devlin let the chief inspector's sordid imagery penetrate his mind. He'd seen enough tenements in London to last him a lifetime. Haunting faces of despair. He wished he didn't remember. Devlin doubted Washington's tenements could be any worse than London's. Nothing could be worse than that. "She's sure she did not recognize her attacker?" he ventured at last.

Callahan shook his head.

"If the back door was left open, then it sounds as if the killer obtained a key and entered that way. If I understand you correctly, the other door was locked and it opened directly into the bordello's hallway. It would have been impossible for the killer to go that way without being seen by this Quinn or the other patrons."

Callahan scowled. "I'd like nothing more than to find grounds to charge that lowlife, Quinn, with murder. But the scurvy rat has an alibi. He was constantly with others during the evening. He was never alone."

"So it seems that the murderer gained entrance up the outside private stairway."

"So it seems."

"Correct me if I'm wrong, Chief Inspector, but that sounds like the killer not only knew about the stairway but also had access to the key. Unless he forced the lock. Was the lock tampered with in any way?"

"None that we could tell."

Callahan leaned back into his brown leather chair and surveyed Devlin carefully. Devlin wasn't sure, but he thought he detected the faintest hint of interest rather than hostility in the gaze. Probably too much to hope for, he thought, and decided not to push his luck. "If you'll forgive an amateur's speculation, the fact that the door was locked might point to someone of Chester's acquaintance who knew of his private pastimes and had access to the key," Devlin suggested ingenuously.

Callahan smiled; a trifle condescendingly, Devlin thought. "Thank you, Mr. Burke. We had already arrived at that conclusion. It seems that Chester kept the key on a gold ring, along with several others. And according to his Senate assistant, the Senator often left the ring in his top desk drawer, unlocked." He watched Devlin's obvious interest, then added, "But, we also found the lock to be fairly old and loose. It wouldn't have taken much to work it open. Consequently, someone *without* access to the key could also have entered, with a little effort, of course." He gave a dark smile.

Devlin felt his momentary elation fade. "Well, that certainly leaves a wide range of potential suspects," he deliberately jibed. "I've heard that Senator Chester had a great many enemies."

"Perhaps so, but not every one of them would be rash enough to commit murder."

A very cold spot centered in the middle of Devlin's gut. The chief inspector's use of the word "rash" told him more than he wanted to know. Freddie was definitely at the top of Callahan's list of suspects. "Well, you've certainly got your work cut out for you, Chief Inspector. I admire your tenacity. And I also want to thank you for your cooperation." Devlin rose from the purgatory of a chair, not wanting to drag out his visit. He sensed that Callahan had told him all he was going to, commissioner or no.

Callahan rose, but stayed behind his desk, not bothering to escort Devlin out. "I hope we've satisfied your curiosity, Mr. Burke."

"You've been most helpful, Chief Inspector." Devlin forced a smile. He was about to attempt a quick exit when Callahan's office door swung open and a rotund, bald police sergeant burst into the room. Obviously excited about something, his face was flushed. He didn't even glance at Devlin, but addressed the chief inspector in a heavy brogue.

"Chief Inspector, she's here again. This time she saw the <u>uniform</u>. Says she saw someone hidin' it in a dark place. Sweet Jesus! I'm beginnin' to think the woman's possessed!"

Callahan's face colored swiftly. "That will be enough, Sergeant! I told you not to mention that to anyone." He shot a glare in Devlin's direction.

"I'm sorry, sir," the sergeant said, not appearing the least bit contrite. "It's just that the woman's given me a fright, she has. It's not natural for her to know about such things. First, the murder, now this—"

"Sergeant, I said *enough*! Go back to your desk immediately."

"What shall I tell her, sir? She insists on talkin' with you."

"Tell her I am too busy to listen to her 'visions' or whatever she calls them. Hallucinations, is more like it. Product of a disturbed widow's imagination. She should spend her time in church instead of gallivanting about town with this foolishness. Tell her I cannot receive her now, but she can write up the stories and leave them at the desk. Perhaps that will help her exorcise these delusions."

At the word "exorcise," the ruddy-faced sergeant blanched. Crossing himself, he hastily exited, closing the door behind him.

Devlin pondered Callahan's angry outburst. It was obvious that the chief inspector was furious the sergeant had let slip an important piece of information. The killer had apparently worn some kind of uniform during the attack and that uniform had now been found. But who on earth was this disturbed widow he had referred to? And how had she known about the murder?

There were too many questions for Devlin to resist so he decided to risk Callahan's wrath himself and ventured, "Exactly who is this woman you are referring to, Chief Inspector?" He deliberately avoided the subject of the uniform, not wishing to press his luck. "What sort of visions has she had?"

Callahan snorted. "Some deluded widow who claims she 'sees' things. Hysterical female. Says she receives these 'visions.' She came to the station the night of the murder and claimed she had seen the attack in her head, while she was in her home on Lafayette Square. Wanted to know if the young girl was alive or not." He shook his head in obvious disgust. "Can you imagine that? Poor misguided creature. She has nothing useful to occupy her time, so she invents these fantasies. If she had remarried like a proper lady, she would be surrounded by a respectable family now and not be traipsing into a police station in the middle of the night, scaring my desk sergeant half to death with her wild stories."

Devlin felt the hair on the back of his neck stand on end. Chief Inspector Callahan might cavalierly dismiss this woman's so-called abilities, but Devlin did not. He had been present in London two years ago when the famous psychic Robert James Lees led Scotland Yard to the very door of the man he claimed was the Ripper—only to be ignored. Devlin's pulse began to race. What had this woman seen in her visions?

"Have you considered the possibility that this woman may have indeed seen something ... in her own special way, I mean. Might she not have some valuable information, which could lead to the culprit's capture? Perhaps you should talk with her," he suggested gently.

He was met with a look of such exquisite scorn Devlin swore he felt his toes curl. Callahan's reply dripped with the sarcasm of a closed mind. "Feel free to interrogate the widow yourself, Mr. Burke. I'm sure you will find her stories most enlightening. Now, if you will excuse me, I must attend to business." He gestured none-too-subtly to the door.

Devlin kept his mouth closed, trying to exit with a shred of dignity intact after being dismissed as if he were an intellectual pygmy simply because he suggested taking the woman's claims seriously. Surveying the large, high-ceilinged room that served as the station house receiving area, Devlin anxiously searched for the woman but saw only the wretches brought up on charges. They sat sullen and silent on the benches lining the walls.

He sought out the sergeant, who was shuffling through some papers, seated at his high desk. Devlin peered up. "Excuse me, Sergeant. If you would be so kind, could you tell me the name of the woman you mentioned previously and where I might reach her?"

"Certainly, sir. Her name's Amanda Duncan." The sergeant glanced toward Callahan's office then leaned over his desk to whisper. "I'd be careful if I was you, sir. She's not normal, that one. She makes my blood run cold whenever she comes in here." He wagged his bald head.

Intrigued, Devlin asked, "Does she report these visions often, Sergeant?"

"Oh, every few months, or so. Sometimes it's a lost child she claims she's seen. Sometimes a runaway spouse. Sometimes ... "his ruddy face paled again. "Sometimes she tells the inspector where to look for people after they're dead." He shivered.

"Does the inspector pay any heed?"

"Oh, never, sir. How could he? Visions and some such." He leaned forward again, and confided in a sinister tone, "Such things smack of witchcraft, if you ask me, sir. It's the Devil's business she's dabbling in. Not right. Not right at all."

Devlin kept his opinions to himself. "Could you tell me where I might find this poor, misguided creature?"

"Most probably, you can find her right outside if you step lively, sir. She just left for her carriage."

Devlin bolted for the door. He had to speak to this woman. She may have seen something, perhaps the murderer's face. He heaved his shoulder into the heavy oak door that lead from the solid red brick building and raced down the cement steps leading to the sidewalk. Several hansom cabs were drawn up before the station house, and Fifteenth Street was filled with passing carriages and carts. A Heurich beer wagon rumbled heavily past, filled with barrels of the local brewery's finest.

Blast! What if he'd missed her? Devlin quickly surveyed the people clustered on the sidewalk, searching for an older woman probably dressed in widow's weeds. He saw only two women nearby. One was a peddler and appeared to be engaged in her trade. The other was definitely not a peddler but neither was she wearing black. Instead, she was stylishly dressed in the latest spring color, a gown of robin's egg blue, as fashionable as his own sister's. He also noticed a coachman was about to open her carriage door.

Devlin quickly approached the slender woman and doffed his hat. "Pardon me, madam. Forgive my impertinence, but I was told by the precinct sergeant that I would find a lady by the name of Amanda Duncan outside, about to enter her carriage. Do I have the pleasure of addressing her? Might you be she?"

The woman turned and glanced up at Devlin from beneath the swooping brim of her gauzy, beribboned hat. He was momentarily taken aback by the direct blue gaze that met his.

"I am Amanda Duncan, sir. What is it you wish?"

Devlin disguised his surprise at meeting Inspector Callahan's "disturbed widow." He broke into a smile. "Forgive me, madam, but I must confess that Inspector Callahan's description does not do you justice." Observing the woman's skeptical expression, Devlin quickly became serious. "Permit me to introduce myself, Mrs. Duncan. My name is Devlin Burke. I frequently travel to Washington to visit family and supervise investments for my brother, the Earl of Devonshire. However, this time, an urgent family issue has caused me to involve myself in this sordid business regarding Senator Chester. I was just inside questioning Inspector Callahan concerning the murder. It appears you have some knowledge of this distressing occurrence."

A faint smile played with Amanda Duncan's lips. "Did Inspector Callahan say that?"

"Not in those precise words."

"I rather thought not."

"Mrs. Duncan, let me say I do not share Chief Inspector Callahan's disbelief in knowledge of the sort you possess. I was hoping you would be good enough to share with me the information your visions revealed."

"You do not find the thought of clairvoyant visions disturbing, Mr. Burke?"

"Not at all, Mrs. Duncan." Devlin assumed a thoughtful pose, for she was observing him carefully. "I have always made it a point to keep an open mind in all matters of natural and physical science. Some might disagree, but I believe the universe has many secrets, and we have only begun to discover them."

"'There are more things in heaven and earth, Horatio, than are dreamt of in your philosophy.' Would you agree, Mr. Burke?"

Devlin grinned. "Along with the Bard, I do, indeed." Her scrutiny continued, so Devlin strove to be as charming as he knew how, which was considerable. "I realize this is the height of impertinence, Mrs. Duncan, but I would be ever so grateful if you would grant me the favor of answering a few questions. It would only take a few moments of your time. The Willard has an excellent afternoon tea. Would you care to join me?"

Amanda leaned her white gloved hands on the handle of her delicate, blue silk parasol and observed Devlin for a long moment. Devlin couldn't tell if she was considering his suggestion or not. Her expression gave nothing away. He noticed her coachman was eyeing him suspiciously and knew his suggestion bordered on the improper. Bordered, hell! It violated all of Society's rigid rules. Here he was, forcing himself upon a lady in a public street, without being properly introduced, and suggesting she spend the afternoon with him. Grandmother Carrington would be appalled.

To her credit, Devlin noticed that Amanda Duncan hadn't fainted away with shock at the obvious impropriety of his proposal. Somehow, he sensed she wouldn't. Although this stunningly lovely woman appeared every inch a proper Washington lady, she was also a woman who appeared at police stations in the middle of the night and spoke of visions. Most unusual. Devlin gambled that the more daring Mrs. Duncan would grant his request.

"You mentioned family, Mr. Burke. Are you related to Senator Chester?"

"Not at all. I am here visiting my sister and brother-in-law, Winifred and Jonathan Carrington."

"Indeed." An expression of interest crossed her face. "I congratulate you. Jonathan Carrington is one of the few honorable men in the Senate. You are favored by family, Mr. Burke."

Pleased that his credentials had met with her approval, Devlin ventured, "That is why I am here, Mrs. Duncan. It is a matter concerning my family. Our reckless young nephew was unwise enough to become embroiled in one of Senator Chester's nefarious schemes. Unfortunately, he did not take his losses well and publicly chastised Chester. Now, we fear he has become a possible suspect in Inspector Callahan's eyes. That is why I wish to speak with you. I—"

Amanda cut him off, concern clouding her face. "I'm afraid I cannot help you, Mr. Burke. I understand your family's dilemma, but there are others to be considered. If you will excuse me." She abruptly turned to her carriage.

Startled, Devlin stepped forward, ignoring a warning look from her coachman. "Please, Mrs. Duncan, do not dismiss me just yet. Let me explain—"

The coachman blocked any further entreaties as he settled Amanda into her carriage. He shut the door in an authoritative manner before he climbed to his seat above. Amanda leaned her arm on the open carriage window. "I'm sorry, Mr. Burke, but I cannot jeopardize the safety of that young woman who survived. Your nephew could indeed be the villain."

Devlin approached as close as propriety would allow and gazed earnestly at her. "You do not know him, Mrs. Duncan. He is foolish beyond belief, weak-willed, and abysmally stupid at times, but Freddie is no murderer. I swear to you he is not." Devlin thought he glimpsed a spark of compassion in her eyes for one brief moment.

"I wish I could help you, Mr. Burke," she said softly. "But my loyalties are to the young girl. Besides there is nothing I can add to what the police already know. I never saw the face of the murderer in my vision. I am sorry."

With that, she tapped once, and the carriage driver cracked his whip. The coach sped away, leaving Devlin standing on the pavement.

CHAPTER SIX

Devlin stared after the coach as it waited its turn to enter the steady stream of carriages and wagons rumbling along Fifteenth Street. A multitude of unanswered question still buzzed in his head.

Amanda Duncan had been gracious enough to allow his questions under the most improper circumstances. But instead of proceeding cautiously, Devlin had bungled badly. He'd shown only his concern to save Freddie. It was clear Mrs. Duncan's concerns centered on protecting the young girl who survived the attack. And it was obvious from the apprehension he'd glimpsed in her eyes that she wasn't about to divulge any information on the girl.

Damn! He simply had to speak with her again. If for nothing else, then to apologize for his bad manners. But, where to find her? The chief inspector had mentioned she lived on Lafayette Square. If Devlin remembered correctly, that lovely park-like area of Washington sat directly across Pennsylvania Avenue from the President's House. And it was lined on three sides with brick row houses.

Devlin smacked the silver head of his cane into his gloved palm in frustration. He certainly couldn't go knocking door-to-door in that prestigious neighborhood. How would he find her?

His gaze caught the back of Amanda's gray carriage as it lurched into the crowded street traffic, and an idea suddenly came to him. Devlin didn't have to think twice. He rushed to the first hansom cab waiting in line and yanked open the door. Pointing toward the street traffic with his cane, he asked, "Can you follow that gray carriage up ahead, cabbie? It's the one right behind the brewery wagon. I'll make it worth your while."

"Right you are, sir. I've got him in my sites," the cabbie said as he cracked a whip over his horse.

Devlin sat in the hansom cab and watched as Amanda Duncan stepped from her carriage and walked up the black wrought iron steps of her red brick row house. He'd instructed the cabbie to park a little way down H Street so as not to be noticed. He observed the distinctive architectural details of Amanda Duncan's Federal style home, the decorative trim above the windows and door. Then the front door opened and Mrs. Duncan disappeared inside.

Deciding not to delay lest he talk himself out of this even-more-improper act, Devlin withdrew a large bill from his wallet and exited the cab. The cabbie exclaimed his gratitude as Devlin headed toward the trim row house. Meanwhile, he rehearsed some rational explanation for following Amanda Duncan to her home. Discarding one reason after another, Devlin decided to rely on his instinct because it had never led him astray. He heaved the brass doorknocker twice.

After only a few seconds, the door opened to reveal a petite woman clad in a housemaid's long black dress and white frilled apron. A ruffled white lace cap held back her grey curls. Her bright, bird-like gaze swept over Devlin quickly.

"And who might you be, sir?" she asked in a heavy Irish brogue. Somehow, the elderly woman managed to look down her nose at Devlin even though she barely reached his chest.

Devlin smiled his most charming smile, hoping to thaw the diminutive servant's frosty attitude. "Good afternoon, madam. My name is Devlin Burke. Your mistress, Amanda Duncan, and I spoke earlier this morning regarding some business. Would you be so kind as to inquire if Mrs. Duncan has a moment to receive me? I have but one question to ask, and I promise I will be brief."

Devlin watched the frost turn to ice on the little maid's face. Her wrinkles froze in place. Once again, his British accent had sealed his fate. These American Irish seemed determined to dislike him.

"And what sort of business would you be discussin' with my mistress, if you don't mind my askin'?" she inquired in a frigid tone.

Actually, Devlin did mind, but knew enough not to let on. He reached inside his vest pocked and, with a flourish, handed her a calling card. "I am the financial advisor to my brother, the Earl of Devonshire and am here in Washington to oversee my family's investments. And to visit with my sister who is married to Jonathan Carrington, the junior senator from Maryland." Devlin hoped his favorable family connections would save him. Otherwise, the little maid might not allow him entry.

The maid frowned as she read the card. "Wait right here while I ask. . ." Pausing, she turned her head as if listening. "Are you certain, madam?" she called behind her. Another pause. Then the maid turned to Devlin, and with an aggrieved sigh, opened the door to allow him entry. She held out her hand for his hat. "The parlor is down the hall and to your right, sir." Devlin couldn't miss the emphasis she placed on the word.

He gave her a gracious nod as well as his hat and strode down the hallway before the maid changed her mind. Devlin spied Amanda Duncan standing in the parlor, waiting for him. At least she wasn't scowling. He took that as a good sign and gave her his most gentlemanly bow.

"Mrs. Duncan, you are incredibly kind to receive me. Let me first apologize for my earlier breach of propriety. My concern for my nephew allowed me to temporarily forget my good manners, and for that, I am sincerely sorry."

"You are forgiven, Mr. Burke. We all go to great lengths to protect our families," Amanda said, gesturing to a midnight blue armchair. "Please have a seat."

Neither Devlin nor Amanda Duncan had the chance to sit, however, because the little Irish maid swept into the room. She fixed Devlin with a disapproving glare. "What's all this about breaching propriety and forgetting manners? Did this gentleman say something improper to you, madam?"

Devlin held his tongue and waited for Mrs. Duncan's answer. He wasn't about to open his mouth. He'd only put his foot in it.

"Not at all, Bridget," Amanda replied calmly. "He merely asked me a question as I was leaving the station house."

Instead of being appeased, Bridget stared at Devlin, clearly horrified. "Saints preserve us! You mean he approached you on the street without a proper introduction?"

Devlin did his best not to flinch under Bridget's withering glare. He could certainly feel its heat.

Amanda continued as calmly as before, as if she was used to her maid's emotional outbursts. "He did introduce himself, Bridget. And as you heard yourself, Mr. Burke is here in Washington to visit his family and conduct his business." Turning to Devlin, she gestured once more to the armchair. "Would you care for tea, Mr. Burke?"

Devlin gratefully sank into the inviting velvet. "Thank you, Mrs. Duncan. I would love some tea."

"Madam, I must protest," Bridget continued.

"There is no need, Bridget, I assure you. Now, go tell Matilda to prepare a tea tray for us, please," Amanda said, her tone calm, but firm.

Bridget glowered at Devlin once more, but did as she was bid, muttering none too softly, "Lord have mercy upon us all," as she left.

Amanda glanced at Devlin with a smile. "You must forgive my housekeeper. She's been with me since I was an infant. Consequently, she's fiercely protective. I fear I am too lax with her at times, but I simply cannot bring myself to scold her. I hope you weren't offended by her outburst."

"Not at all, Mrs. Duncan. Bridget was entirely in the right. My behavior was inexcusable outside the station house today. I deserved her tongue-lashing."

Amanda observed Devlin for a moment. "You said you had something to ask me, Mr. Burke. I'll be happy to answer if I can, but as I said earlier, I did not see the assailant's face in my vision. Just a shadowy dark figure."

This time Devlin chose his words carefully. "First, let me say that I completely understand your desire to protect the safety of the young girl who survived the attack. And I assure you, I have no intention of jeopardizing that safety. Not at all. I simply want to prove my nephew's innocence. And I thought the two of us could help each other with our mutual concerns."

Amanda looked at him with obvious interest. "How so?"

"You want to protect the girl from further harm, and I want to find the real killer of Senator Chester. If I succeed and the police arrest him, then the young girl will be safe forever."

Mrs. Duncan glanced toward the tall windows. Devlin followed her lead and glimpsed the President's House across the square and the avenue beyond. He also took the opportunity to glance around Amanda Duncan's elegantly appointed parlor. Moss green velvet draped the lace-curtained windows, a rich mahogany writing desk sat beside a corner window, and mahogany tables bordered a deep blue velvet settee. Walnut bookcases filled with volumes lined one wall, and gilt-edged oil paintings adorned the other walls.

"You make a good point, Mr. Burke," she said, returning her attention. "But I'm curious as to how I could help you in your search for Senator Chester's killer."

Devlin took a deep breath before answering. "I propose the two of us work together to search for clues as to this vicious killer's identity. I have a fair amount of detecting skills and have actually helped the constabulary in Devonshire ferret out wrongdoers. And I've interviewed several London investigators over the years. I believe that if we combine my analytical skills with your psychic abilities, we could uncover information that would lead us to the real perpetrator of this crime."

"I do not summon my clairvoyant visions, Mr. Burke. They come unbidden whenever they choose. It is a gift that I receive, not a skill that I have mastered."

"I understand, Mrs. Duncan," Devlin continued, encouraged to see that he'd piqued Amanda Duncan's interest. He could tell from her expression. "But I have been present in London with other clairvoyants and psychics, and sometimes they receive additional visions when they are in the vicinity where a crime took place." He deliberately paused and watched her face. If shock replaced the curiosity, then Devlin knew he'd be ushered out before he even had a chance to drink his tea.

Amanda fixed her gaze on Devlin. "What are you suggesting, Mr. Burke?" she asked in a quiet voice.

Devlin paused before answering, making sure his voice was as calm as hers. "Would you be willing to accompany me to the scene of Senator Chester's murder? Perhaps you could sense something more of the killer's identity."

Amanda stared at Devlin, her eyes wide, not saying a word. Devlin held his breath, praying that she would agree. Her face didn't reveal a trace of emotion, save surprise.

"Are you familiar with the area of Washington where the crime occurred, Mr. Burke?"

"Yes, Mrs. Duncan, I believe it happened in a rather unsavory neighborhood called Murder Bay. Trust me, I shall ensure that you will not be exposed to any disreputable characters. I propose we visit the, uh . . . establishment during the morning hours when the likelihood of the most objectionable persons being present would be considerably—"

"Holy Mother and all the Saints! I cannot believe my ears!" Bridget's sharp voice sliced through the room. The little housekeeper stood in the archway where she'd obviously been listening. "Madam, I knew he was no gentleman! Not at all—at all. To make such a wicked suggestion! He is a *knave*, to be sure. I recognize a rogue when I see one. Even one disguised in expensive Savile Row tailoring."

"Now, Bridget," Amanda soothed.

Devlin had to give Bridget credit. Her eye was as sharp as her tongue. But this time he decided he simply must defend his honor as a gentleman. He leaned forward in the chair, his hand on his breast.

"Mrs. Duncan, I swear to you, my suggestion was entirely innocent of any base motives. I seek only the truth in this tragic event. And I would never expose you to any situations which would cause you distress---"

"*HA!*" Bridget scoffed, fists on her hips.

"Bridget, that is enough," Amanda said in a firm tone. "I believe Mr. Burke's intentions are entirely honorable. His motive is solely to prove his nephew's innocence. He's simply trying to search out the identity of Senator Chester's murderer. And for that, he needs my help."

Bridget turned to her mistress, clearly appalled. "Madam! You cannot be serious. You simply cannot set foot in that wretched area of the city."

"It seems Mr. Burke and I have mutual goals, Bridget. I want to ensure that young girl's future safety. Mr. Burke wants to clear his nephew of police suspicion by finding the real culprit." She glanced to Devlin. "If I help him in that endeavor, then both goals will be assured."

Devlin couldn't believe what he was hearing. Amanda Duncan was obviously considering his suggestion. "Absolutely, Mrs. Duncan—"

Bridget cut him off again. "Madam! Might I remind you that your reputation has already been tarnished by your work with the good Sisters of Saint Anne's. Going with them into those filthy tenements is horrible enough, but this. . ." She gestured wordlessly for a change.

Devlin saw his chance and took it. "Bridget, I assure you that I am sensitive to your mistress's situation. That's why I am proposing that we make this foray as brief as possible and in the early morning hours, when the reprobates are off the streets. Secondly, I suggest that Mrs. Duncan disguise herself by wearing a hooded cloak, which would conceal her identity from all curious eyes."

Bridget was apparently taken by surprise at Devlin's suggestion. However, he glimpsed a hint of a smile from Amanda Duncan.

"You see, Bridget. Mr. Burke's intentions are completely above board. Plus, he has made an eminently practical suggestion. I have decided to help him with his investigation." She glanced to Devlin. "When do you suggest we make this trek into the nether regions, Mr. Burke? I have tomorrow morning free."

"Tomorrow would be perfect, Mrs. Duncan," Devlin replied, elated at her cooperation. Glancing to a clearly fuming Bridget, he decided it would be wise to provide insurance. So he addressed the outraged housekeeper. "Why don't you accompany us, Bridget? That way you will be able to assist me in my efforts to protect your mistress. The two of us will provide a formidable defense against any and all reprobates."

Clearly taken aback, Bridget stared at him, then her mistress.

"That's an excellent idea," Amanda chimed in. "You'll come with us, won't you, Bridget?"

Straightening herself taller, Bridget regained some of her bluster. "Of course, I will, madam."

"Excellent. It is settled, then." Devlin spied another servant approach bearing a silver tray. Afternoon tea.

"Thank you, Matilda," Amanda said to the woman with skin the color of honey. "Your timing is perfect. Mr. Burke and I have just negotiated a challenging business venture."

"Hmmmmh!" Bridget gave a derisive shrug, then went to clear a place for the tray. There, she busied herself with the tea service.

Once Amanda and Devlin had both been served, Amanda held up her cup to Devlin and smiled. "Congratulations on a successful negotiation, Mr. Burke."

Devlin responded in kind. "To diplomacy, Mrs. Duncan."

CHAPTER SEVEN

Amanda peered at the brick row houses and buildings lining Thirteenth Street as their hired hansom passed by slowly. They looked no different from many street blocks in Washington, save for dirtier windows and lack of paint on the shops. Morning had dawned cloudy and chilly, which made Amanda grateful for the wool cloak Bridget dug from the back of the closet.

Devlin's prediction proved true. No reprobates could be seen on the streets. The only citizens Amanda spied walking about were laborers, washerwomen, peddlers and deliverymen.

"There, near the corner," Bridget announced triumphantly, pointing through the other coach window. "A red pitchfork, you say? I say it's the sign of the Devil himself."

Amanda spotted the crude red-painted pitchfork on the door to the Devil's Eye tavern. The tavern's dingy glass had the words "Beer and Spirits" in faded blue paint.

Devlin rapped on the side of the coach with his cane. "Pull in front, cabbie," he ordered. The cabbie pulled to a stop directly in front of the tavern. Devlin exited quickly as the cabbie handed over the dismount stool.

"Let me assist you, Bridget," Devlin said, extending his hand.

Ignoring him, Bridget pulled a ladies scarf from the pocket of her coat and turned to Amanda. "Here, my dear. Let me wrap this around you so none of these degenerates can catch a glimpse of how pretty you are." She proceeded to wind the silk scarf around Amanda's neck and face.

"I won't be able to breathe, Bridget," Amanda said in muffled protest as the silk covered the lower half of her face. "The hood will be sufficient."

Bridget finished wrapping the scarf and tied it snugly at the back of Amanda's neck. "Now, that's better. We don't want these wretches getting any ideas and following you home." Then, refusing assistance, she alighted from the coach. "I'm fine, Mr. Burke. See to my mistress, instead."

Amanda didn't bother to reply. She simply pulled up the hood of her cloak and allowed Devlin to help her from the coach.

"An excellent idea, Bridget. Suitably swathed in wool, no one can glimpse your mistress." Devlin ushered both women to the sidewalk before approaching the driver. Reaching into his vest pocket, Devlin pulled out his wallet. "Now, my good man, could you kindly point out the other establishment I spoke to you about earlier?"

The cabbie glanced from Devlin to Amanda and back again, then he sheepishly pointed to the drab row house adjacent to the Devil's Eye. "That's the place, sir."

Devlin handed over a large bill. "And would the proprietor, Quinn, be on the premises; do you know?"

The cabbie shrugged. "Should be. He's always around somewheres."

"I will pay double that amount if you wait for us while we conduct our business."

The cabbie's eyes lit up. "Yes sir. I'll be here."

Devlin approached Amanda and Bridget again. "I think it would be best if you two ladies stay behind me while I inquire about this Quinn fellow." He shepherded them towards the foot of the row house's front steps.

Amanda watched as Devlin hastened up the steps and rapped on the scarred wooden door with his cane. There was no response. Amanda glimpsed a woman approach on the sidewalk, carrying a large empty basket on her hip. She wore a bright print kerchief around her head and a worn apron, which was still white despite its obvious wear.

After a minute, Devlin rapped on the door again and waited. Again, there was no response.

The washerwoman stopped a few feet from Amanda, glanced at her then at Devlin, who was scanning the street, clearly impatient. "If yer lookin' fer Joey Quinn, he ain't awake yet," she called to Devlin. "I know that fer a fact, cuz I do his washing."

Amanda stepped forward. "Is there anyone else in the house who is awake?"

The middle-aged woman squinted at her and leaned forward. "What was that again? I couldn't hear you, ma'am."

Amanda was about to dispense with the silk mask when Devlin bounded down the steps. "Thank you, madam. We'd appreciate your help. Do you know if there's anyone else in the residence we could speak with?" Once again, he reached for his wallet and withdrew some large bills. "It would be well worth their time, I assure you."

The woman's pale blue eyes grew to the size of silver dollars. "Lord have mercy," she exclaimed, staring at the money. "I'll be glad to find out for you, sir."

"Thank you, madam. I appreciate your assistance," he said and handed her a large denomination.

The laundry woman stared at the bill, turning it over in her hands, then looked up at Devlin, her face looking younger than before. "Thank you, sir! I'll go wake him up meself if I have to." With that, she stuffed the bill into the front of her blouse then scurried down the sidewalk to a narrow passageway and disappeared between buildings.

Amanda moved the silk enough to speak clearly. "You don't know how much you helped that woman, Mr. Burke. A washerwoman earns only pennies a day for back-breaking work."

"Oh, but I do, Mrs. Duncan. I have seen the misery of the London slums firsthand. I imagine those in Washington are equally wretched." He caught her gaze. "But then, I gather from Bridget's earlier statement that you have first-hand knowledge of that, yourself. I commend you, Mrs. Duncan. There are too few people who actively try to help the less fortunate. Save for the pennies they put in the collection box on Sunday."

Surprised by his statement, Amanda was about to reply when Devlin's raised hand cut her off. The sound of loud voices could be heard coming from the partially open door above.

"Time to swathe yourself again, Mrs. Duncan. I sense the promise of reward has roused this Quinn. Stay here, please, while I deal with him." Devlin sped up the steps again just as the front door opened.

A swarthy, unshaven man stood in the entryway. He pulled his trousers' suspenders over his grey undershirt and surveyed Devlin. "I'm Joey Quinn. I hear yer lookin' fer me. What is it ya want?"

Quinn's gaze swept over Amanda, and she felt chilled despite the wool.

Devlin withdrew more bills from his wallet. Quinn stared at them with a practiced eye, counting. "I was told by the police inspector that Senator Chester met his demise in your establishment last week. I would very much like to inspect the room where he expired, if I may." Devlin held the bills closer to Quinn's face. Close enough to smell.

Instead of grabbing the money as Amanda expected, Quinn scowled at Devlin instead. "You with the police or something? I already told them everything I know."

"This is a family affair," Devlin said in a reassuring tone. "It has nothing to do with the police."

"What do you want to see the room fer? We just got it cleaned up again. Ain't nothing to see."

Devlin nodded his head toward Amanda and Bridget. "I'm accompanying members of the family who simply want to see where their loved one died so tragically. They're hoping it will bring them some peace." His tone had become solicitous.

Quinn eyed Amanda and Bridget again. "All right. You can go on up and take a look." He snatched the bills from Devlin, counted them quickly, then stuffed them in his pocket as he stepped into the foyer. Gesturing for them to follow, he yelled up the stairs. "Everybody stay in yer rooms, ya hear? We've got visitors!"

Devlin raced down the front steps and offered Amanda his arm. Bridget, however, stalked up the steps quickly, sturdy umbrella raised in ready position. Quinn stared at the belligerent housekeeper, puzzled. However, his expression changed as Amanda entered the foyer.

Quinn screwed up his face. Pointing toward Amanda's silk mask, he demanded, "Here, now. What's wrong with her? She sick or something? I can't risk my girls catching anything."

Devlin's cane swatted Quinn's arm away quickly. "Do not insult the lady. She's merely overcome with grief. That is all."

Amanda placed her gloved hand over her mouth and bent her head, making muffled tearful sounds.

Quinn rubbed his arm and scowled at Amanda and Devlin again. "All right. You can come in fer a few minutes, that's all." He started toward the rickety looking wooden staircase against the wall. "Follow me."

Bridget led the way, umbrella *en garde*.

"Well, done, Mrs. Duncan," Devlin whispered over Amanda's ear as they followed in Bridget's wake.

Amanda worked the silk looser. "Thank you, Mr. Burke. I sensed Mr. Quinn needed further persuasion."

Quinn led them down a narrow hallway, its dingy clapboard walls broken on both sides by closed wooden doors. Amanda assumed they were all bedrooms. There was a sweet smell detected. Stale perfume. Her heart was beating rapidly at the thought of being in a place like this. A brothel in the midst of Murder Bay. The same sort of place Sister Bernice spoke of with such fear and trepidation. Amanda couldn't believe how ordinary it looked. No different from many of the rooming houses she'd visited with the good Sisters.

She glimpsed someone peering through a crack in the doorway as they passed. Amanda turned to look, but the door closed swiftly. There were five rooms on this floor alone. How many were below? Were there women behind every door?

Quinn stopped at the end of the hall and opened the door to a room. "This is it. I'll give you five minutes to pay yer respects." He waved them inside.

Devlin waved another bill beneath Quinn's nose. "We'll need ten minutes at least, maybe more. The bereaved wishes to say some prayers."

Quinn grabbed the bill and rolled his eyes. "All right, all right, just don't get loud and carry on, ya hear?"

Devlin ushered Bridget and Amanda into the barren room. He began to slowly walk around, while Bridget positioned herself near the door. The better to keep an eye on Quinn. Amanda stepped farther into the room, surveyed the frame bed with flimsy counterpane, a small washstand with pitcher in the corner, and battered wardrobe against the wall. She stared at the bed and the floor. No sign of blood as she had seen in her vision. In fact, a shaft of sunshine fell across the floor now. No darkness. All signs of murder had been wiped away.

But Amanda could still feel it. A strange chill rippled through her. She walked around the room. The feeling got stronger. She approached the bed. The chill clutched at her inside now. Amanda quickly stepped away.

Her heart was pounding. She turned her back to the door. Quinn was watching them intently, leaning against the doorjamb, arms folded. Amanda removed her gloves and yanked the silk from her face. She needed to catch her breath. She felt hot despite the chill.

Devlin bent down and picked up something small from the floor. He examined it for a moment. "It looks like one of your clientele lost a button. It appears to be from a uniform. There's an insignia and the letters 'USA.'"

"Probably from an Army uniform. Some of the old soldiers still wear them now and then," Quinn observed.

"That's strange. It's been twenty-five years since your war ended," Devlin said, walking toward Amanda. "Strange that the veterans would still wear their uniforms."

"Naw, it ain't," Quinn said, shaking his head. "They wear 'em whenever they come marchin' on the Capitol. Got an increase in pay last time they did."

Devlin stood right in front of Amanda, blocking Quinn's view. "Did you sense anything more, Mrs. Duncan?" he whispered.

"I felt a chill, that is all." Amanda met his concerned gaze. "But the closer to the bed I got, the more intense the feeling became. It was almost as if I felt their . . . their fear."

"Well, this button must be from the uniform you saw in your later vision, Mrs. Duncan. Examine it yourself." Devlin placed it in her palm.

Amanda held the brass button, and touched it with the tip of her finger. Suddenly a new sensation rushed through her. She caught her breath as the murder vividly flashed before her eyes again. The images tumbled one after another. The shadowy killer falling upon the Senator, slashing away. The girl screaming, the killer racing from the room. But this time, the images continued. The killer racing from the room, down the stairs, crashing through the crowds and past a tavern, bumping into a man with a gold tooth who yelled after him. The killer running until he reaches a broad avenue. Carriages, and then nothing. The vivid images disappeared as quickly as they came. Suddenly Amanda felt dizzy, lightheaded, and grabbed Devlin for support.

"Mrs. Duncan, are you all right?" Devlin grabbed her arm, clearly concerned. "You had another vision, didn't you?"

"Yes, but stronger than before," Amanda whispered. "New images this time. I saw the murderer run into a man in the street. He had a gold tooth." She pulled herself straight. "Forgive me; I don't know what came over me."

Devlin released her. "I do. It was the button that conjured up these new images. I've seen it happen in London with other gifted psychics."

"Madam, are you all right?" Bridget asked, rushing up.

"Here now, what's the matter with her?" Quinn barked. "You told me she wasn't sick."

Devlin held up his hand. "There's nothing wrong. The lady was simply grieving, that's all."

Amanda pulled up her silken mask again. "We may leave now. I have finished my prayers," she said, loud enough for Quinn to hear.

"As you wish, madam." Devlin offered his arm and escorted Amanda from the room.

"It's about time," Quinn growled as he led them down the hallway.

Amanda glimpsed two doorways ajar this time. One was open more than a crack, and she spied a woman with bright reddish hair staring at her. Amanda caught her gaze for a brief second before the woman closed the door.

"Where was the man with the gold tooth?" Devlin asked as they descended the stairs.

"He appeared to be outside in the street, near a tavern. The attacker rushed down some stairs and ran into him."

Quinn stood beside the front door and made a grand gesture outside. "Glad to be of service," he said with a sneer.

Bridget scowled at him once before stalking out, umbrella up and ready should Quinn make a false move.

"What's she so angry about?" Quinn jerked his head toward the departing housekeeper.

Devlin reached for his wallet again. "Tell me, Mr. Quinn, I assume there are stairs leading to the street from that room above, right?"

"There may be," Quinn eyed the bills Devlin counted out.

Devlin waved two large denominations before Quinn's face. "And would you happen to know a tavern-goer who has a gold tooth, perchance?"

"Maybe, maybe not."

"Was it a gold tooth or a missing tooth, madam?" Devlin asked.

"I saw a large gold tooth in the front of his mouth," Amanda said, clearly.

Quinn's eyes narrowed. "Say, who are you? Are you one of them witchy women who see things, or something? You get out of here right—"

Devlin slammed Quinn against the door before he could finish his sentence. Shoving his cane under Quinn's chin so hard his eyes began to bulge, Devlin leaned into his face. "How dare you insult this lady," he rasped. "Apologize this second or I'll thrash you within an inch of your life."

Clearly terrified at Devlin's threat, Quinn tried to speak but couldn't. Devlin moved the cane away. Quinn choked out an apology. "I. . .I. . . apologize. . .madam. . .no offense."

"That's better," Devlin leaned back but kept his fist on Quinn's chest, holding him against the door. "Now, do you know a tavern-goer with a gold tooth or not?"

Quinn coughed twice before answering. "Yeah. . .that's gotta be. . .Smitty. You can find him at the. . .Devil's Eye every night."

"Thank you," Devlin said in a cold voice. Then he tossed two bills on the floor and extended his arm to Amanda.

Amanda glanced over her shoulder once more and caught sight of the redheaded woman standing at the top of the stairs. Amanda wasn't sure, but she thought she spotted her smiling.

"Let us get you into the carriage, Mrs. Duncan, and safely back to Lafayette Square," Devlin said as they approached the sidewalk. "I will seek out this Smitty fellow at the tavern tonight."

Amanda saw the cabbie holding the door as Bridget scrambled inside. She turned to Devlin as he was about to help her into the carriage and yanked off the scarf. "Make sure you ask him if he caught sight of the man's face. I sense he did. The villain ran into him and nearly knocked him over. I think this Smitty called after him, too."

"Rest assured I will interrogate Smitty thoroughly. If he knows something, I will find it out," Devlin promised as he helped Amanda step into the carriage.

The cabbie slammed the door and climbed back into his seat above. Amanda leaned out the window and smiled at Devlin. "I believe you will, Mr. Burke. Your methods are quite persuasive, if a bit unorthodox."

Devlin acknowledged her compliment with a smile and a nod. "Thank you, Mrs. Duncan. That reprobate deserved nothing less."

"I wish I could accompany you this evening, perhaps I could sense something else," she said, surprised at her own comment.

"Madam!" Bridget gasped, clearly appalled. "You can't be serious! One excursion into this cesspool is sufficient."

Devlin grinned. "I quite agree, Bridget. Your mistress should stay safe at home with you. You've done more than enough, Mrs. Duncan. There would be no one to interrogate without your clairvoyant information." Tipping his cane to his hat, he backed away from the coach. "Take them to 1510 H Street, cabbie. Straight away, mind you."

"Aye, sir," the cabbie said, grabbing the reins.

The coach rumbled into the traffic on D Street, turned around, then drove onto Thirteenth Street again. A brief ray of sunlight filtered through the window and onto her rose taffeta gown. Spring was being capricious this year. Flitting between warm and cool, flirting and teasing.

Amanda leaned back against the cushions. She was tired for some reason. Tired and exhilarated at the same time. Amanda didn't know what to make of it. She'd never felt like that before. Perhaps it was the knowledge that she was contributing to the search for this vicious killer. That was new. Inspector Callahan had always dismissed any information she brought to him. All those trips to the police station these past three years had been for naught. But, now. . .now the information her visions brought forward was being taken seriously. At last. She was finally using her gifts as she was destined to.

"I'll have Matilda make us some tea as soon as we return, madam. And perhaps there's a sliver of her apple pie. Oh, delicious, it was. Would you like that, madam?"

"Yes, pie would be fine, Bridget," Amanda replied, barely listening. The coach had turned onto Pennsylvania Avenue and out of the edges of Murder Bay. Amanda took in a deep breath of crisp spring air and admired the bright red tulips and purple crocus edging a garden nearby. It was like she was seeing them for the first time.

CHAPTER EIGHT

"That's him, that's Smitty," the bartender said to Devlin, leaning over the scarred wooden bar top. He pointed to a heavy-set balding man, a fringe of black hair ringing his head.

Devlin eyed the man who entered the crowded Devil's Eye tavern. It was hard to see through the smoke haze and the dim light. Several men standing at the end of the bar greeted Smitty with backslaps and laughter. Unfortunately, Smitty had his back turned to Devlin so no teeth, gold or otherwise, were visible.

"Thank you," Devlin said and surreptitiously handed the bartender a large bill. The bartender glanced over his shoulder and swiftly pocketed it. Devlin drained his glass of the local Heurich's dark beer then slid the man another bill across the smooth wooden surface of the bar. "Could you please tell Smitty I'd like to speak to him?"

The bartender dropped the white towel he'd been using to wipe the bar over the money before he pocketed it. "Consider it done, sir," He proceeded to wind his way through the men crowded around the bar stools and tables. The patrons had left Devlin standing alone at the end of the bar. Every now and then, someone would glance curiously Devlin's way. Devlin could feel their gazes even when he didn't see them.

Devlin watched the bartender approach Smitty, lean over and speak to him, pointing in Devlin's direction. Smitty looked Devlin over, then hitched up his trousers and approached.

"Ya want to talk to me, do ya?" he demanded with a skeptical look. A large gold tooth shone in Smitty's top row of teeth.

"Indeed, I do, sir," Devlin said, in his friendliest tone. "I'd like to ask you some questions, if I may. And I'll gladly make it worth your while." He reached inside his jacket and partially revealed his wallet.

Smitty's skeptical look disappeared. "I guess that would be all right. What do ya want to know?"

"Why don't we step outside where it's quieter, all right?" Devlin suggested, moving away from the bar.

"If it suits ya," Smitty said, following Devlin to the door.

Stepping out into the cold spring night, Devlin drew a deep breath. The crisp air filled his lungs, clearing away the haze of cheap cigar smoke. He gestured Smitty away from the groups of men clustering near the tavern entrance.

Smitty stood across from him and folded his arms across his chest. "Okay, we're outside now. So, whaddya want to know?"

"Do you recall the night that Senator Horace Chester was murdered in the bordello next door?" Devlin pointed toward Quinn's establishment beside the tavern. Two men were climbing the steps.

"I sure do. Half the cops in the District were crawling all over the place."

"Did they happen to ask you any questions?" Devlin kept his interest in check.

Smitty screwed up his face. "I ain't talking to no cops. Why should I help them catch that guy."

"So, you didn't see anything, then."

"I didn't say that. I just said I ain't talking to no cops."

Devlin's pulse sped up. "Did you see someone? Someone running away from that house, perhaps?"

He peered at Devlin. "Maybe, maybe not."

Devlin withdrew his trusty wallet and brought out two large denomination bills. Smitty's eyes grew wider in the dark. "Could you please tell me what you saw?" He held the bills in front of him, tempting Smitty.

Smitty looked from Devlin's face to the bills and back again. "He came running down the backstairs outta that room Joey keeps upstairs.

The bastard ran right into me. I yelled after him but he kept running." Smitty pointed down D Street.

Devlin handed over the bills, which Smitty fondled before pocketing them. "Did you get a good look at him?"

"Maybe," Smitty tempted, a larcenous smile on his face.

Once again, Devlin reached for his wallet, withdrew four large bills and fanned them. "These are all yours if you'll tell me everything you saw and heard."

Smitty's eyes lit up. "He was tall and black haired. His face was dark, but funny like. Kind of like he'd smeared something on his face. And he wore an Army uniform. I recognized the same medal on it that my father had on his uniform. Infantry. And a ribbon for Antietam, too. Can't forget that."

Elated at the new information, Devlin handed over the money. "Thank you kindly, Smitty. You've been very helpful."

"Anytime," Smitty said, counting the bills.

Devlin raced around the corner and headed up Thirteenth Street. More people were on the streets now, laughing, talking loudly. He could catch a hansom on Pennsylvania. Devlin couldn't wait to tell Winnie and Jonathan what he'd learned.

"Dev, darling, you smell absolutely dreadful. Wherever have you been?" Winnie demanded when Devlin approached her in the library doorway. She fanned the air in front of her face.

"Forgive me, Winnie, I was ferreting out information on Senator Chester's demise and my search took me to an unsavory area of the city."

Jonathan rose from his chair beside the fireplace, his evening jacket already discarded and his silk cravat loosened. Winnie, however, was still dressed in her dinner gown. "Out sleuthing, I <u>knew</u> it," he crowed as he approached, crystal glass in hand. An amber liquid sloshed invitingly in the glass.

Devlin thought he scented a fine whiskey and was about to ask for some when Winnie leaned over and sniffed him again. She screwed up her pretty face.

"Cigar smoke," Winnie decreed. "And not very good cigars, either. Jameson take his coat immediately and hang it outside. This foul odor will give us all a headache."

"Yes, madam. If you will allow me, sir," Jameson said, barely waiting for Devlin to cooperate before removing his jacket.

"Really, Winnie," Jonathan said with a chuckle. "Let your brother relax for a minute before you start fumigating him. I for one am anxious to hear of his adventures this evening. I'm sure they were far more interesting than our dinner with the tea totaling Midwesterners."

Winnie reached over and pulled off Devlin's tie with a practiced flick of her wrist. Most impressive. Devlin wasn't about to tell his sister about the other women he'd met who had similar talents.

"Well, it has been an adventurous evening," Devlin said, following Jonathan into the library. Winnie was still fanning the air behind him. "And I'd love a glass of whatever you're drinking." He sank into the nearest armchair.

Winnie fanned the air for a moment longer before settling into her chair beside the fireplace opposite Jonathan. A small sherry glass sat beside her.

"My mother's family is from Kentucky, you know. This aged bourbon is our private stock," Jonathan said as he handed Devlin a half-filled glass. "Now, that will rinse the stale beer taste from your mouth."

"How could you tell?" Devlin quipped as he sniffed the rich bourbon's aroma.

"Only a cheap tavern would have both. Now, tell us where you were sleuthing before we both die of curiosity."

Devlin made them wait while he savored the bourbon's smooth burn. "A cheap tavern in the heart of Murder Bay."

Winnie gasped, nearly spilling her sherry. "Devlin! Really?" Her shocked expression quickly changed to curiosity. "What was it like?"

"Singularly dreary. And depressing," Devlin said after a cleansing sip. "Earlier in the day, I'd gotten the owner of the bordello where Chester died to allow me to look around the room."

This time Winnie's jaw dropped in a most unladylike fashion. "*You didn't!*" she exclaimed when she could speak.

"Oh, but I did," Devlin said with a wicked smile.

"Winnie, darling, either put the sherry down or drink it before you spill it on your gown." Jonathan laughed, clearly enjoying his wife's reactions. "I'm surprised the scoundrel allowed you in, Devlin."

"It took a fair amount of financial persuasion before he did."

Winnie drained her small glass and leaned forward in the armchair. "What was it like, Devlin? Were there women there? Did you see them?"

Devlin grinned. "What an unseemly curiosity you have, dear Winnie. You haven't changed a bit since we were children."

"Stop teasing this minute, Dev, or I'll have Jameson take *all* your clothes," Winnie threatened.

"What's all this?" Jonathan asked.

Devlin gestured to his younger sister. "When we were children, Winnie would demand that I tell her all the scrapes that my friends and I would get into. And if I refused, she'd slip into my room when I wasn't there and take all of my clothes. She'd hide them in the garden. In the dustbin. Anywhere. And the insolent wench wouldn't give them to me until she had her way."

Jonathan threw back his head and laughed. "What a minx you were," Jonathan said after he'd laughed loudly.

"Oh, she was worse than that," Devlin countered. "She'd get into mischief and blame it on me. It did me no good to accuse her, because no one believed me."

"That's because you were always up to far worse mischief," Winnie said with a complacent smile.

"Naughty girl, Winnie," Jonathan teased.

"Not at all. I was the angel. Dev was the 'devilish' one," she quipped. Jonathan and Devlin both groaned.

"Now, tell us, Dev. Did you see any women in that house of ill repute?" Winnie demanded again.

Devlin took another sip. "I did not see any, but I'm sure they were there. Quinn yelled out for everyone to stay inside their rooms before... before I followed him upstairs." Devlin caught himself before he let slip the word "we."

"Did you find any clues, Dev?" Jonathan asked, serious again.

"The room was bare and had obviously been cleaned, for there were no vestiges of murder. But I did find a button wedged into a floor crack. And Quinn identified it as coming from an Army uniform."

"But wouldn't that make the murderer fairly old?" Jonathan asked, puzzled.

"If the murderer were indeed a veteran of their war. But I imagine there are a lot of uniforms in closets all around Washington City."

"I'm afraid that clue doesn't prove much. The newspapers already said the police had found a uniform."

Devlin savored the bourbon for a minute, debating how to reveal the role Amanda played in his investigation. "That would be true under normal circumstances. But fortunately, I had access to extraordinary information."

Winnie's brows shot up at that. "I've seen that look before, Devlin. And you only use that term when you refer to information you've gained from those psychic friends of yours."

Devlin had to give his younger sister credit. She had a razor sharp mind as well as memory. And she didn't miss a trick. "I never could keep secrets from you, Winnie," he lied with a disarming smile.

"Are you serious, Devlin?" Jonathan leaned forward, matching Winnie's pose. "Have you contacted someone to help you here in Washington?"

"Who was it? Did someone come down from New York?" Winnie continued to probe.

"Yes and no," Devlin couldn't resist teasing. Watching Winnie roll her eyes, he continued. "No, I did not contact any of my friends in New York. I met a gifted clairvoyant here in Washington who had a vision of the grisly murder right after it happened. She alerted the police, but in their ignorance, they paid no heed to her information."

Winnie sat up straighter, and Devlin braced himself for the coming interrogation.

"A woman psychic, you say. Fascinating," Jonathan said, before draining his glass.

Winnie launched herself from the armchair and flew straight as a hawk to the footstool beside Devlin. He had to laugh at her expression—part shock, park intense curiosity.

"Who is she, Dev? Tell us now, or I swear I won't leave you a stitch to wear. Your Saville Row suits will go to the coachman."

Jonathan chuckled. "Winnie, let him draw a breath."

"Well, I was going to protect her privacy. . ."

"Dev!"

"But in the interest of protecting my tailored wardrobe, I'll reveal her identity. On the condition that you both swear you'll keep the lady's privacy. It's my understanding that she has already suffered Society's slights because she has chosen to use her gifts to help others."

"Ahhhh, I believe I heard mention of something to that effect," Jonathan mused.

Clearly fascinated, Winnie leaned forward. "I swear I shall not reveal a word, Devlin. Now, tell me, please. Do I know her? Is she from a Washington family? Are they in the Congress? Are they diplomats?"

"That I do not know yet, but I imagine Jonathan can help with those details. But I recognize a lady when I meet one, and Amanda Duncan is every inch a lady of refinement. When I learned from the police commissioner of Mrs. Duncan's abilities, I dashed over to her home on Lafayette Square and begged her housekeeper for a few minutes of her mistress's time. Mrs. Duncan was kind enough to receive me."

"Lafayette Square, you say? How close to Saint John's Church?" Winnie asked.

"If she is the lady I heard mentioned, she lives only a stone's throw from the church," Jonathan added.

"Do you know of her, Jonathan?" Winnie asked, peering at her husband. "What have you heard?"

"Very little. Only that she's from a prominent Washington family and lost her husband and young child in a train wreck a few years ago. Apparently, she 'saw' the wreck ahead of time, but her husband refused to believe her warnings. Alas, he and the child both died."

Winnie drew back, hand to her breast. "That's horrible! How dreadful. . .to be able to see something about to happen and not be able to save her loved ones. She must have been heartbroken."

Devlin swirled the whiskey in his glass, allowing his sister's comment to sink in. Winnie, as always, had gone to the emotional heart of the matter. Amanda Duncan's grief over losing her family so tragically must have been a turning point in her life.

Jonathan broke the somber mood. "From what little I've heard, that's precisely why the Widow Duncan removed herself, so to speak, from Washington Society. Apparently, after mourning her family for two years, she stopped attending social functions entirely. Senator Jefferson told me she's devoted her life to helping the less fortunate in the city through charitable works. I've heard she even helps the Catholic Sisters in their work in the tenements."

"How extraordinary," Winnie said, clearly impressed.

"Did Mrs. Duncan see the murderer's face in this. . .this vision you spoke of?" Jonathan probed.

"Alas, she did not," Devlin shook his head and took a sip. "But when I brought the button I found in the bordello, it brought on another vision, and she saw the killer escape out a back door and run into a tavern-goer in the street. A man with a gold tooth. Hence, my visit to the tavern tonight."

"Fascinating," Winnie breathed. "Did she have the vision right in front of you, Dev?"

He finished off the whiskey. "Yes, she did, and it was extraordinary. She had no idea she possessed psychometric gifts, but I recognized them from accompanying other gifted London psychics in their investigations."

"However were you able to identify one man in a crowded tavern?" Jonathan asked as he walked to the library's liquor cabinet.

"Ahhhh, that's because I used Mrs. Duncan's information to inter-rogate the brothel owner, Quinn. Again, he supplied the man's name and where I might find him. For a price."

"So, Mrs. Duncan gave you the clue to find the man in the tavern who saw the killer escape, correct?" Winnie summarized.

"Did you find the man, Devlin?" Jonathan asked, as he refilled Devlin's glass.

"Of course, he did," Winnie answered before Devlin had a chance. "Otherwise, he wouldn't be sitting here smiling like the Cheshire cat. He'd be all somber and quiet."

"You know me too well, dear sister," Devlin replied before tasting the whiskey. "Consider yourself fortunate, Jonathan, that you did not have a razor-sharp younger sister who excelled in analyzing your every mood."

"Ah, yes, but I married her, remember?" Jonathan said with a chuckle as he sipped his family's prized whiskey. "I swear Winnie can read my mind. It's positively unnerving."

"Now, you know why I'm a confirmed bachelor," Devlin said, raising his glass to her and joining in Jonathan's laughter.

"Let's get back to the tavern-goer," Winnie said, clearly refusing to be distracted. "What did you learn from him, Devlin? Did he see the killer?"

"Most definitely. The culprit ran right into the man and he got a good look at him. Unfortunately, the killer had smeared something on his face, to disguise himself, no doubt. But Smitty did recognize several medals on the Army uniform. But, as I said, there are probably thou-sands of uniforms hanging in closets throughout the city." Devlin took a deep drink this time.

Jonathan spoke. "What will you do now, Devlin?"

Devlin pondered for a moment. "I think I'll follow up on your sug-gestion and pay a visit to Senator Sherwood Steele. Considering he's the one with the most to gain from Senator Chester's death, I'd like to take a measure of the man."

"I can help you with that. I'll stop in Steele's office tomorrow morn-ing and ask his secretary to make an appointment for you." Jonathan took a deep sip of the whiskey. "Now that Steele's advanced to the

Chairmanship of the Commerce Committee, he will be the recipient of any and all bribes to learn which tariff legislation will survive the committee. Men are willing to pay dearly for that information, because they can make a fortune on Wall Street with it."

"Privileged information is always devoutly to be wished," Devlin said.

"Plus, there is something even more important being considered. Crucial regulatory legislation is presently before the committee. Antitrust legislation. Many have much to lose if that bill becomes law."

Devlin sipped his whiskey, then mused over his glass. "And some might resort to murder to make sure it doesn't."

CHAPTER NINE

"I'm so glad you stopped in, Amanda. Francie is doing much better. She was actually talking with Sister Rosemarie who stayed with her last night," Sister Beatrice said, beckoning Amanda inside the convent foyer.

"I'm so glad to hear that," Amanda said, following the nun down the convent hallway.

"In fact, Father Tom told the police detective that Francie was doing better. Detective Donnolly came by this morning to ask her some questions."

Amanda's pulse began to race. "Did Francie remember anything about the night of the murder?"

The little nun paused in front of a door at the back of the hallway. Two sisters hurried past them, their voluminous white robes rustling softly. Amanda nodded to both as they passed.

"She remembered a few things, but I'm afraid the sheer terror of the attack kept her from remembering it all. Which may be a blessing," Beatrice said as she opened the door.

Amanda followed after her. The small bedroom was barren except for the bed where the young dark-haired girl lay. An oil lamp sat on a wooden table beside the bed. A rosary lay beside the lamp. Francie looked first at Sister Beatrice, then Amanda with a surprised expression.

"Francie, you're looking more rested, my dear," Beatrice said with a smile. "Did you take a short nap after Inspector Donnolly's visit?"

"Yes, Sister," Francie said in a breathy whisper.

Francie's neck was wrapped with strips of white cotton, and Amanda spied only a trace of blood edging the bandages. So much better than the blood-soaked bandages she'd seen when Francie was first brought to the convent. Her skinny little body looked so frail as she lay on the metal frame bed.

Sister Beatrice sat on the bed and patted Francie's arm. "I wanted you to meet someone else who's been watching over you. This is Amanda, and she's a tremendous help to all of us here at the convent."

Francie's blue eyes widened, and she looked Amanda up and down, her expression of amazement. "You're. . .you're a nun?" her raspy voice croaked.

Amanda smiled as she approached. "No, Francie. I simply help out the sisters whenever I can. And I'm happy to see you looking so much better. We were all worried about you."

Francie's eyes widened even more. "You. . .you were here when the doctor brought me?" she asked in a whispery voice.

"No, but I came shortly afterwards, when Sister called me. We've all been concerned about you. And it's wonderful to see you doing so much better. Sister told me you even spoke with the police detective today."

Sister Beatrice patted Francie's arm. "Amanda and I wondered what the detective asked you. Were you able to remember anything about the man who attacked you?"

As if the memory brought a chill, Francie pulled the bedcovers up to her chest and sank back on the pillows, an anxious expression. "I couldn't really see. . .his face was dark and all. . .I can't remember much. It's all mixed up in my head."

Amanda sat on the other side of the bed. "I understand why you can't remember, Francie. When we see something horrible, we block it out of our minds. We don't want to see it," she said in a reassuring voice.

Francie's wide blue eyes locked on Amanda and she slowly nodded her head. "He came out of nowhere. . .I don't know how he got there. That door is always locked."

Encouraged by Francie's statement, Amanda decided to try and see if another memory could be drawn out. "Tell me, Francie, did Senator Chester recognize the man? Did he call out his name perchance?"

Francie's expression changed, and Amanda thought she detected a glimpse of recognition, then it was gone. Francie closed her eyes for a long moment. Then she opened them and shook her head.

"I think the Senator recognized him," she said in her raspy voice. "He called out something, but. . .but I can't remember what it was. All I remember is that knife." She squeezed her eyes shut and shivered, sinking down lower into the covers.

"That's all right, dearie," Sister Beatrice comforted her. "You've been through a frightening ordeal. You just rest and think about getting better."

"I'll try, Sister. How. . .how long can I stay here?" Francie croaked, her face anxious again.

"Why, you can stay as long as you need to get well, Francie," Sister Beatrice replied. "Then we'll find a suitable place for you."

Fear claimed Francie's face this time. "You mean I have to go back to Quinn's? Please, Sister, don't send me back there!"

"No, no, Francie. We'd never send you back to that horrible place," Beatrice reassured. "I promise. I simply meant we'd find suitable employment for you. With a family, perhaps."

Amanda felt her heart squeeze as she watched the fear on Francie's face disappear and amazement take its place. "You won't ever have to sell yourself again, Francie. Sister Beatrice and I will see to it. I promise you."

Again, Francie locked her gaze on Amanda. "You swear?"

"I swear to you," Amanda promised, holding the girl's desperate gaze. "You'll never have to go back to Joey Quinn's place again. Or any place like it."

Relief shimmered in Francie's eyes along with tears and she glanced away, murmuring a whispery "Thank you."

"Come now, you should rest some more, dear. We don't want to overtire you," Sister Beatrice said, as she and Amanda both rose from the bed.

"I'll visit you again, Francie," Amanda promised as she paused in the doorway. "Meanwhile, you concentrate on healing and getting your strength back."

"I'll try. . ." Francie said, glancing toward the window. "But I'm worried about my younger sister, Daisy. Sometimes Quinn would let me see her at the tavern next door. I don't know what she's heard. And I'm, I'm afraid of what my father might do if he hears what happened."

"Don't worry, Francie," Sister Beatrice reassured. "I'll make sure we get over to your house in Snow's Court and check on Daisy."

"Oh, would you, Sister? I'd be so grateful," Francie croaked until her voice gave way. She held her hand to her throat and coughed.

"We've overstayed. No more talking for a while, my dear. Sister Rosemarie will check in on you later," Beatrice said, following Amanda out the door.

"What did Francie mean about her father?" Amanda asked as she walked down the hallway beside Sister Beatrice.

"Bill Kelly is a brutal man, God help me, but he is. And Francie is understandably concerned that he may start to beat twelve-year old Daisy in one of his drunken rages like he did her, and Anna, their mother." Beatrice fingered the crucifix around her neck, but said no more.

She didn't need to. Amanda was already sensing what Francie's home life had been. "Please let me know when you and the other sisters are going into Snow's Court, will you, please? I'd like to go with you and check on Daisy myself."

Beatrice paused at the convent front door and smiled at Amanda. "Of course, we'd be glad to have you come with us. I'll let you know later this week, perhaps."

Amanda opened the door herself, then hesitated on the threshold. Something else tugged at her inside. "There's no chance that Francie's father will learn where she is, correct? You told me the detective said he wouldn't release Francie's name or whereabouts to anyone except the police."

"That's right. Detective Donnolly assured me that no one other than the authorities would know where Francie was recuperating. There's no need for concern, Amanda. Francie is safe with us," Beatrice said with her motherly smile then closed the door.

Amanda walked back to her waiting coach. Mathias was holding the coach door open. Unfortunately, Sister Beatrice's words did not erase the uneasy feeling that tugged at Amanda inside.

Devlin paused before entering Sommersby Public House. The building was still a handsome example of the Georgian style brick homes that were scattered about Washington. The more popular Federal style architecture dominated most of the prestigious areas of the city, but there were pockets of Georgian and other styles dotted about the city as well. Devlin always had a fondness for Georgian architecture. His family's home in Devonshire was a fine example of the period style. The Sommersby Public House looked to be the perfect setting for gentlemen who wished a quiet meal.

Since Sherwood Steele had suggested they meet for lunch in the city instead of his office in the Capitol, Devlin had assumed Steele wanted to keep their meeting quiet and would choose a discreet location. After all, everyone on Capitol Hill knew that Freddie had been interviewed by the police in connection with Senator Chester's murder. And everyone in Washington also knew by now that Freddie was related to Jonathan and Winnie. Gossip seemed to spread on the balmy spring breezes that teased Washingtonians with April's promise.

Devlin pulled open the heavy door and was taken aback by the noisy atmosphere that greeted him. Sommersby Public House was not a quiet refined establishment at all. It was a tavern, and it was filled with men. Several men stood at the bar, drinking their lunch obviously. But the tables scattered about the tavern were filled. And not with gentlemen of the Senate, either. Devlin observed that all of the men were workingmen, judging from their attire. Rough jackets and coats, caps, overalls, shirtsleeves rolled to their elbows. Everyone was dressed as if he'd just come in off the street, all except one man seated at a table in the corner beside the paned glass windows. The man glanced at Devlin and beckoned him over as he rose from the table.

"Senator Steele, I presume?" Devlin said with an ingratiating smile and extended his hand to the tall grey-haired man.

"Guilty," Steele said, his thin moustache curving up with a semblance of a smile. "And you're Jonathan Carrington's brother-in-law, I take it? Please join me." He gestured to a chair.

Devlin doffed his hat and sat, noticing a serving plate of empty oyster shells and an equally empty beer glass in front of Steele. "How are the oysters?"

"Delicious. This is the last month until autumn, you know. There's no 'R' in May," Steele said with a chuckle, referring to the coming warm months. "And they have a fine stout which goes down as smooth as any of old man Heurich's brew."

"An excellent suggestion," Devlin said, as Steele signaled a passing waiter. Waiting until Steele had given an order for a double order of oysters and crackers and stout for both, Devlin decided to ease his way into the conversation, hoping to work up to questioning Steele about Horace Chester. "I appreciate your meeting me, Senator. My brother, the Earl of Devonshire, has instructed me to get to the bottom of this unpleasant business. As you can imagine, our family is considerably disturbed by the accusations which have attached themselves to our nephew."

Steele leaned back into the curved wooden chair, observing Devlin with dark eyes. "I can imagine they are. Tell me, Mr. Burke, Carrington inferred you were the financial advisor for his wife's family. You must make several trips to New York, then. To keep track of Wall Street's machinations, that is."

"Yes, I do. The vagaries of the Stock Market require constant vigilance," Devlin replied, following Steele's lead in the interest of congeniality, deciding his credentials were being assessed.

"I thought you might. Well, then, you must have several friends and advisors in the investment business on whom you depend for advice," Steele said as the waiter approached with a tray.

Devlin sensed he knew where this conversational turn was going and waited until their oysters and stout were served before following Steele's lead. He took a sip of the dark stout before answering. "There are several advisors I depend upon. Good advice is hard to come by, as you're aware, I'm sure. Especially in a fluctuating market like this one."

Steele gobbled down two large oysters with a loud slurp before replying. "That it is, Mr. Burke. So I would appreciate your keeping me informed as to any sudden market movements." He took a deep drink of his stout before fixing his dark gaze on Devlin. "Any <u>unexpected</u> market movements, if you know what I mean."

Devlin did, indeed. Senator Steele certainly didn't waste any time in requesting a bribe for meeting with him. Advance notice of a company's financial situation was prized information. A great deal of money could be made on a company's sudden rise or fall, if the investor knew ahead of time.

He finished off two oysters himself then sent Steele a knowing smile. "I certainly do, Senator. And I will be sure to let you know if a profitable opportunity appears." He raised his glass to the corrupt politician across from him, hoping the stout would wash away the bad taste of the words in his mouth.

"I appreciate it, Mr. Burke," Steele said before draining his stout and signaling for another.

Devlin sampled more oysters, enjoying their slithery wiggle down his throat. Now that Steele's business had been taken care of, Devlin felt no compunction to be subtle. He settled back into his chair and looked Steele in the eye. "And I would appreciate any information you might have as to possible suspects in the Senator's murder. What enemies did Chester have? Who would hate him enough to kill him?"

A sneer curled Steele's thin lips. "That would be a long list, Mr. Burke. Chester cheated more men than there are in Congress. Both houses. Many men have wished him dead. Businessmen, landowners, countless investors, speculators, and any congressman or senator who'd had dealings with the man. Several of my Senate colleagues would have gladly done the bloody deed if they'd had the spine." He slurped down another oyster.

Surprised by Steele's blunt answer, Devlin probed. "You mentioned investors and speculators. Can you recall if any of those reside in Washington?"

Steele gave a derisive snort. "Far too many. Once someone comes to the Capital City, they're smitten, and they never want to leave." He lifted his stout and drank.

"Do any of them possess the spine to do the deed?" Devlin asked.

"Several, but the one who lost the most was Raymond Miller. Chester wiped the man out. Miller lost everything in one of Chester's schemes." He smirked at Devlin. "Just like your nephew Freddie Livermore."

Devlin's dislike of Steele was growing by the minute. He doubted there was enough stout in the city to wash away his distaste of the man. "Anyone else that comes to mind?" he continued. "How did you and Chester get along?"

Steele's dark eyes narrowed into slits. "Don't think you've fooled me for a moment, Burke. I'm sure you're already aware of Chester's and my stormy history in the Senate. You're here hoping to glean something that might point in my direction. But it won't work." The light in his eyes turned malicious. "You see, I was with several friends at a musicale at the National Theatre that evening. So, there are plenty of witnesses to my whereabouts. Unlike Freddie." A deep laugh rumbled out of his chest.

Devlin held Steele's contemptuous gaze until the senator returned to his oysters. However, Devlin had lost his appetite. Knowing that nothing more of value could be learned from this devious politician, Devlin took a last drink of the stout, grabbed his hat and cane, and pushed back his chair.

"I thank you for your time, Senator, and for your recommendation of this restaurant. The oysters were delicious. And I appreciate your candor."

"I was happy to be of assistance," Steele said with an oily smile. "And you're right to be worried about your nephew. From what I've heard, Freddie accompanied Chester on more than one of his forays into Murder Bay."

Devlin held his tongue as he felt his heart sink. "Thank you, Senator, and a good afternoon." He turned and strode to the door before he lost patience. Behind him, Devlin heard Steele call, "I'll be expecting that advice." Devlin gritted his teeth and pushed out the door.

CHAPTER TEN

"I tell you, Winnie, it was all I could do to remain in the man's presence long enough to question him." Devlin paced the library carpet. "A thoroughly despicable sort. I'm surprised you didn't smell his stench when I returned."

"Do sit down and have some tea, Devlin. You need to relax," Winnie advised as she perched on her armchair beside the fireplace. "I've fixed it with extra cream. The way mother did when we were all wrought up about something."

Devlin took another two laps about the library then collapsed into an armchair. "How does Jonathan abide dealing with these politicians? I'm surprised he's kept his sanity." He spotted the cup of tea and drank it down in two gulps. The creamy flavor did bring back memories—and relaxed him a little. Winnie was right.

"There, now. I can tell you're calmer," Winnie observed. "Now, Let us look on the bright side. Disgustingly corrupt Senator Steele did provide you with a potential suspect. And If I know you, Devlin, you'll be checking into this Raymond Miller."

"Yes, of course, I will. And I'll start at your upcoming soiree this week. I'm sure you and Jonathan have invited plenty of senators who can provide even more details as to those who Chester wronged. According to Steele, that included practically everyone in the entire Congress!"

Winnie poured another cup of tea, added a healthy dollop of cream and brought it to Devlin. "Everyone we've invited has replied they will attend."

"Testament to your stellar reputation as one of Washington's most charming hostesses."

"Thank you, dear," Winnie said, patting her curls in a gesture Devlin had watched since childhood. "More importantly, it should provide you with sources to probe."

Devlin drained his teacup and licked the last taste of rich cream from his lips. "Have you heard from Freddie today?"

"No, I haven't, as a matter of fact. Perhaps I should send a message to the Willard and have him call." Winnie sank into her chair and took a sip from her teacup.

"Don't bother, Winnie. I'll check in on him. I haven't spoken with Freddie in two days. Considering how the gossip is flying around this city, I imagine he's holed up in the hotel, hiding." Devlin scowled little. "Rather, he should be."

"Now, Dev. . ."

Jameson appeared at the library door then. "Madam, a Mrs. Amanda Duncan is here to see you. Do you have a moment to receive her?" He walked over to Winnie, silver tray in his hand. A single white calling card lay on the tray.

Devlin almost laughed at his normally non-plussed sister's reaction. She nearly dropped her teacup.

Winnie quickly scanned the card. "Of course, Jameson. Please show her in. And have Annie bring us another tea tray. With those pastries, too." Jameson nodded and disappeared down the hall. Winnie turned to Devlin with a mixture of surprise and delight. "Devlin! Do you have any idea what this is about? How extraordinary. I was *so* hoping to meet her."

"I have no idea, dear Winnie. I did tell her that I was visiting you and Jonathan. Perhaps she's making a social call." Devlin rose from his chair as Jameson ushered Amanda into the room. Winnie fairly leapt from hers.

Devlin approached Amanda and gestured to his sister. "Mrs. Duncan, how delightful of you to pay us a visit. Winnie, let me have the privilege of introducing Amanda Duncan of Lafayette Square. My sister, Winifred Carrington."

"Welcome, Mrs. Duncan," Winnie greeted as she hastened across the room to take Amanda's hand. "I'm delighted you've come. Devlin has spoken so highly of you."

"I hope I'm not intruding," Amanda said as she paused in the middle of the library.

"Not at all, Mrs. Duncan," Devlin reassured, escorting Amanda to a nearby armchair. "In fact, my sister, Winnie, has been most anxious to meet you."

"I assure you, I would not have disturbed your household so near the dinner hour if it weren't important," Amanda said as she sank into the chair, her lavender crepe de chine skirts gathering about her.

Devlin chose a chair closest to Amanda. She was clearly concerned about something. He detected the same worried look in her eyes he'd seen the first day he'd met her outside the police station. "Mrs. Duncan, please tell us what has you so concerned. Perhaps we can help."

"Yes, please," Winnie chimed in.

"I've just spoken with one of the sisters at Saint Anne's and they are caring for the young girl who survived that vicious attack." Amanda glanced down. "They have moved her to a secluded location for her well-being."

"How is the poor thing doing?" Winnie asked.

"She's healing slowly, even though it's still hard for her to talk. But the sisters told me that the police detective investigating Senator Chester's murder questioned Francie this morning." Amanda paused. "Apparently she told him she didn't really see the man's face, but she remembered that Chester called out something when he saw his attacker. Francie cannot remember if it was a name. I'm sure the sheer horror has blocked it out of her mind."

"That's understandable," Devlin said, watching Amanda's face.

"I'm worried that the killer will try to find Francie. After all, he doesn't know she cannot remember the name Chester called out." Amanda's deep blue gaze shifted from Devlin to Winnie and back again. "I'm frightened for Francie, Mr. Burke."

"I can understand your anxiety, Mrs. Duncan, but Francie is safe. . ." he paused, then gestured to Winnie. "I can attest to my sister's ability to keep a secret, Mrs. Duncan. If not, I would have been disowned years ago. Do I have permission to tell Winnie the details?"

"I swear I will not share them with a soul," Winnie said, hand over her heart. "Not even my husband." She leaned forward, clearly curious.

Amanda glanced at Winnie then back. "Of course, Mr. Burke. Senator and Mrs. Carrington's reputation for honesty and integrity are well known in Washington. I trust them. And you have my permission to share the details with your husband, Mrs. Carrington."

Devlin thought he glimpsed a hint of a smile at Amanda's lips. "The young girl, Francie, is being cared for by the sisters of Saint Anne's at their own convent," Devlin told an enraptured Winnie. "And only the police and those whom the sisters have chosen to tell know of her whereabouts." He turned to Amanda. "So, you should not be concerned, Mrs. Duncan. No one else knows about Francie. In fact, only a few of us know that she's alive."

To his surprise, Amanda didn't look relieved. Instead, she reached into her small purse and withdrew a folded paper. It appeared to be newsprint.

"Unfortunately, that's no longer the case, Mr. Burke. This article appeared in this afternoon's *Evening Star*. Now, all of Washington will know." She unfolded the newsprint and held it up for Devlin and Winnie to see.

The black bold type proclaimed: "Young Girl Survives Maniac's Murderous Attempt!"

"Oh, dear," Winnie exclaimed, then gestured to the servant who entered with the tea tray. "Sally, before you serve tea, could you ask Jameson if the afternoon newspaper has arrived, please?" Sally nodded and scurried wordlessly from the room.

Devlin stared at the headline and frowned. Damn. Mrs. Duncan's fears were well-founded. "Now I see the cause of your concern, Mrs. Duncan. But I believe that Francie is still safe because no one knows who she is or where she is recuperating."

"What about those people at. . ." Mrs. Duncan hesitated. "At the place where the murder occurred? Wouldn't someone there know where she was taken?"

"Let us hope not, Mrs. Duncan," Devlin said, trying to assuage Amanda's concern while his own was surfacing.

"Here, you go, ma'am." Sally handed the newspaper to Winnie then turned to the tea service.

"It's on the front page, where everyone will see it," Amanda said.

Winnie spread open the paper and scanned it, then drew back. "I'm afraid you're right, Mrs. Duncan. Look, Devlin. This is awful. The press is still trying to frighten people."

Devlin spotted the article immediately. Right on the front page and above the fold. Prominent display. "Yellow journalism at its best," he said, then tossed the paper aside.

"I confess I am hoping your investigative efforts are bearing fruit, Mr. Burke. This monster needs to be identified and arrested before he can do further harm. Did you question that man at the tavern you spoke of?" Amanda accepted a teacup from the young blonde housemaid and nodded her thank you.

"Yes, I did. And you do not have to shy away from admitting your contribution to this investigation, Mrs. Duncan. Winnie has always kept informed of my various sleuthing efforts."

"Yes, indeed, Devlin has worked with numerous gifted psychics in London and in New York," Winnie explained. "And I've always demanded to know everything. I find it fascinating."

Amanda smiled. "You are among the minority, Mrs. Carrington. Most people are horrified by the idea of otherworldly information."

"The fear and ignorance of small minds," Winnie said, with a dismissive wave of her hand. "I find your decision to use your gifts to help others to be admirable. Devlin told us that you had provided the information about the man with a gold tooth who saw the killer when he escaped in an alleyway. And Devlin did not waste any time following up on it. In fact, I had to fumigate his entire wardrobe after his evening at the tavern."

Devlin wished his sister didn't feel the need to go into such detail, but he saved his breath. "Yes, I was amazed dear Winnie let me sleep in the house that night. But it was worth the aggravation, because my meeting with Smitty at the tavern yielded valuable information. He identified two of the medals he saw on the uniform and confirmed that the man had dark hair and had smeared something dark on his face. An obvious attempt to disguise himself."

"Did Smitty recognize the man?" Amanda asked, her teacup still in her lap.

"No, he did not. So I used Jonathan's connections to start another line of investigation. Today I spoke with Senator Sherwood Steele, hoping to learn some of Chester's enemies. Unfortunately, the list seems to be endless."

"You actually spent time with Senator Steele?" Amanda asked with a look of amazement. "I'm surprised you're not drinking something stronger than tea." She lifted her cup.

Devlin laughed out loud at Amanda's quip. Winnie joined him. "Well, I intend to remedy that later in the evening."

"Jonathan had warned Devlin that Sherwood Steele was every bit as corrupt as Horace Chester, but more clever in his attempts to conceal it."

"However distasteful the experience, I did learn of someone who bore Chester a great deal of ill will. A man named Raymond Miller. A businessman, I believe. Apparently Chester cheated him out of a considerable amount of money."

"Chester cheated Raymond Miller out of his entire fortune," Amanda observed. "My late husband was acquainted with Miller in various business organizations in the city. This happened several years ago, and from what I've heard, Miller was never able to recover financially."

"According to Steele, this Miller was quite vocal in his hatred of Horace Chester. And Miller still resides in Washington," Devlin added.

"Perhaps he decided to act on his hatred," Winnie mused.

Devlin finished his tea as Jameson appeared in the library doorway. "Excuse me, madam, but a note arrived for Mr. Burke."

"Thank you, Jameson," Devlin said, taking the note and slipping it from its envelope. As he read, Devlin wished that he had had something stronger than tea. The note was from Freddie.

Uncle Devlin, the police were here to question me again. Please come quickly. I'll be in the parlor sitting room.

Good Lord! Detective Donnolly had questioned Freddie again. That meant the police had new details about the murder. And Freddie no doubt did not hold up well.

"Ladies, I apologize to you both, but I must leave for an important meeting. Financial matters require my immediate attention," he lied as he rose from the chair.

Amanda placed her cup on the table. "I really should leave as well. I have imposed upon your good will long enough. Thank you both for allowing me to share my concerns about Francie."

Winnie leaned forward, her hand outstretched. "Oh, please don't go, Mrs. Duncan. I would love to hear more about the work you're doing with the good Sisters of Saint Anne's. Our dinner plans are later this evening and Jonathan is still at the Capitol."

"Yes, Mrs. Duncan, do not rush off," Devlin said, giving a nod to Jameson. "Stay and enjoy your time with Winnie. I promise I will keep you apprised of what I learn."

"I have an even better idea," Winnie chirped. "Why don't you come to our soiree tomorrow evening? We would love to have you. And you'll get to watch Devlin do his sleuthing among the many guests."

Leave it to his clever sister to come up with something brilliant. "That would be wonderful. Please say you'll come, Mrs. Duncan. Besides, with all those senators about, you might pick up something from one of them."

A slow smile spread across Amanda's face. "How very kind of you to invite me. But I haven't been, shall I say, involved in Washington Society for approximately four years. I'm not sure I would be welcome to return. Washington doesn't take kindly to being snubbed."

Winnie sat up straight. "Do not concern yourself, Mrs. Duncan. From what I have experienced, Washington can be easily wooed. I am convinced that everyone will be as impressed with you as Devlin and I are. You've endeavored to make a difference in the lives of our city's less fortunate. That is more than admirable."

"True, but you forget that my unique talents are not universally admired. Some of Washington's social arbiters may not appreciate my attendance."

Winnie lifted her chin in what Devlin recognized as her defiant pose. "They have not been invited to this gathering. Those who will attend will be fascinated by your sense of purpose as well as your courage to defy Society's dragons and Washington's iron-clad rules. And I predict that those so-called arbiters will be consumed with curiosity when they hear of your triumphant social return, and distressed because they were not included."

Amanda laughed softly. "Mrs. Carrington, I fear you exaggerate the impact of my presence."

Winnie gestured. "Please, call me Winnie."

On that congenial note, Devlin decided to take his leave. "I bid you *adieu*, ladies," he said as he turned to leave. The meeting that awaited him would be far less congenial than the one he was leaving.

Devlin spotted Freddie the moment he entered the Willard's gentlemen's lounge. Two empty glasses sat on the table beside him and another one sloshed carelessly as Freddie rose unsteadily to greet his uncle.

"Devlin, thank God you came," he said, louder than Devlin wished. The rest of the sitting room was filled with other well-dressed gentlemen speaking in hushed tones. Devlin spied waiters offering decanters of various spirits to the men relaxing there.

"Lower your voice, Freddie," Devlin said tersely as he sat in the closest chair. "We do not want to share this conversation with others."

Freddie glanced down, chagrined. "Yes, yes, quite right."

"I hope you're sober enough to recall what transpired during the police visit. Was it Inspector Donnolly again?"

"Yes, the little man in the ill-fitting suit with the large moustache." Freddie took another drink.

Devlin signaled a passing waiter. "I'll have what the gentleman is drinking, but he will not need another." The waiter nodded and scurried off. "Now, Freddie, tell me exactly what Donnolly said. Or as close as you can remember."

Freddie leaned forward, his arms resting on his legs, fidgeting with the half-filled whiskey glass in his hands. "He informed me that police now have witnesses who have confirmed that I accompanied Senator Chester to Joey Quinn's bordello twice during the last six months."

"Do you know who these individuals might be?"

Freddie scowled. "Both of them are undoubtedly congressional aides from Chester's office. They often went along on Chester's evening adventures."

"So, they would be reliable witnesses, I take it?"

"Yes, unfortunately. They've both worked for Chester for years and have accumulated many friends in the Capitol."

Devlin pondered while accepting a glass of whiskey from the waiter. Mrs. Duncan had been right. He needed something stronger than tea this evening.

"Be honest with me, Freddie, how did you react when Donnolly told you about the witnesses?"

Freddie stared into his glass. "Not very well, I'm afraid. The man caught me totally off-guard. I didn't know how to respond at first. Especially when he started badgering me with questions."

Going from bad to worse, Devlin thought as he sipped the whiskey. "What sort of questions?"

"He asked me if I still maintained that I was asleep all night at the Willard. Considering the other men's statements, that is." Freddie tossed down the rest of the whiskey. "Then he went on to ask if I wanted to get anything off my chest. Insufferable little man. I could tell he was delighting in my predicament."

"I'd hardly call this a predicament, Freddie. It's clear that Inspector Donnolly considers you his prime suspect."

Freddie's belligerent pose disappeared, and the boyish, scared face appeared. "Please, Uncle Devlin, help me! That policeman has targeted me. I. . .I don't know what to do."

"He's targeted you for good reason," Devlin replied in a low voice. "You publicly threatened Chester and you have no alibi for the night of his death. That makes you suspect number one in Donnolly's book, no doubt. As for what to do, you need to stay here in the Willard and stay away from people who might draw you into conversation. Particularly strangers. They may be newspaper reporters and will publish every word you'll say. Meanwhile, I'll continue my investigation into the other men who may have wanted Chester dead."

"Ohhh, thank you, Devlin, thank you so much," Freddie gushed.

"Don't thank me yet," Devlin said, swirling the whiskey in his glass. "I've learned the list is endless, so the search may go on longer than we wish. Meanwhile, you must stay here and out of trouble. Do you understand, Freddie?"

"Y-yes," he murmured, docilely.

"I'm concerned about the appearance of guilt which is attaching itself to you, Freddie. It's evident that Inspector Donnolly is circling you like a hungry wolf. If he visits again, I want you to get a message to me immediately. I want to be there if Donnolly returns to question you."

The look of gratitude on Freddie's face was almost childlike. "Thank you, Devlin. That makes me feel infinitely better knowing that you will be there."

Devlin sipped his whiskey, wishing his anxieties were as easily assuaged.

CHAPTER ELEVEN

Devlin took a glass of Bordeaux from a passing server's tray as he sidled up beside Jonathan in the parlor doorway. "That white-haired gentleman speaking to Senator Remington, is he the Senator Crawford from Michigan you spoke of earlier?" Devlin asked, gesturing toward the fireplace where two men were deep in conversation.

"Yes, he's probably congratulating Remington on his ascension to New Jersey's senior senator," Jonathan replied as he sipped from the wine glass. Various couples drifted about the parlor and formal dining room. "Crawford and Chester were bitter enemies for years."

"Was he the one who confronted Chester in the Senate last year?'

"Yes, indeed. And he's made no secret of the contempt he felt for Chester." Jonathan glanced around and leaned toward Devlin, lowering his voice. "Did you happen to spot the article in this evening's newspaper about the carriage driver? Seems he went to police after he'd heard gossip in the streets about police finding a uniform. Apparently, he picked up a man in a uniform that night only two blocks from the bordello in Murder Bay and drove him to Pennsylvania Avenue and Fifteenth Street. He said the man got off just past the Willard and went down an alley beside the hotel."

Devlin took a sip as he watched Jonathan and Winnie's soiree guests mingle with each other. The Carrington housemaids passed amongst the guests with trays that offered buttery Dutch cheeses and strong English cheddars as well as delicate pastries stuffed with savories and spiced meats. Brandy-soaked tea cakes filled other trays, followed by tray after tray of wines.

"Yes, I saw the article, and I'm certain that cannot be coincidence. I think the killer deliberately chose to dispose of the uniform disguise in the alley behind the Willard in order to incriminate Freddie."

"Hmmmmmm, you could be right," Jonathan mused, as a couple strolled down the foyer heading his way. "Meanwhile, I must tend to guests. Good luck with your sleuthing."

Devlin edged into the parlor again, hoping to approach Senator Remington once the elderly gentleman from Michigan had finished venting his vitriol over the departed Chester. In the half-hour he'd been strolling among the Carrington guests, Devlin had yet to hear one kind word expressed over the departed Chester. He appeared to be universally despised, if that was possible.

Sipping the fine Bordeaux again, Devlin noticed the elderly Crawford gesturing intently, still irate. Remington listened politely to the older man, no trace of impatience on his face. Devlin noted that Remington appeared to be near his own age of mid-thirties.

"Is Senator Crawford still haranguing?" Winnie approached, wine glass in hand.

"I'm afraid so. I've been hoping to have a moment with Remington, myself. He was at the Capitol that evening, and I'd like to hear his side of Freddie's altercation with Chester. And he took Freddie to his private club afterwards. I'm sure he knows details of that evening that Freddie has forgotten."

"Well, I think Senator Remington needs assistance. I'll rescue him, and you can step in and provide more pleasant conversation." Winnie snatched a glass of wine from a maid's tray. "Here, give him this. It may loosen him up a bit. Remington has always appeared a bit shy and withdrawn to me."

With that said, Winnie sashayed over to the two senators. Another Crawford harangue was in progress. Devlin strolled behind her. He had to admire Winnie's style. Boldness and beauty. Clearly exercising Hostess privileges. His sister looked especially lovely in a rose pink gown with deep-cut décolletage. Devlin sincerely appreciated the current dressmakers' designs of women's gowns.

"Senator Remington, you'll have to forgive me, but I simply must steal Senator Crawford from you for a while," Winnie declared, slipping her arm through Crawford's possessively. "There is another couple that is absolutely dying to hear about Senator Crawford's Michigan properties. You'll excuse us, won't you, Senator?"

"Uhhh, who. . .what. . .?" Crawford sputtered, clearly confused.

Remington, however, appeared relieved. "Of course, Mrs. Carrington, I understand completely. Give your wife my regards, senator," he said to Crawford as Winnie escorted him away.

Devlin noticed that *hostess* Winnie was every bit as bossy as *Younger Sister* Winnie. He smiled, watching a bewildered Crawford being led out of the parlor and down the hall. Who knew where Winnie might take him? Devlin lost no time in approaching Remington.

"My sister thought you might need this after your conversation," Devlin said with a friendly smile as he offered Remington the glass of wine. "The Bordeaux is quite good."

"Why, thank you," Remington said, clearly surprised by Devlin's gesture. "I hope it wasn't too obvious that I was flagging a bit under Crawford's long litany. He had a contentious relationship with my former colleague, rest his soul." He lifted his glass.

Devlin sipped his wine. "It's quite amazing that Senator Chester appeared to be universally despised. I don't believe I've heard one kind word expressed about him so far this evening. That's extraordinary."

Remington's mouth twisted. "Yes. I'm afraid my former colleague did not encourage friendship. Rather, he saw relationships as forms of competition, and he was bound to win at all costs." He took a sip of wine and nodded. "I concur. The wine is excellent. I must ask Mrs. Carrington which suppliers she patronizes. My wife and I have seen our social obligations increase, as I'm sure you understand. In fact, she's scouting among the other senate wives gleaning information." He shook his head with the hint of a smile.

"By the way, congratulations on your elevation to the senior senate position for your state," Devlin said. "I predict your social calendar will be full. And your dining partners will be barely able to contain their relief."

This time, Remington actually smiled. "Your candor is refreshing, Mr. Burke. A welcome change from most of my colleagues. With the exception of Crawford, of course. At his age, he's generally allowed to rant away with no restrictions. Everyone excuses his behavior."

"By the way, Winnie, Jonathan and I want to express our gratitude to you for your kindness to our nephew. Thank you for taking him to your club following his altercation with Chester. You were able to provide a cool head and talk sense to the impetuous lad. Plus, remove him from Chester's presence."

"You're more than welcome, Mr. Burke. I was happy to help Freddie. He was clearly overwrought and incensed over Chester's duplicity. I'm not surprised he assaulted Chester." Remington shook his head. "In the five years I've been in the Senate, I've seen countless men duped and swindled by Horace Chester. The schemes varied, but the results were always the same. Each investor or businessman was skillfully fleeced of every available dollar. It sickened me to watch it. I tried to warn anyone who asked that Chester was not to be trusted. Alas, far too few listened. The allure of riches was too powerful. Like an aphrodisiac."

Devlin had witnessed the same situation himself as he moved through the world of High Finance. Far too few investors made their decisions based on reason and facts alone. Too many allowed emotion to drive them. And the most powerful emotion was greed. It *was* an aphrodisiac, and its aroma wafted through the investment world like perfume. Floating on rumor. Once scented, the vulnerable chased after the newest fortune to be made. Most ended in ruin.

"Quite honorable of you to try, Senator. It's been my experience that when it comes to money and the making of it, the most sensible men often lose their senses. Would you please indulge me and relate all the events of that evening? Starting when you first saw Freddie at the Capitol."

"I'd be happy to, Mr. Burke. I'll repeat everything that I told the police detectives when they interviewed me." He took another sip of wine. "I had taken a liking to Freddie from the moment I met him at the Capitol. He's a bright young man. And I'd tried to warn him away from listening to Chester's investment advice. Unfortunately, Freddie paid no heed. Once he was ensnared, it was too late. Freddie, like others before him, was soon bankrupt. I felt sorry for him, so I offered to set up a meeting between Freddie and Chester to see if there was any way Chester could help Freddie salvage something so he wouldn't be wiped out."

This was the first time Devlin had heard any of these details. Freddie apparently had blocked them out. "Indeed, I have not heard mention of any meeting. How did it turn out?"

Remington frowned. "Disastrously, I'm afraid. Chester was intractable, and when he walked away, well, that's when Freddie attacked him."

"Could you describe the actual attack? Did Freddie strike Chester?"

"Freddie raced after him and grabbed Chester around the throat, then threw him to the floor and proceeded to thrash Chester until several men pulled him off."

Devlin flinched inwardly. It was even worse than he'd originally imagined. He shook his head. "How could Freddie do something that stupid?"

"It was obvious Freddie was acting in sheer rage. He'd relied upon Chester's advice and had been bankrupt because of it. Then, Chester callously dismissed his complaints and turned his back on him. I must admit Freddie showed more backbone than most of Chester's victims."

Devlin wished Freddie had less backbone and more brain. "Unfortunately, that backbone has caused him to become a suspect in the police investigation of Chester's murder."

"How is Freddie holding up?" Remington asked, his tone solicitous.

"Fairly well, considering the circumstances. He's at the Willard, keeping to himself for a change. Thank you for taking Freddie to your club afterwards and getting him out of Chester's sight. I imagine the man was livid."

"Oh, yes. Chester threatened to press charges, he was so mad. One of his congressional aides, however, soothed him and enticed him to visit his favorite bordello instead. That's when I took Freddie away to my club, hoping he'd calm down over dinner. It took the whole evening as I remember, but Freddie eventually calmed himself. He grew

SCANDALS, SECRETS, AND MURDER

fatigued, so I took him by carriage to the Willard, walked him inside and to the elevator for him to go up to his room. Then, I departed for my own home."

"And what time was that?"

"Approximately eleven o'clock. Perhaps a little later."

"That was very kind of you to go to all that trouble, Senator. Again, let me express my family's appreciation for assisting Freddie on that dreadful evening."

"Well, I was happy to help him. As I said, I'd always liked Freddie and had tried to warn him away from getting involved with Chester, but unfortunately, he didn't pay attention. Chester was a powerful persuader, especially when he smelled money."

Devlin was about to ask Remington some of the names of others who'd been duped, but another couple suddenly approached them.

"Excuse me, Mr. Burke, but Senator Brown looks like he has something on his mind as well. Perhaps we'll have a chance to talk at another one of these delightful Carrington soirees." Remington gave him a polite smile, his gaze already drifting to the approaching couple.

"Certainly, Senator. You've been more than patient with my questions. Thank you again." Devlin stepped away from the fireplace with a nod to the couple. He'd gladly leave the politicians to themselves.

Strolling into the hallway, Devlin glimpsed Jonathan gesture to him. Depositing his empty glass with a serving girl, Devlin smiled and nodded at passing guests until he reached Jonathan's side. "It appears your entire guest list has arrived, Jonathan. I had to weave my way down the hall."

"Yes, it appears so. However, I will need your assistance before I greet the latest arrival. Is that lovely lady in the foyer Mrs. Amanda Duncan, perchance?"

Devlin glanced to the front entry and observed Jameson taking Amanda's dark blue evening cloak. Her gown was deep robin's egg blue and was quite stylish, if not the latest design. Amanda Duncan looked stunning. Her chestnut curls were upswept with a lacy comb.

"Yes, that is she," he replied, curious as to Jonathan's reaction. It came quickly.

"My word. I was rather expecting a careworn widow to appear this evening, not this gorgeous creature. How delightful for you to find a gifted psychic who wasn't dressed in tweed."

Devlin heard the tease in Jonathan's voice. "You're quite right. And I believe this evening will prove to everyone in attendance that her absence from Washington Society has been their loss entirely." Devlin caught Amanda's searching gaze and gave her a welcoming smile as he and Jonathan approached. "Mrs. Duncan, we're so pleased you could come. Let me present to you my brother-in-law and our host, Senator Jonathan Carrington. Jonathan, Mrs. Amanda Duncan of Lafayette Square."

"Senator, I am honored that you invited me this evening," Amanda said with a warm smile.

Jonathan scooped up Amanda's extended hand with both of his. "The honor is entirely ours, Mrs. Duncan. Winnie has not ceased praising you and all of your charitable endeavors. She was quite impressed, as am I."

"You are very kind and charitable to say so, Senator," Amanda replied.

"Winnie mentioned your busy schedule has kept you away from the Washington social scene for a while, so I will let my brother-in-law assist you in your re-entry, so to speak. You and he can venture forth amongst the politicians together. Provide each other moral support." He placed Amanda's hand on Devlin's offered arm just as Jameson welcomed another couple into the foyer.

Devlin wrapped Amanda's arm around his. "I'm ready if you are, Mrs. Duncan. Shall we go forth into the political sea? No dragons are in sight."

Amanda laughed softly. "Lead on, Mr. Burke."

Devlin escorted Amanda down the hallway and into the parlor, which was more crowded than before. He noticed heads turning as they passed; appreciative glances from the gentlemen and curious ones from the ladies. Amanda appeared oblivious. "Would you care for a glass of Bordeaux, Mrs. Duncan? It's quite nice."

SCANDALS, SECRETS, AND MURDER

"Perhaps another time, Mr. Burke. Since I've been out of the arena for a while, I fear I've lost some of my former skills, such as keeping wine in the glass and my tongue in check at the same time."

Devlin laughed at that. "I'll admit that's a challenge for us all."

"Devlin Burke, is it?" a male voice asked from behind them. "You're Carrington's brother-in-law from England, I'm told."

Devlin and Amanda turned to see Senator Crawford and a silver-haired woman observing them intently. "Yes, indeed, Senator Crawford. You and I have not have been introduced, but your reputation precedes you, sir. I take it this lovely lady is your wife?"

Senator Crawford stood even taller under Devlin's praise. "Yes, indeed. And may we inquire as to who this lovely lady is you're accompanying?"

Devlin felt a slight tension in Amanda's arm as she gave the Crawfords a radiant smile. "Let me introduce Mrs. Amanda Duncan of Lafayette Square. She's recently become acquainted with the Carrington's, and my sister, Winnie, insisted she join us tonight." He patted Amanda's arm in a brotherly fashion. "She's been out of the Washington social whirl for a spell."

Mrs. Crawford lifted her snub nose. "You're a widow, correct? Wasn't your husband Reginald Duncan?"

Again, Devlin felt the slight tension in Amanda's arm, but there was none in her voice. "Yes, I am, Mrs. Crawford. I lost my husband and young daughter four years ago."

"I'm so sorry..." Senator Crawford began, only to be interrupted by his wife.

"Train crash in the Midwest, wasn't it?" Mrs. Crawford continued, her bird-like gaze targeting Amanda like a worm in a garden.

Devlin couldn't believe the rudeness of the woman's question and was about to deflect it with a comment. But Amanda spoke with the same calm composed voice. "That is correct, Mrs. Crawford."

"Tragic, simply tragic," the Senator wagged his head.

Devlin decided to remove Amanda from any more of this interrogation. He gestured to the sitting room across the hall. "I believe the harpist will be performing—" Unfortunately, the rest of his sentence was lost beneath Mrs. Crawford's next interruption.

"Why have you waited so long to return to your social obligations? Traditional mourning is only two years."

It was all Devlin could do to refrain from scowling at Mrs. Crawford. Amanda, however, continued to answer the rudeness with grace. "I found that I needed more time to heal from my loss. So I devoted my efforts to helping the Sisters of St. Anne's in their charitable work. And I discovered that turning my attention away from myself and toward others provided the balm I sought."

"An admirable decision," Devlin said quickly before Mrs. Crawford could voice another insensitive question. "Senator, Mrs. Crawford, you'll have to excuse us. I noticed my sister beckoning. Enjoy the evening." He swiftly steered Amanda from the parlor and away from further aggravation. "I apologize for exposing you to that unforgivably rude exchange, Mrs. Duncan. It appears that dragons do lurk in this murky political sea."

"No apologies necessary, Mr. Burke," Amanda replied giving him one of her warm smiles. "I was prepared for some confrontation once I returned to the arena, and it's actually a relief to have the first joust over and done with."

Devlin felt his aggravation dissipate with laughter. "Your metaphor is apt, madam. You handled the old harridan superbly and with more grace than she deserved. I'm amazed at your patience. I do not suffer fools gladly."

"Well, I have learned to tolerate them, at least," she replied as they entered the sitting room.

Devlin noticed several rows of chairs set out in preparation for the evening's musical entertainment. Some were occupied already. He was about to escort Amanda to a seat, when Winnie hastened over to them. How women moved so quickly with yards of silk surrounding their legs, Devlin never quite understood.

"Devlin, you are supposed to be sleuthing about," Winnie proclaimed, taking Amanda's other arm. "I have scores of people I want Amanda to meet before the harpist begins."

Devlin reluctantly allowed Winnie to steal Amanda away. "Be sure to steer clear of any more dragons, would you, please? Mrs. Duncan's already been subjected to Mrs. Crawford's rudeness."

"It was nothing, I assure you," Amanda replied.

"Worry not. These people are civilized," Winnie gave a dismissive wave as she escorted Amanda toward two couples beside the piano.

No one could move through a social gathering as swiftly and efficiently as dear Winnie, and still leave each couple convinced she was raptly attentive to their every word. Amazing ability. No doubt Mrs. Duncan would meet more people in an hour than she'd no met this last year.

Devlin took the moment to choose another glass of Bordeaux as a server passed. Strolling into the hallway, he scanned the room, calculating which senators he had yet to meet. He noticed Jonathan speaking with Jameson, who gestured toward the foyer. Jonathan noticed Devlin and beckoned him over.

"Devlin, I think you'll like to accompany me while we welcome the latest guests. The tall, balding man on the right is Senator Buchanan of North Carolina. And instead of his charming wife, Buchanan is accompanied tonight by a man named Raymond Miller."

Devlin glanced to the foyer, observing the tall, broad shouldered, dark-haired man who stood beside Buchanan. "Indeed? That's a coincidence. I've been wanting to meet Raymond Miller. Sherwood Steele mentioned that he was embittered over his financial undoing at Senator Chester's hands."

"Yes, I recall your conversation with Steele. I, too, agree it's quite a coincidence that this Miller would appear here tonight as Buchanan's guest. I wonder what Buchanan is up to?"

"Shall we find out?" Devlin suggested as they started down the hallway.

"Senator Buchanan, how good of you to come," Jonathan greeted as he and Devlin walked up to Buchanan and guest. "And Jameson told me you've brought a guest. Your name is Miller, sir?" He extended his hand first to the senator, then to Miller.

"Raymond Miller," the man said, clasping Jonathan's hand.

"Yes, I thought you and Mr. Burke might enjoy meeting Raymond. It seems you share some mutual interests." Buchanan's thin lips curved into a small smile.

Devlin extended his hand to both men. "Devlin Burke. I am Senator Carrington's brother-in-law. Delighted you both could join us this evening."

Buchanan's light eyes flitted over Devlin. "Ah, yes. The visiting London financier. I've heard you have quite the knack for investments, Mr. Burke. We should talk sometime."

Devlin bowed his head slightly. "You are too kind, Senator. I'd be happy to speak with you anytime." Glancing to the tall man who stood beside Buchanan. He thought he detected a slight smirk. "Mr. Miller. I'm glad to make your acquaintance. Are you from Washington as well, or visiting?"

The smirk became a full-fledged sneer. "I've been in Washington for a lifetime, Mr. Burke."

"If you gentlemen will excuse me, I must return to my duties as host. Please make yourselves comfortable and enjoy the evening." Jonathan gave the men a polite nod then moved toward the foyer again where Jameson was helping another couple with their evening cloaks.

"Gentlemen, why don't we move away from the busy hallway, where we can converse more easily." Devlin gestured toward the parlor.

"You and Raymond have much in common, Mr. Burke," Buchanan said as he accepted a glass of wine from a server. "He, too, was deeply involved in Wall Street for years. But he's been working as a lobbyist for the last year. He used to handle a great many clients for the financial firm of Hastings and Sons. I believe that's the same firm your nephew Freddie was employed by, correct?"

"You're correct. Freddie was an investment advisor until recently when his fortunes drastically changed, I'm afraid."

Raymond Miller snorted. "I'll say. I heard that Chester used the same scheme on your nephew that he'd used on me years ago. The bastard ruined me." Miller snatched a wineglass from another passing tray and tossed down the entire contents in one huge gulp. "The New York investment houses wouldn't touch me after that. I was lucky to obtain this position."

Devlin observed Miller closely. Resentment seethed out of the man in a palpable cloud. What was his reason for coming tonight? Did he merely want to share his tale of personal destruction with others who would understand? An opportunity to vent his anger at mistreatment at Chester's hands? If so, this gathering would definitely provide many a sympathetic ear. Chester had no supporters in this group, Devlin had found.

"I'm extremely sorry to hear that Chester ruined your life the way he has ruined our nephew's," Devlin said. "From what I have learned, the man was an abomination as a senator and a despicable human being."

Miller gave another derisive snort, and grabbed the last glass of wine from a nearby tray. Down, it went in a second. "Tell your nephew I understand his desire to seek revenge on the bastard. I only wish I had acted on my impulses."

Miller's comment gave Devlin pause. "I appreciate your concern, Mr. Miller, but our family is convinced that Freddie is innocent of that heinous attack perpetrated on Senator Chester. Freddie was asleep in his hotel room at the Willard when it occurred."

Miller laughed in Devlin's face, while Buchanan simply snickered. "Yes, we had heard that Freddie was sleeping soundly only hours after he'd assaulted Chester in the halls of the Capitol. Somewhat hard to believe, wouldn't you say, Mr. Burke?"

Devlin looked Buchanan in the eye. "I assure you, sir, that Freddie is telling the truth. I spoke with him that following morning and I had to awaken him from a sound slumber."

Miller gave another distasteful snort. Again, Buchanan simply smirked. "I see. Well, I hope you obtain excellent legal counsel for the lad." His gaze shifted across Devlin's shoulder. "If you'll excuse us, I want to introduce Raymond to Senator Jones. We'll speak later, Mr. Burke."

Devlin watched Buchanan and Miller move away toward the sitting room. If he had his way, he and Senator Buchanan wouldn't speak anytime soon—if at all.

CHAPTER TWELVE

"Please make yourself comfortable. I'll return shortly with your cognac," the slender brunette said, as she escorted Devlin into an inviting, tastefully decorated parlor.

"Thank you, my dear. That would be perfect," Devlin replied, watching the lovely nymph in the diaphanous gown disappear down the hallway.

As he entered the room, Devlin noticed two other gentlemen sat comfortably relaxed against velvet settee cushions, already enjoying a beverage. Feet on hassocks, both were coatless with shirtfronts open as his was. The well-appointed parlor's gaslights were lowered, and a soft warm glow bathed the room. Devlin sank into a nearby armchair and awaited his cognac as well as his charming late evening companion.

After he'd gotten Amanda safely in her carriage and on her way home, and the last of the Carrington's guests had left, Devlin shared his thoughts with Winnie and Jonathan about Raymond Miller's visit. Jonathan agreed that Miller had come more to malign Freddie than to express concern. But what was Buchanan up to, he wondered? Jonathan confirmed that Buchanan was more schemer than anything else. Not one to lust for money, power seemed the key to Buchanan's desires.

Instead of joining Winnie and Jonathan for a late night brandy, Devlin had chosen a late night walk instead. He needed to let his thoughts sort themselves out before he could enjoy a brandy—or any-one else's company for that matter. After an hour of walking a gas lit Connecticut Avenue, bathed in shadows now that the trees had leafed out, Devlin had found himself nearing Dupont Circle and a familiar location.

Nestled in the midst of similar brick rowhouses along N Street, conservative in all appearances, was the most private club in all of Washington. A sophisticated Parisienne, Genevieve, maintained an elegant establishment with the choicest brandies, the finest cigars, and the most provocative female companionship the discriminating gentleman of taste could desire. The women at Genevieve's were cultured as well as beautiful, and the clientele was composed of some of the most powerful men in Washington—as well as the wealthiest.

Devlin rested his head on the cushioned chair. His evening of interviews had provided only one thing that was certain. Horace Chester was universally despised for his greed and corruption and just as equally feared for his ability to take revenge upon those who stood in his way. Many men were glad that he was dead. But, who had possessed the backbone, as Miller put it, to do the deed? Devlin had left the gathering with more questions than answers.

"The brandies are quite fine here, Mr. Burke," a man's voice spoke from across the room.

Devlin glanced over to the grey-haired gentleman who sat on a burgundy settee. He thought he recognized the man. "Excuse me, sir, I believe we've met, but—"

"Alan Hagan," the older man replied with a smile. "I was one of Jonathan and Winnie's guests this evening."

Senator Hagan was Jonathan's mentor in the Senate. An honorable man. "Ahhh, yes, Senator. Now I remember. Jonathan speaks quite highly of you."

"Jonathan is a fine young man and an excellent Senator. He'll be quite the leader one day." Hagan took a sip from his glass. "Would you care to join me? I see the young lady returning with your cognac."

"Why thank you, Senator, I believe I will." Devlin crossed the room and chose the armchair next to Senator Hagan.

"Your cognac, monsieur," the nymph's lightly accented voice changed the syllables. She handed Devlin the glass of amber liquid. "I'll be close by, if you wish my company. . .again." She gave him a winning smile.

"Thank you, my dear. I'll bear that in mind," Devlin said with a grin.

Senator Hagan chuckled. "Sophie is quite a lovely sprite, isn't she?"

"Yes, indeed, and an excellent listener. I confess I was quite wound up from an evening where the conversation centered on various accounts of the late Senator Chester's venal activities."

Senator Hagan's smile disappeared. "Ah, yes, our disreputable former colleague. It is good that they're taking his remains back to New Jersey for burial. I doubt there'd be any mourners here."

Devlin swirled the cognac in his glass and sniffed its rich aroma. As pleasant as the surroundings were, he shouldn't miss an opportunity to glean more information. "From what I've heard, Chester's greed and vindictiveness were responsible for many a man's ruin, financially and politically."

Hagan sipped his brandy, his kind face creasing with scorn. "That is true. But some of the men were as greedy as Chester, and their greed helped bring on their own ruin. Men like that unpleasant individual who accompanied Senator Buchanan tonight, Raymond Miller. He was arrogant and obnoxious while he still had his family fortune to waste on Wall Street speculation. I'm amazed it lasted as long as it did, before he frittered it all away. Fool. He'd ignore honest advice and search out the schemers and corrupt financiers. Miller was always one to cross over the line of ethical investing. I'm sure you know what I mean, Mr. Burke. It's no accident he and Chester found one another. I'm sure Chester saw him coming."

"It's Devlin, Senator. And I agree that Miller is a most disagreeable sort. I spoke with him when he arrived with Senator Buchanan. His hatred of Chester was palpable, and it seems his only reason for attending was to rage against Chester."

"Yes, that's true, but he also came to try and inveigle others to look favorably on his client company's fortunes. He's representing a smaller railroad line in the Midwest. Miller knows that there is more governmental legislation working its way through committees in the Senate that will affect the railroaders' fortunes. As well as most industrialists."

His interest piqued, Devlin asked, "Which legislation would that be, Senator?"

Hagan swirled his brandy. "The Senate is attempting to craft anti-trust legislation that is long overdue. The greed of some of our biggest industrialists is beyond all proportion. And their desire to control markets for their products has stifled competition. The time has come to rein in these behemoths." He took another sip. "Reform is long overdue, Devlin. We must bring these corporate robber barons to heel. Otherwise, they will gain a stranglehold on American industry. Competition is healthy for business, and yet, that is what these men seek to eliminate at all cost. They're interested solely in their individual companies' success, ignoring the fact that more competition means more success for the entire system and serves the country's interest."

Devlin pondered what Hagan said. He had observed the same situations and had come to some of the same conclusions that Hagan had. However, there was one difference. Devlin was an investor; consequently, he was looking for successful investments to secure his family's financial well-being.

"I agree, Senator Hagan. Some of these industries do not operate as efficiently as before. Take the railroads for example. At first, their scramble to acquire each other and consolidate operations resulted in better operations, and I might add, profits to their investors. But then, other men wanted to share in that profitable pie. Suddenly, there were small rail companies popping up from the East Coast to your Midwestern states, laying parallel tracks to the larger lines. All in hopes that they'd be bought out at a high price. Consequently, the railroads' profitability has declined because of it."

"No one has ever argued the efficiency of the railroads' monopolies, but it's the cost that's the issue. The price of shipping freight has constantly risen. Farmers and businessmen all over this country have no choice but to pay the charges. Otherwise, they cannot get their goods to markets in the East and Midwest. I tell you, Devlin, something needs to be done."

"You certainly make a compelling argument, Senator," Devlin said. "And as a prudent financial observer, I agree some reforms to the present situation are necessary. However, as an investor who is responsible for guarding the wealth of my family's estate, I have to be careful. If this legislation you speak of becomes law, then I will need to observe your markets carefully to make sure the reform efforts do not result in ruin. Our family has significant assets invested in your American industries."

Hagan smiled. "A candid financier. How refreshing."

Devlin returned his smile. "I strive to be honest and forthright in all my dealings, Senator, even the financial ones. There are sufficient profits to be made for shrewd investors. One does not have to lose ones' soul in the search for wealth."

Hagan observed Devlin for a moment. "Why don't you join my wife and me for dinner at our home tomorrow evening? I believe you'd find our guests' company pleasurable as well as stimulating. There are others who share some of your concerns as well as the reformers. In fact, young Theodore Roosevelt from New York will be joining us. It should be a lively evening. He's been making quite a splash here in Washington since he was appointed Civil Service Commissioner last year. There is no one more passionate about reform than Teddy."

"I'd be delighted to join you, senator. Thank you for inviting me. It sounds like a stimulating evening, as you said."

Just then, Devlin noticed the nymph-like Sophie draping herself across a settee across the room. She cast a languid look Devlin's way. Obviously, this evening has more stimulation in store.

"If you'll excuse me, Senator, Sophie looks a bit lonely. I think I'll keep her company for a while," Devlin said as he rose.

Senator Hagan laughed softly in reply.

CHAPTER THIRTEEN

Amanda tugged at the gray muslin bonnet that covered her hair, tucking her curls beneath. Following after Sister Beatrice, she lifted the skirts of her plain muslin dress and stepped through the mud that remained from this morning's shower. Workmen and tradesmen, washerwomen and peddlers walked past Sister Beatrice and Amanda with barely a passing glance.

Twenty-fifth Street was crowded. Occasionally, someone would mutter a quick, "Bless you, Sister," as they hurried by. Everyone who walked the street knew where Sister Beatrice was headed. *Snow's Court*. One of Washington's many alleyway slums, filled with deteriorating wooden dwellings that were packed with several families each. All of the buildings were hidden neatly behind respectable brick row houses that filled all four sides of the block, concealing what lay behind.

As they entered the alleyway leading to the interior blocks of Snow's Court, Amanda noticed the people around her. They looked different than the other workers who occupied the outside streets. These people were thinner, their faces paler and gaunt, and their clothes were not much better than rags. Torn and dirty. But it was the expression on their faces which wrenched Amanda's heart. Despair.

An unshaven older man carrying a box on his shoulder glanced toward Amanda and started walking beside her through the alley. "Well, ain't you a pretty one," he said, leaning over close enough for Amanda to smell his rank odor and his foul breath.

Amanda did not reply, but picked up her pace behind Sister Beatrice. However, the man did the same, keeping up with Amanda.

"Don't hurry off, pretty thing. Why don't you come with me instead? You'll—"

Sister Beatrice turned then and sent the man a beatific smile, while she continued walking. "Go on about your work, good sir, and we shall be about ours. Bless you."

The man took one look at the crucifix Beatrice held in her hand and immediately backed up. "Sorry, Sister," he mumbled.

Amanda caught up with Sister Beatrice and walked beside her as they neared the end of the alley where it opened onto Snow's Court. The rank odors of urine and excrement and unwashed bodies floated out to greet them before they arrived.

They walked out of the alley's darkness and into the bright sunshine of the interior court. *Such a beautiful spring day and such a wretched view*, Amanda couldn't help thinking.

Old, dilapidated wooden rowhouses were crowded together side by side. Once they faced the outside streets and were well-kept. But as brick rowhouses began to replace the wooden ones, those older flimsy structures were literally shoved to the back of the lots to make room for the new ones. Eventually, those old neglected rowhouses became a neighborhood of their own, completely separate from the nice homes facing the carriage filled streets.

"Francie's house is in the middle of this stretch," Sister Beatrice said, pointing ahead of them. She started off at her usual fast pace, Amanda right beside her.

"You'll recognize Francie's little sister, won't you?" Amanda.

"Oh, yes. She looks just like Francie, but she has blonde hair like her mother, Anna, had. Dear Anna." Beatrice didn't say anything else as they walked along.

Up ahead, Amada spotted a Negro woman exiting one of the dilapidated dwellings and walk toward them. She wore a white shirtwaist blouse and dark blue skirt, and she had on a flat brimmed straw hat. Altogether, she was much better dressed than anyone else milling about the crowded court. She also carried a straw basket.

The woman nodded to Sister Beatrice as she passed by. "Sister, how are you doing today?"

"Grateful that I can still do the Lord's work, Miss Agnes."

"Amen to that, Sister," Miss Agnes said as she passed by. Nodding to Amanda, she said, "Morning, Miss."

"Good morning to you," Amanda replied with a friendly smile. Normally, she didn't see many smiles in Snow's Court. "Who is that woman, Sister? Is she with one of the churches?"

"That's Agnes Fisher, and she's with the large Baptist church over on New York Avenue. Bless her heart. She's been coming over here to the court as long as I have. Tending to her flock." Slowing her pace, she pointed to a rundown faded green dwelling. "Here we are. Let's hope Daisy is around. Usually she's helping the other family that lives upstairs—or staying out of Bill Kelly's way."

Amanda followed Beatrice up the steps and waited to see if their door knock was answered. Amanda looked around her. Several scrawny children were scribbling in the dirt with a stick in front of the house next door. One of them glanced over his shoulder toward the alley then quickly averted his eyes.

Sister Beatrice knocked on the door again. Amanda thought she detected a slight movement inside the front window, but the pane was so dirty she couldn't be sure if she saw anyone or not.

Suddenly the door opened and a skinny, disheveled little girl stood in the entry. Her blonde hair was matted and dirty and was tied back with a shoelace. She barely looked ten years old. She stared up at Sister Beatrice with an expression of wonderment.

"Sister! Oh, Sister, I'm so glad you came! Do you know where Francie is? Please tell me, please, please! I'm so scared something happened to her. Do you know where she is, Sister?"

Sister Beatrice reached down and gave Daisy a hug. "Daisy, it's so good to see you. How are you, dear? Have you eaten today?"

Daisy shook her head. "Not yet, Sister. Papa said he'd try to bring me something tonight. The woman upstairs gave me a cracker. Do you know anything about Francie? Have you heard anything? I wanted to go over to . . . to the house where Francie works and ask them. I haven't seen her in over a month! She's never waited that long before. I'm scared, Sister! Maybe something happened to her. Maybe. . .maybe that crazy man got her!"

Tears suddenly filled Daisy's blue eyes and spilled down her pale cheeks. Amanda's heart broke, watching Daisy's anguish. She was the same age that her own daughter would have been had she lived. Yet how pathetic and hopeless this poor little wretch was. She was clearly starving, judging from her bony arms and legs that showed clearly through her torn cotton dress.

Sister Beatrice glanced to Amanda then back to Francie. "I've heard that Francie is safe and out of harm's way, Daisy. So you shouldn't worry. And she's not working in that house any more, so you stay away—promise?"

Instead of promising, however, Daisy started jumping up and down. The loose soles on her shoes flopping. "Where is she? Where is she? Oh, please tell me Sister! Please, please! I miss her so! Please, please!"

Amanda couldn't bear the child's pleas. "Could we possibly take Daisy?"

Beatrice glanced to Amanda, and Amanda saw the uncertainty in her eyes diminish. "Perhaps we can take her for a short visit—"

"Yes, Sister! Yes, please take me! Please!" Daisy interrupted, still jumping up and down. Her eyes alight.

"Daisy, if we take you to see your sister, you must promise me you won't tell your father where you've been. When do you expect him home?'

"Papa won't be home until late this afternoon. I promise I won't tell. Cross my heart!" Her tiny hand made an "X" on her chest.

"All right, then, come along," Sister Beatrice took Daisy's hand and headed down the front steps. "We'll go right this minute, so Sister Teresa can bring you back before anyone misses you."

Daisy fairly leaped down the stairs beside the petite nun, Amanda following behind once again. This time Amanda surveyed the people milling around the interior of Snow's Court, and she deliberately paid attention to loiterers who might be watching.

That evening, Sen. Hagan's home

Devlin looked around at the faces of the three men who encircled him in Senator Hagan's parlor. Two were Hagan's closest colleagues in the Senate, Alfred Dunn and Warren Ingram. The other man, Robert Johnson, was a sitting judge on the Federal Appeals Court for the District, another long-time friend of Hagan's. Devlin had found them to be unfailingly blunt in their opinions of the corruption that infected the Senate. And unsparing in their condemnation of the men who continued and protected the many practices. Devlin decided to take the risk of being perfectly honest about his quest for information.

"Gentlemen, I agree. Something needs to be done to curb the complacent attitudes of your peers toward these corrupt practices. In fact, I accepted an invitation for lunch with Senator Sherwood Steele last week, and I was amazed that he would actually bribe me before I'd even finished my meal. Turned me off those fine oysters entirely."

Dunn snorted, his grey mustache twitching. "Sherwood Steele is as much a cancer on the Senate as Chester ever was. Every bit as corrupt."

"Why on earth would you meet with Steele?" the older Judge Johnson asked before he sipped his whiskey.

"Yes, and why would he bribe you?" balding Ingram probed, red wine sloshing in his glass.

"Yes, tell us, Devlin," Dunn urged, then took another drink of the amber liquid in his glass.

Devlin glanced over his shoulder at the ladies clustered about the piano. Senator Hagan's wife was showing them an oil painting she'd recently acquired. He lowered his voice and leaned forward a bit, so as not to be overheard.

"I lunched with Steele because I was curious as to his whereabouts on the night of Chester's murder. I confess it was brazen of me to do so, gentlemen, but I'll leave no stone unturned in the search to discover Chester's killer. My family and I are convinced our nephew, Freddie, is innocent. He was asleep at the Willard the entire night. Alas, he has no witnesses to that fact."

All three gentlemen stared intently at Devlin. No one spoke for a moment.

"That may have been brazen, but it was damnably shrewd of you, Burke," Judge Johnson said. "Steele and Chester had been enemies for years, and Steele openly lusted for Chester's chairmanship."

"Precisely why I met with him. I wanted to see how the man reacted when I probed him." Devlin took a sip of a very fine dry sherry.

"Well, don't keep us on pins and needles, Devlin," Dunn prodded. "How did Steele respond?"

"He laughed in my face. Then, proceeded to tell me he'd guessed my reason for meeting him, and added, with a smirk, that he was with a group of friends at the National Theatre that night."

"That sounds like Steele," Ingram said, sipping his wine.

"But he did tell me about Raymond Miller's ruination at Chester's hands, and added that Miller has continued to rail about Chester ever since." Devlin took another sip. The ladies were stirring a bit, he noticed. Dinner might be announced any moment. But, they were still missing a dinner guest.

"That's an apt description of Miller, I'll say that," Dunn agreed. "But I wonder if he would actually resort to murder. His tirades seem to me to be blowing off hot air, that's all."

"I agree," Judge Johnson chimed in. "I've been acquainted with Miller here in Washington for years. I doubt he's smart enough to plot such a daring murder."

Dunn gave a short laugh. "Well, that is the truth. This crime was well thought out."

Delighted that they were following his lead, Devlin quickly continued. "Precisely, gentlemen. I've done a bit of work with London investigators over the years, and it appears to me that Chester was murdered by someone who knew him, because the door that led to the outside stairway was always locked. But Chester apparently kept the key on his key ring. Now, I'm assuming he did not carry a huge key ring around the

Senate chamber all day. So, that leaves the possibility that someone who knew Chester's habits and knew of the key ring could have gained access to the key and had a copy made."

"Hmmmm, that sounds plausible," Dunn said, rubbing his chin.

"Yes, indeed," Judge Johnson agreed. "And it would have to be someone who was regularly seen in the Senate Office Building so his appearance would cause no notice."

"Exactly," Devlin nodded his head, encouraging more comments.

"I concur that it is a splendid theory, Burke," Ingram said. "But don't limit your investigation to the Senate alone. Chester's enemies were spread far and wide. And I personally know of someone else Chester ruined. Ruined the man and his entire family. Broderick Wray. Chester cleverly stole the Wray family's railroad last year. Nearly drove the entire family into the poor house. Wray's father committed suicide a month afterwards. Tragic. Now, there's a man with revenge on his mind." Ingram drained his wineglass.

"Yes, you're right. And I remember seeing Wray a couple of weeks ago here in Washington at a meeting of railroad men. Poor devil. He used to be one of them. Now he's working for the state of Indiana lobbying the railroads for better shipping rates." He wagged his head in obvious sympathy.

Devlin's ears perked up at that. "A couple of weeks ago, you say? That would be the week that Chester was killed. Most intriguing."

"I imagine you'll be lunching with Broderick Wray soon; am I right, Burke?" Ingram asked, with raised brow.

Devlin smiled. "Indeed, you are, Senator." Devlin smiled as the gentlemen around him chuckled. He was about to ask a question when a man about his own age with dark hair and a bushy mustache marched up to their group. Peering at them through his spectacles, the new arrival's face burst into a huge grin. Devlin was struck by the sheer size of the man's smile. He had the biggest teeth Devlin had ever seen. This must be Theodore Roosevelt, the missing dinner guest.

"Here, now, I hope you gentlemen are telling a joke," Roosevelt announced to them all. "I love a good joke. Haven't heard a new one in weeks."

"Well, actually, Teddy, we were simply egging on our new acquaintance, Devlin Burke," Senator Dunn said, clapping Devlin on the shoulder. "He's Jonathan Carrington's brother-in-law and an English financier, to boot. Just your sort of fellow."

"Jolly, good. I feel like I'm back home in New York," Roosevelt joked. "I'll ask Hagan if Burke can be seated next to me. Perhaps he can make some suggestions for my portfolio to help offset the losses I had with those Western blizzards."

"We saw him first, Teddy," Ingram countered with a grin. "We'll all be picking Burke's brain over dinner."

"Good Lord, man, you make it sound like Devlin's a dish on the menu," Judge Johnson chortled.

All of the men laughed loudly at that, Roosevelt the loudest of all. Devlin had to laugh, just watching Roosevelt. He seemed to bounce in place instead of standing still. Most amusing.

Senator Hagan walked up to the group then. "Gentlemen, I can tell you're up to no good. You're laughing too loud. Come along, it's time for dinner."

"In that case, we'd best leave Roosevelt in the parlor," Dunn teased. "He'll have us all laughing before the soup."

Devlin decided to join the fun. "When will the roasted Devlin be served? Before or after the soup?"

The men all threw back their heads and guffawed. Once again, Roosevelt was the loudest.

Roosevelt leaned over his empty dinner plate and lowered his voice. His audience around the table held absolutely still. "I proceeded to fire at the braves until they pulled rein. Then they leaned down beside their ponies, their rifles at the ready."

Mrs. Hagan caught her breath. "Oh, goodness. What did you do then?"

"Well, madam, I aimed my rifle and fired at each one of them again." Roosevelt took a sip of his wine but said nothing more, despite his audience's rapt attention. Devlin noticed Roosevelt's wife, Edith, sat observing her husband with a benevolent smile. No doubt, Mrs. Roosevelt had heard these stories over many dinners.

"Well, tell us, Teddy. What happened next?" Mrs. Dunn asked.

"Madam, that's when I exercised great political wisdom. I turned my pony around and raced hell-for-leather out of Sioux Territory," Roosevelt said, flashing his toothy grin.

The Hagan dinner table exploded with laughter. Devlin couldn't remember when he'd met such an engaging and entertaining man as Theodore Roosevelt. Teddy, as everyone called him. Devlin hadn't presumed, having just met the man, but he had to admit that he was impressed with Roosevelt. If for nothing else than his sheer exuberance. The man barely could sit still for dinner.

"I can see you now, Teddy," Hagan said as he poured wine into Mrs. Dunn's glass.

"I'll take some more of that Cabernet," Dunn said, handing Hagan his wineglass. Other dinner guests took up the invitation as well.

Devlin decided to seize the opportunity. He leaned over to Roosevelt and spoke quietly. "I hope your losses in the Western blizzards weren't too severe. I've met other investors who were wiped out of their Western holdings entirely."

Surprisingly, Roosevelt lowered his voice to match Devlin's tone. "I'm afraid mine were equally severe. I've been hard-pressed to keep the Western lands at all. To be frank, it's put quite a strain on us. Edith and I maintain our family home, Sagamore Hill, back in New York, you know. That's why we're forced into quite a modest situation here in Washington."

"What have your advisors counseled you?" Devlin said, surprised by Roosevelt's forthright response. "Surely with your family connections, you have the best financial minds in New York for advice."

Roosevelt's huge teeth flashed again. "I'm afraid it's not a matter of connections, my good sir. It's a matter of money. That's what's lacking." Then he gave a short laugh at his own expense. Devlin had to join in.

"Devlin, your brother-in-law mentioned that you fancied yourself an amateur scientist," Senator Dunn said, leaning back in his chair. "If so, then you might be interested in attending some of the lectures at the Smithsonian Institution. I read that a professor of astronomy will be speaking this week. There are several of us who like to attend the lectures. Perhaps you'll join us."

"Why, yes, Senator, I'd be delighted to join you. I'm always fascinated to learn more about the natural sciences and those of the outer world as well. Thank you for inviting me."

"Yes, do come along," Roosevelt encouraged. "The lectures are excellent."

Senator Ingram took the bottle of Cabernet that his host offered and poured himself another glass. "Science aside, Devlin. I want to know exactly, what did Sherwood Steele want for a bribe?"

"Oh, Warren, really," Ingram's striking wife scolded. "Must we discuss the disreputable Steele's tawdry activities over dinner?"

"Dinner's finished, my dear," Ingram said with a grin, lifting his glass as his wife shook her head.

"This isn't a jest?" Roosevelt asked, his face suddenly somber, no longer smiling. "Senator Steele actually bribed you?"

"I'm afraid so," Devlin replied, holding his wineglass as Ingram refilled it. "In exchange for answering my questions, Steele wanted me to inform him whenever I heard news of a company's imminent success or failure. I'm assuming he wanted advance notice so he could make appropriate investments in the company. Either betting on its stock price to rise or fall. Probably by using the popular option contracts."

"Son of a—" Hagan blurted before his wife waved her hand. "Not at the dinner table, Alan," she chided.

"Why are we surprised?" Judge Johnson said, looking around at his friends. "We all knew Steele was no better than Chester."

"What is it the French say? 'The more things change, the more they stay the same,'" Dunn said with a wry smile.

"What will you do?" Roosevelt asked, intently focusing. "You're not seriously going to give him the information, are you?"

"I have a better idea," Ingram suggested. "Why don't you steer Steele in a completely wrong direction? It would serve him right."

Devlin looked across the table. "I'm afraid I couldn't deliberately mislead an investor, even someone as odious as Sherwood Steele. I'll simply ignore him instead. I sense Senator Steele isn't used to being ignored, so that will annoy him far greater than losing money."

Laughter floated around the table, and once more Roosevelt's was the loudest of all.

CHAPTER FOURTEEN

"I confess, I'm worried about Daisy, Father," Amanda said to the middle-aged priest who was standing beside her in the outside courtyard behind the convent. "She's skin and bones. Clearly, she doesn't have enough to eat every day. Look at her." Amanda gestured to Daisy who was walking through the small manicured courtyard, picking flowers. Francie sat on a chair beneath an apple tree that was heavy with blossoms. The sweet scent floated on the air.

"You're right, Amanda. That's why the sisters have been feeding her these last two days. Trying to get some solid food into the child."

Amanda watched Daisy choose another larkspur from Sister Geraldine's flower garden. Sister Geraldine had told Daisy she could pick as many larkspurs as she wanted. Daisy carefully arranged the flowers in a small bunch and brought them to her sister.

Francie responded with a big smile and drew Daisy to her chest in a hug. Amanda was glad to see that the wrappings around Francie's throat were diminishing in thickness. A sure sign that her wounds were healing.

Daisy snuggled closer to her sister, wrapping her skinny arms around Francie. At least now, Daisy's hair was clean and shiny, Amanda noticed. Young Sister Teresa had washed and combed Daisy's hair on yesterday's visit. And she'd mended the tears in Daisy's dress.

Amanda felt a tug on her heart, watching Daisy and Francie. "All of you have been wonderful to bring Daisy to see Francie these last two days, but watching them together makes my heart ache, Father. These sisters belong together. Surely there's a way we can bring Daisy here permanently."

Father Tom shook his head. He looked much older than his forty years. *Too many Francie's and Daisy's to worry about*, Amanda thought.

"I wish there were, Amanda. But we can't just take the child away from Bill Kelly. Even though he's a drunkard, he's still her father."

"But I fear he'll start to beat Daisy now that Francie isn't around to deflect his anger. She was sending him money for Daisy. Now, Kelly may turn his hand to her."

A pained look crossed the priest's face. "Let us pray he doesn't Amanda."

Father Tom's advice didn't bring Amanda any solace. She'd given up depending on the Almighty's mercy years ago. Even though April sunshine streamed throughout the courtyard, Amanda felt a slight chill run through her. She glanced to Francie, who was clapping hands with Daisy in a childhood game. The chill increased.

Concerned that her clairvoyant sense was sending her a warning, Amanda shared her fears. "Father, I'm still concerned for Francie. The newspapers have published her survival, which will surely frighten the killer. He knows Francie heard whatever name the senator called out. The killer may be out looking for Francie right now. I'm worried about her safety."

"Francie's safe here with us, Amanda. She's never alone. And once she's healed, we'll move her to another convent out in the Virginia countryside. The man who's responsible for Chester's murder will never find Francie. Not with us protecting her. And the Lord. Francie is under the Lord's protection, too." He gave her a kind smile.

Amanda didn't feel relieved. Her extra sense was sending her a signal. She knew it. That chilled feeling meant danger. And it was always right.

Devlin paused in front of a glass display case. Senator Dunn slowed to examine the display as well. A large buffalo skull and hide were spread out beneath the glass.

"We should bring Teddy over. He's shot one of these beasts when he was out West," Dunn said.

"I'm not surprised," Devlin said with a smile. "I'll wager he shot the beast as it was charging."

Dunn chuckled. "I believe he did. The man is amazing, I'll grant that."

"He has more energy than any man I know," Devlin said, observing Roosevelt rounding up others to join him in the lecture room.

"That he does." Dunn looked across the Smithsonian's Great Hall. "Devlin, you'll have to excuse me. I've spotted a congressional aide who's been dragging his feet with my document request. I must pin him down. I'll make sure I'm in the lecture on time."

"Certainly," Devlin said, checking his gold pocket watch. Ten more minutes before the astronomy professor began speaking. Plenty of time to peruse more of the Smithsonian's interesting displays. The London Museum was grander and larger to be sure, but there was something exciting about watching a young museum explore the world around them. And bring it all for everyone to see.

As he strolled between two glass cases, Devlin noticed a vaguely familiar face. The man was thin and his face pinched, with a high forehead. Devlin strolled closer. It was Senator Buchanan.

Immediately, Devlin began running the other evening's conversation through his head again, and he was still annoyed. However, Buchanan obviously knew Raymond Miller well. Perhaps this accidental meeting before the lecture would allow Devlin to ask some of the questions that had been bothering him.

He strolled over to the display of Indian tomahawks and spears, an impressive feathered headdress lying beside the weapons. "Senator Buchanan, how good to see you again. Are you here for the astronomy lecture?" he asked as he drew closer.

Buchanan looked up and assessed Devlin in a swift glance. The slightly arrogant twist to his lips resembled a smile. "Ahh, Mr. Burke. I see you have an interest in science, too."

"Yes, indeed. I try to attend as many lectures as I can, whether in London, New York, or Washington. Your museum has some interesting exhibits."

"I agree. Is this your first visit to the Smithsonian?"

"Not at all. I visited a decade ago when I was here with family. Winnie and Jonathan had become engaged." Devlin thought he detected a slight tightening along Buchanan's jaw, but it was gone in an instant.

"I've heard you visit Washington often, Mr. Burke. How do you like our fair city?"

Devlin wondered why Buchanan was discussing him with others. "Yes, I'm here quite frequently, as a matter of fact. I oversee all the financial investments for my brother, the Earl of Devonshire. So, it requires my constant attention. Washington is a pleasant change from New York's colder climate. Plus, Wall Street's winds can be chilly."

Buchanan's lips twisted in that smirk Devlin remembered. "Yes, I imagine that's true. And the social scene has become more animated over the years. Many of New York's finest families spend the Season here now. Washington's warmer winters are much more conducive to late-night festivities. And I imagine your many acquaintances have kept your dance card full."

Devlin wasn't sure what Buchanan meant by that. His comment sounded vaguely like an insult, but Devlin forced a smile anyway. "I am fortunate to have made many friends here."

"Yes, I heard you even dined with the so-called Inner Circle the other night. Congratulations, Burke. Senator Hagan is very selective about his dinner guests." Buchanan's thin lips lost their smirk.

Devlin sensed that Buchanan had never been invited. There was an unmistakable trace of resentment on his pinched face. "Indeed, it was an enjoyable evening." Devlin said in a pleasant voice. Devlin had hoped to glean some information from this conversation, and instead, he was the one being interrogated.

Buchanan peered down his nose at Devlin, even though he was shorter. "I've also heard that you're probing everyone you've met about Chester's enemies. I assumed you're searching for a viable suspect in order to distract the police from your nephew."

Devlin did his best not to look surprised. Buchanan was uncanny. It was like he'd been spying on Devlin. Listening in on conversations. And Buchanan had correctly surmised Devlin's reason for doing so. Devlin wasn't used to having his motives and actions scrutinized. He found it more than annoying.

"Yes, Senator, I have been inquiring into Senator Chester's activities. But my search has more to do with finding the truth than deflecting suspicions about Freddie."

The smirk returned. "I think you'd best spend your time preparing your family for the reality of your nephew's disgrace. No amount of social connections can remove the stain of guilt from the young man. He clearly attacked Chester in a fit of rage. I was present when he first assaulted Chester in the Senate hallway, and I have testified to the police that he was acting like a madman, completely oblivious to anything other than inflicting harm upon Horace Chester."

Devlin stared at Buchanan, completely unprepared for his vituperative statement. "You're entitled to your opinion, senator. But the police deal with facts, as do I."

Buchanan gave a derisive snort, but said nothing.

Devlin decided he would leave this unpleasant man's company before he said something cutting. However, he wanted to come away with something.

"In case it hasn't occurred to you, senator, there were several other men in Washington that night who had even stronger reasons to hate Horace Chester than Freddie. Not the least of them would be your friend, Raymond Miller."

This time, Buchanan didn't bother to smirk. He simply laughed. "Unlike your nephew, Mr. Burke, Raymond Miller has an alibi. He was with me most of that evening, then spent the rest of the evening with one of Washington's charming hostesses. Evening hostesses, that is. I'm sure she'll be glad to corroborate Miller's presence if you inquire."

Devlin strove not to let his disappointment show. "That is indeed interesting," was all he could manage at the time.

"Yes, isn't it?" Buchanan smirked, then turned on his heel and walked away, without so much as a "good evening."

Devlin scowled after him. Damnation, he detested that man.

CHAPTER FIFTEEN

Bridget pinned her modest black hat in place. "Madam, I don't understand why I have to wait for the dressmaker to finish these alterations. They will take the seamstress a fair bit of time. I have things to do here which need my attention."

"I realize that, Bridget, but I want this gown to be finished quickly. You can leave the other two with the seamstress. Now that I've re-emerged into Washington's social scene, my wardrobe needs attention. I took stock of the ladies' gowns at the Carrington's soiree the other evening and knew that alterations were necessary."

Bridget opened the door and gave her mistress a smile. "Well, waiting for alternations is a small price to pay to see you taking your rightful place in Society, my girl. I've prayed for this day for quite a while."

"Not to discourage you from your prayers, Bridget, but my decision to rejoin Washington Society has less to do with the Lord and more with Mr. Burke's family's intercessions. Senator Jonathan and Winnie Carrington are every bit as charming as I've heard."

"Well, at least that roguish man has been good for something other than improper suggestions. I'll give the devil his due, I suppose. But, mind you, I'll still keep my eye on him," Bridget said as she trotted down the front steps, umbrella in its customary attack position. Mathias was already waiting at the carriage door; the box of gowns was on top the coach beside his seat.

Amanda watched until Bridget was safely in the coach and Mathias had driven away before closing the door. Then, she scurried down the hall into the library. Opening a lower cabinet, she removed a large upholstered carpetbag, then hurried upstairs to her bedroom. As she quickly unfastened her crepe de chine gown, Amanda sincerely hoped that the elderly Sister Florence was still recuperating in her bed at the convent. That way there would be no reason to open Sister Florence's closet door—and be surprised at what was missing.

Tucking her chin down in the manner of Sister Beatrice, Amanda strove to unobtrusively observe the people walking the streets around her. As she'd noticed on her last trip to Murder Bay, most of these people did not appear to be loitering about during the warm April midday. Washerwomen lugged heavy baskets of clothes about. Peddlers rolled carts in the street, singing their familiar chants for sharpening knives and scissors. Laborers looked to be returning to their worksites after a lunch at the many nearby taverns. The Devil's Fork had a hand-painted sign in the window advertising a dozen oysters and beer for lunch.

"Good day to ya, Sister," a woman said as she walked by, a basket of apples over her arm.

Amanda gave a polite nod in reply. Gathering the voluminous skirts of Sister Florence's white habit, Amanda sidestepped a pool of dirty water on the sidewalk. She knew it was wrong of her to confiscate a sickly nun's attire, but it was the only way Amanda could return to Murder Bay and not look suspicious or out of place. Religious sisters and priests of various faiths were seen regularly on the streets of Washington, tending to the needs of their flocks. And return to Murder Bay, Amanda must. She had questions.

Two younger workingmen stepped out of the Devil's Fork tavern as she passed. Amanda tucked her chin again and quickened her pace. She heard one man say something, and the other responded with a guttural laugh.

Approaching the dingy green row house that served as Joey Quinn's brothel, she gathered the bulky skirts and hurried up the steps. Amanda knocked on the door twice in quick succession.

"Sister, whatever you do, stay away from there," one of the men taunted as he walked by. "We don't want those girls converting any time soon."

The man's companion hooted with laughter as they both continued their saunter down D Street. Amanda ignored them. The door slowly opened, and a tall woman with reddish hair stood on the doorstep. She wore a blue cotton dress exactly like so many of Washington's shop girls and office employees. The woman's blue eyes popped wide when she saw who stood outside.

"Holy Saints!" she exclaimed. "What in Heaven's name are you doing here, Sister? Are you lost?"

Convinced that her disguise had passed all muster, Amanda said, "Pardon me, Miss. I'm looking for Joey Quinn's establishment. Is this it?"

The woman rolled her eyes. "God in Heaven, Sister! What would you be looking for him for? He's the devil, himself. If you're trying to convert Joey, save your prayers. He's not worth saving."

"I'm not looking for Mr. Quinn," Amanda continued, lowering her voice and leaning closer. "I'm looking for someone who is, uh, employed here. I have some questions to ask concerning that young girl who was attacked two weeks ago."

The woman stared at Amanda, then glanced over her shoulder inside the house. Motioning Amanda back, she closed the door behind her. "Let's talk outside, it's better." Then she beckoned Amanda down the front steps and onto the sidewalk beside the curb. "Now, what is it you want to know, Sister?"

Amanda thought she recognized the woman as the one she'd glimpsed standing at the top of the stairs, smiling as Devlin Burke man-handled Joey Quinn. "Did you know the young girl, Francie?"

"Yeah, I knew her. Sweet little kid. Not cut out for this kind of work, pardon me, Sister. I was the one who went over to the convent and asked Sister Beatrice if Francie could stay there. Are you one of the Sisters of Saint Anne's?" She peered at Amanda.

Amanda bit her cheek and nodded her lie. "Thank you so much for rescuing the poor girl. You saved Francie's life—"

"Say it ain't so, Lizzie," an unshaven workingman taunted as he passed by. "Don't join up. We'll miss ya."

Lizzie fixed him with a jaundiced expression. "Keep it in yer pants, Eddie," she replied. Eddie simply cackled as he sauntered down the sidewalk. "Sorry to be talkin' like that in front of ya, Sister. Sometimes ya just have to put 'em in their place. How's Francie doing? Last week, Sister Beatrice said she was healing up pretty well."

"Yes, she is," Amanda said, adding a "praise the Lord" for good measure. "We're all delighted that Francie is healing, but we're concerned as well. As you know, the newspapers printed that a young girl survived the attack. That means the murderer knows Francie is alive. And we're worried that he may come looking for Francie."

Lizzie frowned. "You're right, Sister. I'd thought about that myself."

"That's why I'm here, to warn you to be watchful for anyone who seems too curious about the girl who survived the attack. None of us knows who is guilty. Could you please send a message to the convent if anyone comes around asking questions?"

"Of course, Sister," Lizzie nodded sympathetically. "I'll be sure to keep an eye out. And I'll warn the, uh, the other girls as well."

"Bless you, my dear," Amanda said, lifting Bridget's crucifix in emphasis.

"Here, now, what's all this?" an unfortunately familiar voice came from behind Amanda.

She turned quickly and saw Joey Quinn walking up to them. Quinn looked Amanda up and down, and she felt chilled.

"What's a nun doing here, Lizzie?" he demanded as he strode up, facing off with Lizzie.

Lizzie's chin came up. "She's with one of the sisters at the convent where we took Francie. What's your name, Sister?"

"Sister. . .Sister Mary," Amanda grabbed for a name. "And I simply came to express our concerns for Francie."

Joey screwed up his unshaven face. "It's a shame that skinny little thing didn't attract that much attention when she was working here. This is the second time this week someone's come asking about her." He gave a disgusted snort.

Amanda went cold all over. Her sense was right. The killer *was* searching for Francie. "Did. . .did the person identify himself?"

Quinn narrowed his dark eyes and rubbed the black stubble on his chin as he peered at Amanda. "You look familiar. Do you have a sister or something that worked here?"

Amanda grabbed for something. "No, my good man. All of us at Saint Anne's look a little alike after awhile. Doing the Lord's work, you know."

"Hmmmmmmmm," was all he said, still scrutinizing Amanda. She swallowed, fearful he'd recognize her from the earlier visit with Devlin.

"Come on, Joey. Tell us," Lizzie prodded. "Who was the man asking questions about Francie?"

Quinn shrugged. "I don't remember his name. He was dressed all proper like and said he was with Senator Chester's office. They'd taken up a collection for the young victim of the attack and wanted to know where to deliver the donation. So, I told him Bill Kelly was Francie's father, and he lived in Snow's Court. He could take the money there, but Francie wouldn't see a dime of it. Kelly would drink it up."

Amanda strove to keep from allowing her rising panic to show in her voice. "When was this? Do you remember, Mr. Quinn?"

"A few days ago." He peered at Amanda again. "How'd you know my name?"

"I . . . I . . ."

"Fer Chrissakes, Joey, I *told* her," Lizzie interrupted just in time.

Gathering as much calm as she could, Amanda held up Bridget's crucifix again, hoping her hand wasn't shaking. "Thank you for telling me, good sir. I shall convey the message to Sister Beatrice. And thank you again for your help, Lizzie."

"I was glad to help, Sister. Anytime," Lizzie said with a warm smile.

"Yeah, well, come inside and help me get this place ready fer tonight why don'cha?" Quinn chided, giving Lizzie's arm a yank.

"I'm coming, I'm coming," Lizzie retorted. "What's yer hurry?"

Amanda raised her hand in a quick wave of goodbye before hurrying across D Street. She lifted the full skirts to quicken her pace. She could find a hansom cab on Pennsylvania as she had when she'd left Lafayette Square. Sister Beatrice and Father Tom must be alerted as soon as possible.

Devlin hastened across the green of Lafayette Square. It was such a lovely spring day and he'd walked all the way from the Carrington's home on Connecticut at a fast clip. He wanted to apprise Mrs. Duncan of the new information he had gathered since the soiree. Devlin also used the long walk to sort through his thoughts. He'd learned much in that short time.

Several well-dressed couples strolled through the lovely symmetrical park. Women who Devlin surmised to be governesses supervised young children at play. Two small girls were rolling hoops while another two boys raced each other over the green. Meanwhile, squirrels scampered out of the way or sat on the branches of the tall oak trees, loudly scolding the park's visitors for disturbing their rituals of stealing seedlings.

Devlin paused briefly to admire the sunlit view of the blossoming apple trees interspersed with the maples lining Jackson Place and H Street. As he did, he noticed a hansom cab draw up to Amanda Duncan's home. A visitor? Perhaps he should return another time.

His thoughts changed the moment Devlin spied a white-garbed nun emerge from the cab and hasten up the steps. Instead of ringing the bell, however, the nun appeared to unlock the door. Surprised that Mrs. Duncan had given one of the sisters a key to her home, Devlin was even more curious as to why the good sister was arriving by cab. Most of the various religious orders he'd observed in Washington were walking, not hiring hansom cabs.

Devlin waited a minute then bounded up Amanda Duncan's front steps. His curiosity got the better of him. And a new worry. Perhaps Francie had taken a turn for the worse, and one of the sisters was here to notify Amanda. Myriad scenarios popping into his head, Devlin rang the door chimes and waited. And waited.

Strange. Surely, the good sister wouldn't be all alone in Amanda's home, would she? He thought he spotted a slight movement of the lacy white curtain at the tall windows bordering the front door. The door finally opened, and Amanda Duncan stood there, her chestnut hair arranged in an unusual fashion, heaped upon her head.

Devlin immediately doffed his hat. "Mrs. Duncan, I hope I haven't disturbed you, but I wanted to share what I have learned since we last spoke at the soiree—" The rest of his sentence disappeared when Devlin noticed Mrs. Duncan was dressed completely in white in what looked for all the world to be a nun's habit. "Begging your pardon, Mrs. Duncan, but your attire is quite curious. I spied a nun exiting a hansom cab only a few moments ago and enter your home, and I—"

"Please come in, Mr. Burke, before my elderly neighbors get too curious," Amanda said, beckoning him inside.

Now that Devlin had a closer view of the garment, he was convinced. Amanda Duncan was the nun. He couldn't wait for the explanation. "Good Lord, Mrs. Duncan, have you taken orders?" he jested.

"Not at all, Mr. Burke," Amanda said with her winning smile. "I simply needed a disguise that would arouse no suspicion or questions. I had. . .an errand to run this morning."

Devlin stood, holding his hat and cane, waiting for the rest of the explanation. "An errand that would require a disguise? Exactly where did this errand take you, if I may ask?"

Amanda fixed him with a no nonsense look. "I returned to Joey Quinn's establishment. I wanted to ask one of the women who worked there if anyone has come around asking questions about Francie, and—"

Now, it was Devlin's turn to interrupt her. He stared at Amanda, incredulous. "Mrs. Duncan! I cannot believe you returned to that den of iniquity in the midst of Murder Bay! Do you realize how dangerous that was?"

"Yes, Mr. Burke, that's why I wore a disguise."

"Disguise or not, I cannot believe you did something so reckless!" he blurted, horrified that Amanda Duncan had been walking the streets of Murder Bay alone with only some good sister's habit as her protection. "What if that swine, Quinn, recognized you? I shudder to think what might have happened."

"Thankfully, he did not, because I share your concerns about Joey Quinn's nature."

Devlin shook his head. "I cannot believe you took such a risk."

"Neither can I, Mr. Burke," Amanda admitted. "But it did yield important information. I spoke with one of Quinn's women, Lizzie, and—"

The front door burst open then, and there stood Bridget, Mathias right behind her. Both of them stared at Amanda and Devlin, their expressions registering great surprise.

"What is going on here?" Bridget demanded, gloved fist on bony hip. "Madam, what on earth are you wearing? And why is Mr. Burke here?"

Devlin noticed that Bridget was scowling at him like he'd been up to something, but this time Devlin decided to defend himself. Amanda Duncan would have to fend for herself.

"That's exactly what I asked, Bridget, when I arrived only two minutes ago," he said, gesturing in a gentlemanly fashion to Amanda. "Mrs. Duncan, perhaps you can explain your actions to Bridget more convincingly than you have to me."

"Throwing me to the wolves are you, Mr. Burke?" Amanda asked with raised brow.

"Indeed I am, Mrs. Duncan," Devlin said, nonchalantly. "I cannot scold half as well as Bridget."

Bridget focused her hawk-like gaze on Amanda. "Madam, what have you been up to, may I ask? And what exactly are you wearing? It looks suspiciously like a nun's habit."

Mathias looked from Amanda to Bridget to Devlin, his dark eyes wide with concern. "Excuse me, ma'am. I'll just put this package here for now." He set the box on the floor and hastened out the front door, closing it behind him. Removing himself from the line of fire, Devlin surmised.

To her credit, Mrs. Duncan did not try to dissemble. Instead, she confessed. "Indeed, it is, Bridget. I needed to disguise myself in order to ferret out information. Francie's safety is at stake."

"So that's why you instructed me to wait on the seamstress. It was a ruse to get me out of the house." Bridget's wrinkles clustered together in a formidable frown. "Exactly where, pray tell, were you going that you needed to disguise yourself as a nun?"

Amanda paused. "Near Pennsylvania Avenue."

That answer clearly didn't satisfy Bridget. "Madam, I've travelled that entire avenue and there is no place where you would need to disguise yourself. Exactly where was this place?"

Again, Amanda hesitated. She glanced briefly to Devlin, and he couldn't resist. "I cannot save you, Mrs. Duncan. You had best tell Bridget the truth."

"Really, Mr. Burke," Amanda chided.

"Yes, madam. What is it you could tell this roguish Englishman, but you cannot tell me?"

Amanda sighed and surrendered. "I returned to the Quinn establishment and asked one of the women there if anyone had come around asking about Francie. You know how concerned I've been since the newspapers published..."

"*Holy Mother*!" Bridget gasped. "Madam, I cannot believe you went back to that wretched place!"

"My words exactly," Devlin couldn't resist.

"And. . .and you talked to a common <u>whore</u>! Madam! Have you lost your senses?"

At that, Amanda raised both hands. In the white habit, she looked as if she were about to say prayers. "Bridget, both you and Mr. Burke are correct. *Mea culpa, mea culpa.* I was reckless to venture into that dangerous area of the city even in disguise, but I sensed danger around Francie. And my risks yielded fruit. I learned that someone came to Quinn's bordello earlier this week and asked about Francie."

Devlin lost all interest in teasing Amanda. "Who was it? Did that woman know?"

"Actually, Lizzie did not speak with the man. Quinn said he spoke with him. The man did not identify himself. He—"

"Merciful God! You spoke with that. . .that creature?" Bridget had gone white as a sheet.

Devlin went cold. "Mrs. Duncan, I beg of you, please do not put yourself at such risk again. Quinn is a violent wretch. You should not be near him. He might recognize you."

"Well, he very nearly did," Amanda admitted. "But I talked my way out of it."

"Holy Mary and all the Saints!" Bridget muttered, crossing herself. Then she scrutinized Amanda again. "Madam, is that my rosary?"

Amanda gave her a sheepish smile as she gently removed the rose pink strand of beads and crucifix. "I confess it is, Bridget. I needed to borrow it to complete my ensemble." She handed it over.

Devlin simply shook his head. He was about to start saying prayers, himself, but he'd forgotten most of the ones he once knew. Mrs. Duncan's guile as well as her bravado were astounding. And worrisome. "Exactly what did Quinn say? Did he know the man?"

"No, he did not. The man said only that he was from Senator Chester's office and they had taken a donation for the young girl who survived the attack. And he asked Quinn where he could deliver the donation." Amanda looked at both of them, her anxiety evident. "So, you can see that my concerns were valid. The killer has come looking for Francie."

"All the more reason you should never return to that dangerous place, Mrs. Duncan," Devlin felt compelled to add. "Promise us you will never venture into Murder Bay alone again. The killer may lurk there yet. And you would need more than a disguise to protect you."

"I promise, Mr. Burke," Amanda said.

"Swear it," Bridget demanded.

"I swear that I will never return to Murder Bay unescorted again," Amanda repeated solemnly.

"Very well, then. Now, back to this inquisitive stranger who was asking about Francie," Devlin said. "I shall ask Jonathan to inquire with Senator Chester's remaining staff if anyone in their office had taken a donation."

"Mr. Burke, I believe that to be the killer's ruse to gain information about Francie's whereabouts." Amanda countered.

"I agree, Mrs. Duncan. But we should make sure we don't overlook anything."

Matilda suddenly appeared in the doorway to the parlor, holding a large tea tray. "Mrs. Duncan, ma'am. I heard several voices and I thought you and your visitors would like some tea."

"How thoughtful, Matilda. Frankly, I would love some. Mr. Burke, let us finish this conversation in the parlor. I believe you said you had new information as well. We need to share what we've each learned to better protect Francie." Glancing to Bridget, Amanda added, "Bridget, would you please tell Mathias that I'll be needing the carriage in an hour? I need to alert Father Tom and Sister Beatrice."

"You're going out again?" Bridget asked, clearly disapproving.

"Only to the convent, Bridget, I promise I will return straightaway," Amanda said as she headed down the hallway. "Come, Mr. Burke, let us have tea. We both have much to do."

"After hearing about your adventures this morning, I fear I may need something stronger than tea, Mrs. Duncan," Devlin said, only half joking.

"As you wish, Mr. Burke," Amanda Duncan replied, glancing over her shoulder.

"What do you plan to do next, Mr. Burke? Now that Raymond Miller is no longer a viable suspect. Who's next on your list?" Amanda stirred the sugar into her tea slowly.

Devlin sipped his second cup of cream tea. "I shall try to meet with this Broderick Wray, but I will need Senator Ingram's help with that. An introduction of sorts. I'd like to get a measure of the man. See how he reacts when Chester's name comes up. Then, perhaps I can probe a bit. Follow my instinct, if you will."

Amanda gave him a wry smile. "It sounds as if your sleuthing methods are not too different from my sensing abilities."

"You are too generous, Mrs. Duncan. My instincts have never provided the rich yield of your visions. We would never have thought to suspect one of Chester's acquaintances without them. We'd all believe the press's hysterical 'crazed maniac' as the killer. Your visions pointed to a man who was clever enough to disguise himself. That's no crazed maniac. That's a killer who thought this crime through."

"And has continued to elude us."

"For the time being, Mrs. Duncan. I believe our search will bring him into focus, eventually."

"It's the eventually part that concerns me," Amanda said, frowning. "I don't know how long Francie's whereabouts will remain hidden. Thanks to Quinn, the killer knows to contact Bill Kelly in Snow's Court. From what I've heard of Kelly, he is not a man to be trusted. What if he learns that Francie's at the convent?"

"Perhaps the man who approached Quinn was truly someone from Chester's office who came with a donation. It's not unusual for someone wanting to help," Devlin suggested, trying to reassure her—and himself.

"You do not believe that, Mr. Burke, and neither do I," Amanda said, as she placed her empty cup on the end table beside her armchair. "It was the murderer looking for Francie. I sense it."

"I confess, it is worrisome, and I've always been suspicious of coincidences." Devlin set his empty cup aside. "All we can do is to remain vigilant. You're going to alert Father Tom and the good sisters this afternoon. So, they will be on their guard against any inquisitive visitors."

"Perhaps we should find another place to shelter Francie. Maybe I should bring her here," Amanda mused out loud as she stared out the window into Lafayette Square.

Devlin didn't think that was a good idea at all but knew he must be diplomatic in his discouragement. "It sounds as if Francie's wounds have not completely healed, so moving her might not be wise. And remember, the convent is not a public place where people can come and go as they wish. They need to gain entrance to those cloistered spaces. So her safety should be secure."

"I suppose you are right, Mr. Burke." Glancing toward the stately grandfather clock that stood against the parlor wall, Amanda said, "We should be about our business while the afternoon is still with us. I assume you'll keep me apprised of any new information you learn, Mr. Burke."

"You may depend upon it, Mrs. Duncan." Devlin rose from his chair and smiled. "By the way, there is another reason you should refrain from bringing Francie into your home. I think Bridget has endured enough shocks to her system. I fear this suggestion might bring on an apoplectic fit."

CHAPTER SIXTEEN

Devlin strode into the Willard Hotel lobby. Senator Ingram had described Broderick Wray as a slender silver-haired man with spectacles. Then he specifically added that Wray usually carried his umbrella, no matter the weather.

Scanning the couples who strolled through the Willard's grand lobby at twelve noon, Devlin noticed a lone man standing off to the side of the parlor seating. The man was slender, dressed in black and held an umbrella by his side. Devlin walked up to him.

"How do you do, sir? I'm looking for Mr. Broderick Wray. Would you be he?" Devlin asked politely.

Wray looked at Devlin, a slightly startled expression in his pale gray eyes. "Yes, I am. Are you Senator Ingram's friend, Devlin Burke?"

"Indeed I am, Mister Wray." Devlin extended his hand. "Thank you for taking time to meet with me."

Wray shook Devlin's hand. "Not at all. I'm happy to help any friend of Warren Ingram. He's a good man."

"Would you join me for a brandy?" Devlin gestured toward the hotel's parlor.

"Thank you, that would be very nice, Mr. Burke," Wray said, accompanying Devlin into the elegant–yet-comfortable room.

Devlin doffed his hat and settled into an emerald green velvet armchair in the far corner, a matching armchair sat beside. It was a quiet nook in a crowded room. Several couples were scattered about enjoying the Willard's afternoon tea. As soon as Wray settled, Devlin signaled the waiter. "Two Grand Marnier's, please," he instructed.

"Tell me, Mr. Burke, have you known Senator Ingram long?" Wray asked, peering at Devlin.

"Not long at all, actually. I met him at a dinner party at Senator Hagan's home a few evenings ago. He and I briefly discussed investments and I mentioned my concern about the status of several of the American railroads, especially those on the East Coast and in the Midwest. Ingram suggested I speak with you."

The wary expression on Wray's face softened. "I see. Well, that was very flattering of Senator Ingram to recommend me. What is the nature of your concern, Mr. Burke? Surely not profitability. Our American railroads have been yielding great profits for you and the scores of other English and European investors."

Devlin sent him a friendly smile. "Indeed, so, Mr. Wray. So, you can imagine my concern with this situation of the smaller competing lines trying to cut into the larger rail lines' business by laying down parallel tracks. Such practices drive down shipping rates and prices as well as profitability." He paused to take his brandy from the waiter's tray. "It's most worrisome to those of us who hold large investments in your railroads. Our family's estate holds a sizable position in several of these rail lines."

Wray took a sip, closed his eyes, obviously enjoying the rich taste. "Very fine, very fine," he said in a slightly wistful tone. "Ahhhh, yes, you're correct, Mr. Burke. That situation has proved to be particularly troublesome. But I believe the situation may be alleviated fairly soon."

Devlin's financial instincts snapped alert. "Really? How, so?"

Taking another lingering sip, Wray savored before answering. "I've heard on good authority that J.P. Morgan in New York will take it upon himself to bring order to this situation."

That caught Devlin's attention. "Morgan will get involved? That is very good news, indeed."

Wray gave him a wry smile. "I imagine it is, Mr. Burke. Considering most of your fellow English investors hold your shares through Morgan's company. As you may yourself."

"You are correct on that front, Mr. Wray. We do, indeed."

"So, you can see why Morgan would involve himself. I've even heard it said he's railed against these uncompetitive practices many times." He drained his glass.

Devlin was beginning to like the man. Wray had a quiet competency about him. But, Devlin reminded himself why he had sought out Wray. "Would you care for another brandy?" Devlin asked, signaling the waiter. He hastily finished his own, so as to encourage Wray to have another.

Wray hesitated but a moment. "Why, yes, that would be very nice. Thank you."

Devlin settled into the chair as the waiter scurried off. "You're quite knowledgeable about the status of the American railroads, Mr. Wray. I commend you."

"Thank you, Mr. Burke. I. . .I've spent a lifetime with the rail lines. My whole family has, in fact." His mouth tightened a bit, Devlin noticed.

Softening his voice, Devlin added, "Ingram mentioned that you and your family owned a medium-sized line in the Midwest, Ohio, I believe."

This time Wray's expression hardened and his voice as well. "Yes. . .yes, we did. The line had been in our family for generations. Until that black-hearted bastard stole it."

Devlin was glad the waiter arrived then with the brandies. Hopefully, Wray's tongue would be loosened even more. Wray's gray eyes had darkened to slate. "Yes, Ingram mentioned that travesty. Senator Chester seems to have been a vile creature, indeed."

"He was a monster," Wray fairly hissed, then he took a large drink.

"Ingram said he cheated scores of men. From what I've heard, there were many who would have wanted him dead."

Wray shot Devlin a look. Devlin could see the raw hatred that still blazed in mild-mannered businessman Wray's eyes. The burning intensity was riveting.

"I hope he rots in hell. I only wish I could have been the one who sent him there. His treachery killed my father."

Devlin watched the anger seep out of Wray, hovering like a cloud above him. But what of his open admission he wished he'd killed

Chester himself? "Well, I'm sure the police are working diligently to find the murderer."

Instead of showing uneasiness of any kind, Wray looked Devlin straight in the eye. "They should give the man a medal."

If Wray were deliberately dissembling, then he was a damn good liar, Devlin decided. "Clearly, Chester will not be mourned."

Wray gave a derisive snort and tossed down the rest of his brandy. "If you'll excuse me, Mr. Burke. I believe I need to take a brisk walk. I'm afraid talking about Horace Chester puts me in a foul mood." He rose from his chair.

Devlin immediately followed suit, leaving a large bill on the side table. He grabbed his hat and cane. "I'm sorry, sir, if any of my comments offended you. It is clear that Chester's name brings back painful memories."

"Do not concern yourself, Mr. Burke," Wray said as they walked from the parlor and into the lobby once again. "I enjoyed our meeting otherwise. And I'm glad I was able to allay some of your concerns about our American railroad industry. Rest assured, order will be regained, sir. You may tell your fellow investors that their and your investments will be secure."

"Thank you, Mr. Wray. You were very kind to meet with me. I feel reassured, after hearing that Pierpont Morgan himself will be taking the rail lines in hand." Pausing in the lobby, Devlin thought to ask, "Would you care to join me for dinner, sir? We could continue our financial discussions over a fine rib roast."

Wray glanced toward the Willard's elegant dining room. Devlin thought he spied that wistful expression again. "Another time, perhaps, Mr. Burke. I'm afraid I have lost my appetite. I may stop at a tavern for some oysters after my walk. But thank you for asking." He donned his hat.

"Enjoy your walk, Mr. Wray," Devlin said, extending his hand. Wray shook it more forcefully this time, Devlin noticed. "By the way, where are you staying in Washington?"

Wray gave a small smile and gestured around the lavish lobby. "Right here, Mr. Burke. The Willard brings back more pleasant memories from the past. Good day to you." He tipped his hat then strode out the Willard's front door.

Devlin stood staring after him.

Amanda lifted her cotton skirts from the foul-looking puddle collecting in the Snow's Court alleyway and walked faster, striving to keep up with Father Tom's longer strides. The outdoor privies' stench had ripened in the midday sun and the rank odor assaulted Amanda's nostrils as they neared the inner courtyard.

"There was no need for you to come, Amanda," Father Tom said as they rounded the corner into the crowded inner court. "I'm sure Daisy was simply out of the house when Sister Teresa came by for her this morning. Perhaps playing with some other youngsters."

Amanda wished that were true, but she'd had an uneasy feeling when Sister Teresa returned to the convent and said she'd been unable to locate Daisy when she'd come for her. She'd knocked on the front door of the house Daisy and her father shared with the other families but no one answered, even though Sister Teresa spied faces at the upstairs windows. Sister Beatrice shared Amanda's concern that something might be wrong. Daisy would never miss a visit with her sister, Francie. Thankfully, Father Tom agreed to check on Daisy himself.

"I hope you're right, Father. But I've had a nagging uneasiness ever since I learned that Joey Quinn was approached by that stranger looking for Francie."

Father Tom and Amanda passed a cluster of small boys taking turns with a scarred wooden baseball bat, swinging it in mid-air. One little boy recognized the priest.

"Hey, Father. Who ya lookin' for?" he called, cap shoved back on his black curls.

"Why, hello, Robbie," Father Tom nodded to the bunch. "I was looking for Daisy Kelly. Have any of you boys seen her today?"

Robbie glanced sideways to his friends whose expressions turned solemn. He shook his head. "Daisy hasn't been out today. Mister Kelly came home drunk last night and whipped her pretty bad. We live next door, so I heard her crying."

Amanda caught her breath, her fears realized. "Is she at home now?"

"Yes, ma'am."

Father Tom leaned over and placed his hand on Robbie's shoulder. "Thank you, Robbie. We'll go and check on Daisy. You be a good lad and keep looking out for the young ones, all right?" he said in a warm voice.

"Yes, Father," Robbie nodded, blue eyes wide.

This time, Father Tom's strides lengthened so much that Amanda had to lift her skirts and run to keep up as the priest strode through the crowded court to reach Daisy's house. He took the steps two at a time, Amanda trotting behind him.

Father Tom pounded on the front door loudly with three loud thumps. "This is Father Thomas from Saint Anne's Parish. I've come to see Daisy Kelly. Please open the door."

Amanda's pulse was racing from the running and her heart was pounding out of fear for Daisy. Her eye caught movement at the upper windows and she managed a friendly wave and smile, hoping to encourage an answer. Whether it was Father Tom's pounding or Amanda's wave, the front door opened, and a thin grey-haired woman stared out at them, her face drawn and pale.

"Daisy's here, but she's afraid to come out and see you," the woman said. "Bill Kelly beat her last night because he'd heard she'd gone to see that 'whoring sister.'" Her eyes darted, looking over Amanda's shoulder. "Pardon me, Father, but you may be doin' more harm than good. Takin' her to see Francie and all." She glanced over her shoulder at the children hovering in the hallway, watching. "Bill Kelly's a mean one, he is. Especially when he's drinking, which is most times. He'll hit anything or anyone who gets in his way."

Amanda could feel the woman's fear radiating out of her. She'd probably gotten in Bill Kelly's way and had the bruises to show for it.

Father Tom's face had reddened, either from exertion or anger, Amanda couldn't tell. But she did recognize the priest's no-nonsense tone of voice. "Well, we've come to see Daisy and we're not leaving until we do. So, you'd best bring her out, Sarah."

Sarah stared at Father Tom for a few seconds then acquiesced. "All right, Father." She called over her shoulder, "Daisy! You can come out now. It's all right. It's Father Tom."

Amanda watched as the cluster of children stepped back to reveal Daisy, standing behind them. A protective wall of children. Amanda had to hold her breath so she wouldn't gasp out loud at the sight of Daisy's bruised face and neck showing above her cotton dress.

Father Tom walked into the room and held out his arms as he sank to one knee. "Come, along, Daisy. You know I won't hurt you."

Daisy didn't hesitate. She ran into the priest's open arms and began to sob. Amanda sank down beside Father Tom and patted Daisy gently on her arm. The flimsy cotton dress probably concealed worse bruises beneath.

"There, now, Daisy. You're all right now," Father Tom soothed the sobbing child. "We'll make sure of that."

"I'm sorry, Father. . .I had to tell Papa. He made me," Daisy choked out between sobs. "He. . .he made me tell where Francie was." She buried her tangled head in the priest's chest and cried. "I'm. . .sorry. . .Sister told me not to."

That cold feeling of dread that had been hovering beside Amanda settled over her like a shroud. Her fears were realized. Now, Bill Kelly knew where Francie was. And Joey Quinn had sent a man to Kelly's house looking for Francie. Offering a collection for her welfare. What would keep Bill Kelly from selling Francie's whereabouts?

Father Tom patted Daisy gently. "Don't you worry, Daisy. It's all right. Francie is safe. And you're going to be safe, too." With that, he gathered up the child in his arms and stood up. He fixed Amanda with a determined look. "We're going to make sure Daisy stays safe from now on." Then, he turned toward the door.

Amanda scrambled to her feet. Thank Heaven for Father Tom. Saint Mary's convent was the only safe haven for both of these brutalized girls.

Sarah blanched and walked toward them, hands out. "Where are you taking her, Father? Bill Kelly will fly into a rage."

The priest turned, Daisy snuggled into his arms. Skinny legs dangling on either side of him. "You tell Bill Kelly I've taken Daisy to Saint Anne's for safekeeping. And if he has any objections, he can take them up with me. He knows where to find me."

Amanda sent a clearly frightened Sarah an encouraging look. Unfortunately, Amanda knew it took more than encouragement to protect the defenseless in Snow's Court.

"I should only be a few minutes, Mathias," Amanda said as her coachman helped her from the carriage.

"Yes, ma'am," Mathias said with a nod as Amanda stepped onto the sidewalk in front of Winnie and Jonathan Carrington's Connecticut Avenue grey brick townhouse.

Amanda sped up the steps a little slower now that she'd changed back into her normal ladies' attire. Her sky blue crepe de chine dress gathered at the waist, with a belt cinching it fashionably. Her calling card in hand, Amanda let the brass knocker fall twice. The same proper English butler she'd seen at the Carrington soiree greeted her.

"Mrs. Duncan, I presume?" he asked, in a clipped accent.

"Yes, indeed. I hope I am not disturbing your mistress," Amanda said as she handed him the card. "I merely wished a moment of her time to convey some important information."

"Please come in. I will see if she is available," Jameson said, giving Amanda a slight bow before hastening down the hallway.

Now that the hallway was empty, Amanda could appreciate the décor. A luscious full fern sat on a nearby walnut entry table, its green leafy fronds draping almost to the floor. Oriental carpets with rich maroon and deep blue patterns graced the polished walnut floors.

Jameson reappeared as quickly as he'd disappeared. "Mrs. Carrington will receive you in the library." He gestured down the hallway. Winnie Carrington rose from her writing desk by the window the moment Amanda entered.

"Amanda, how delightful of you to stop by. Please come in. I was about to send you an invitation for dinner tomorrow evening."

"I apologize for interrupting your afternoon," Amanda said, removing her grey kid gloves as she entered. "But I have just heard some very distressing news about the young girl who's recuperating at Saint Anne's convent."

Winnie hastened to her side. "Oh, my, I hope she hasn't taken a turn for the worse."

"Fortunately, not. But it's her future wellbeing that I'm concerned about. I didn't think your brother would be in now, but I hoped you could convey the information when you see him."

"Of course, please sit down, Amanda. We'll have tea, Jameson," Winnie said to the butler who was still hovering in the library doorway.

Amanda sat n a deep blue velvet settee, and Winnie settled beside her. "Now, what has you so concerned, Amanda?"

"I visited the convent this afternoon and learned that Francie's younger sister, Daisy, had not arrived for her morning visit. The Sisters have been bringing Daisy for several days now."

"Yes, I recall your telling me. It's such a shame they have to be separated."

"However, this morning Daisy wasn't at her home. No one answered at the door when Sister Teresa knocked, even though there were clearly people inside the house looking out. Father Tom decided to go to Snow's Court and inquire about Daisy, so I accompanied him."

Winnie's eyes widened. "You are to be commended, Amanda. I have heard stories about the horrible conditions in these alley slums."

Amanda glanced down. She wasn't used to being praised for breaching society's rigid restrictions for genteel ladies. "You're very kind to say so, Winnie. I only help the good Sisters whenever I can. The conditions are wretched, indeed. But this morning I was so worried about Daisy I simply had to go with Father Tom. A young boy told us Daisy's father had learned she'd visited Francie and had beaten her the night before." Watching Winnie flinch, Amanda continued quickly. "We found her cowering with the neighbors, covered with bruises. Father Tom carried her back to the convent where she'll be safe. I hope." Amanda couldn't hide her apprehension.

"Thank Heavens for Father Tom," Winnie exclaimed. "He saved her from that brutish creature."

"Unfortunately, Daisy's father forced her to tell him where Francie is staying. That information was only known by a select few. Now, I fear that drunken father will pass along Francie's location for a price. Mister Burke and I have already learned that a man was asking about Francie's whereabouts, and—"

"What about Francie?" Devlin asked as he suddenly appeared in the library doorway. "Sorry to barge in, Winnie, but I spied Mrs. Duncan's carriage outside and was concerned she'd brought unfortunate news."

"She has indeed, Devlin," Winnie said to her brother as he sat in a nearby armchair. "It appears the young child's brutal father has learned that her sister Francie is staying at Saint Anne's convent. Amanda's concerned he will inform that inquisitive stranger who's been asking about Francie."

"I see." A worried expression crossed Devlin's face. "I can see why you're concerned, Mrs. Duncan. Their father, Bill Kelly, sounds like a drunken reprobate. If that stranger approaches Kelly again, he'll eagerly sell Francie's location for a price."

"My thoughts, precisely, Mr. Burke," Amanda replied. "This is the exact situation I feared would happen. Father Tom and I went into Snow's Court this afternoon and found Daisy covered with bruises. The poor child was terrified of her father, and rightly so. Father Tom took Daisy to the convent to spare her more brutality. He's also promised me that Francie will never be alone. There will be a nun with her all day and night. And Father Tom is only footsteps away." Amanda glanced out into the room. "Both Father Tom and Sister Beatrice have reassured me that both girls will be safe, but I cannot rid myself of this feeling of foreboding."

Winnie reached over and placed her hand on Amanda's arm. "That's understandable, Amanda. You've become extremely fond of these girls, and you're worried." Glancing at Devlin, she added, "Shouldn't the authorities be alerted to this new situation?"

"You're reading my mind, Winnie. I left a message for Chief Inspector Callahan yesterday informing him of the mysterious stranger who's been asking questions about Francie's whereabouts on the pretext of bringing her a charitable donation. Yet, Jonathan's inquiries on Capitol Hill revealed that none of Chester's congressional aides knew anything about a donation." Devlin frowned. "You'd think that new information would catch the chief inspector's interest, but I have had no reply from him."

"Having met Inspector Callahan, I can only surmise he's dismissed your information as idle gossip," Amanda suggested.

A maid entered the library then with a large tea tray. "Thank you, Annie," Winnie said, gesturing to a nearby table.

"I really should be going," Amanda said, stirring in her chair. "I've delayed your afternoon enough. You'll be needing to dress for a dinner engagement this evening, I'm sure."

Winnie gave a dismissive wave. "That's not until later, Amanda. We have time for tea. Plus, we need to hear from Devlin about his meeting this afternoon. Some railroad man who was cheated out of his family's railroad, if I remember correctly."

"Your memory is excellent, as usual," Devlin gave his sister a small smile. "Broderick Wray is his name, and I found him to be an engaging and modest businessman."

"This sounds like the man you mentioned earlier who might be a possible suspect in Senator Chester's murder," Amanda said as she accepted a cup of tea from Winnie.

"Indeed, yes. Chester stole the Wray family railroad a few years ago, and I must say, mild-mannered Broderick Wray fairly seethed with hatred at the mention of Chester's name." Devlin sipped his creamed tea.

"Ahhhh, that sounds like motive to me," Winnie announced, from behind her cup.

"Oh, Wray has more than enough motives to do away with Chester. However, he's also quite vocal in his desire that he wished he'd been the one who committed the act. I found that fascinating. When I probed him more, his gaze never wavered on mine. He declared the killer should be given a medal." He took another sip. "If Wray is lying, he's damnably good at it."

"Do you believe him?" Amanda asked.

"I'm not sure. He would have no reason to profess his desire to kill Chester so vehemently. So, that's puzzling."

Winnie pursed her lips. "Maybe he's simply play-acting to throw you off."

"That thought had occurred to me. But he would have to be as accomplished an actor as he is a liar. Liars often give themselves away. But there's something else that keeps me suspicious of Wray. Like Freddie, he's also staying at the Willard."

"Indeed," Amanda said, observing Devlin. "I find that very interesting, Mr. Burke."

"So do I, Mrs. Duncan. And I believe that Chief Inspector Callahan should be made aware of all the information that has come to light recently. And I intend to make sure the good inspector pays attention when I visit him tomorrow."

CHAPTER SEVENTEEN

Devlin paced the worn wooden floor of the District of Columbia's 15th Street Police Precinct station house. Glancing at his pocket watch again, Devlin counted off the minutes since he'd arrived and requested an appointment with Chief Inspector Callahan. Nearly three hours had passed. Other visitors came and went from the inspector's office, he noticed. Obviously, they had earlier appointments. Or, were considered more important.

Devlin had sat calmly for the first hour, even though the wooden benches lining the walls offered little comfort. Clearly, most of the folk who filled the benches surrounding him were more patient than he. Some had waited nearly as long as Devlin. Other offenders were brought up before the balding desk sergeant in a shorter time. Try as he might, Devlin could deduce no logical order in how the proceedings evolved. But having visited scores of constabularies in England, he knew that each precinct had its own order and procedures. Even if it wasn't immediately obvious.

Completing another lap around the main room, Devlin noticed a uniformed officer leave Inspector Callahan's office, then scurry over to the desk sergeant. The balding little sergeant leaned down to hear what the other officer said. Then glancing at Devlin, the sergeant gave him a sheepish look.

"The chief inspector will see you now, Mr. Burke. I'm sorry it was such a wait. The chief inspector's quite busy, you know."

"I understand completely," Devlin said amiably, striving to look as polite and patient as possible. "Thank you, sergeant." The other officer escorted

Devlin to Callahan's office, knocked once, then hearing a gruff voice answer "Yes", Devlin was ushered into the chief inspector's office at last.

"Mr. Devlin Burke to see you, sir," the officer announced before backing out and closing the door behind him. Callahan didn't even look up from the files he was perusing.

Undeterred, Devlin adopted his friendliest demeanor. "Inspector Callahan, how good of you to see me again," he said, striding across the office, hand outstretched.

Callahan raised his head, glanced at Devlin's hand distastefully, but gave a quick handshake. "What brings you here, Mr. Burke? As I told you before, our investigation is proceeding. You'll be informed of our conclusions when we're finished."

Devlin kept his pleasant expression in place with great effort. "I've come to bring you some new information which has recently surfaced regarding Senator Chester's murder."

Callahan raised one bushy gray eyebrow. "Have you, now? And what new information would this be that has eluded our police detectives?" he asked in a sardonic tone.

"I have been making inquiries amongst some of Senator Chester's colleagues and..."

"As have we," Callahan retorted.

"...and I have learned that there were several others in Washington who had grudges against Chester and regularly spoke with rancor about Chester's nefarious dealings with them. Some were quite vocal in their hatred of the man."

Callahan folded his arms on his desk and gave Devlin a patient smile, like a troublesome schoolboy brought up on truancy. "And who might these individuals be?"

"Raymond Miller, for one," Devlin went on. "He was a prominent Washington businessman and investor until Chester cheated him out of his fortune as well as his family's."

Callahan nodded patiently. "We've already questioned Mr. Miller, and he has an explanation and a witness for his whereabouts that evening, unlike your nephew, I might add."

Striving to maintain his cordiality, Devlin pressed on. "Yes, I was told that he was meeting with Senator Buchanan, then spent the later evening with a woman referred to as a 'hostess.' I wonder if you had questioned the woman to see if Miller was indeed with her the entire night?"

Callahan's smile disappeared. "We were about to interview the woman in question this week."

Devlin wondered if that was true or merely quick thinking on Callahan's part. The inspector clearly didn't take kindly to Devlin's suggestions. "And there is another gentleman who was cheated out of his family's railroad by Chester a few years ago. And I can attest his hatred of Chester is still raw. A businessman named Broderick Wray, who presently works as a lobbyist for the state of Indiana. And, he has been here in Washington for the past two weeks. The same timeframe of Chester's murder. And, Wray is also staying at the Willard Hotel."

Callahan's eyes narrowed and his voice came out tighter than normal. "We've been informed about Mr. Wray, and again, planned to question him this week as well. So, you see, Mr. Burke, we are one step ahead of you."

Devlin doubted that, but didn't let on. "That is gratifying to hear, inspector. I would be interested to learn if Mr. Wray has someone who can testify as to his whereabouts the night of Chester's murder." He deliberately held Callahan's angry gaze.

"Trust me, you and your family will be made aware of our investigation's findings. Is there anything else, Mr. Burke? I'm a busy man."

Devlin let his friendly smile fade. "Yes, there is, inspector. I have heard accounts that an unidentified stranger has been asking around the Murder Bay brothel about the whereabouts of the young girl, Francie, who survived the attack. I have personally contacted the Sisters of Saint Anne's Convent and have learned they are caring for the girl while she recuperates. The good sisters, as well as the rest of us who care about the young girl's safety, are quite concerned that someone was searching out for her whereabouts. And now I have heard that Father Tom from Saint Anne's parish found Francie's younger sister beaten in her home in Snow's Court. The priest has stated that Francie's father, Bill Kelly, is a drunken brute and beat the younger Daisy to force her to tell him where Francie was staying."

Devlin paused to watch his words register on Callahan's face. The inspector did not make an attempt to hide his surprise. "When did you learn this?" he barked.

"Three days ago. And what is worse, I've heard that the brothel owner, Joey Quinn, steered the stranger to Bill Kelly in his search for Francie. Now that Kelly knows Francie's location, the sisters as well as Father Tom are afraid Kelly will tell the stranger for a price. And that stranger may indeed be the killer and come back to remove the last witness to Chester's murder."

Callahan's face flushed and he leaned forward over his desk. "And just how come you are privy to this information, Mr. Burke?"

Devlin gave a nonchalant shrug. "As I mentioned in our previous visit, I have been involved in several police investigations in London. I have a natural inclination for detection, you might say. But I have been kept informed about the activities at Saint Anne's convent by someone who helps the nuns and priest in their work with the city's less fortunate. I'm sure you recall Mrs. Amanda Duncan? In fact, I contacted her at your suggestion, Inspector."

Callahan was clearly taken by surprise, Devlin could tell. The surprise was short-lived, however, and the inspector's face flushed red once more. Callahan slapped both hands on his desk and slowly rose from his chair. He was a tall man, and in his uniform and gold insignia, looked quite imposing.

"I see you've been quite busy since our last conversation, Mr. Burke," Callahan fixed Devlin with a hard glare. "Now, I suggest you stop interfering in official police investigations and return to your Wall Street financial business or whatever it is that you do when you visit our country. The London constabularies may appreciate your meddling in their work, but the Capital City of these United States does not."

Devlin held his ground. "I assure you, Chief Inspector Callahan, my intention was not to meddle, but to insure that the truth be revealed in this murder investigation. I had the distinct impression you and your detectives had convinced yourselves of my nephew's guilt and were disinterested in pursuing other viable suspects."

Callahan's face darkened. "That is a bald-faced lie. Your nephew remains the chief suspect because he publicly threatened and attacked Senator Chester only hours before the murder was committed. Your nephew, Freddie Livermore, had a reason to kill Chester, had knowledge of where Chester would be that night, and had the opportunity to commit the crime. And need I remind you, that your nephew also has absolutely no alibi for that evening. That, Mr. Burke, makes him the number one suspect in my book."

The force of Callahan's anger was considerable, but Devlin didn't blink. "I also spoke with Senator Remington and he confirmed that Freddie was with him that evening at his club."

"Only until eleven o'clock, Mr. Burke," Callahan sneered. "Senator Remington told our investigators that he delivered your nephew to the Willard at eleven o'clock. The Senator made sure your nephew was safely inside the hotel, then he returned by carriage to his own home on Connecticut Avenue, arriving by midnight. And Joey Quinn found Senator Chester murdered a little after midnight. So, you see, Mr. Burke, your nephew, Freddie, had ample time to leave the Willard, go to Quinn's brothel, and commit the crime."

"As did the other two gentlemen I mentioned, Inspector," Devlin insisted in a cold voice. "I'm curious if you will question them with the same thoroughness that you have demonstrated with my nephew. Broderick Wray also was at the Willard, and I believe he is here in Washington alone. Can someone vouch for his whereabouts?"

"We don't need you to tell us how to conduct our investigation, Mr. Burke," Inspector Callahan said in a derisive tone. "Now, I suggest you stop maligning honest businessmen and face up to the fact that your wastrel nephew is shamelessly using you and hiding behind his well-connected family in hopes he can escape being charged with murder." With that, Callahan marched across his office and yanked open the door, holding it wide. "As I said before, Mr. Burke, I am a busy man. Good day."

Devlin gathered up his dignity and marched out of Chief Inspector Callahan's office, wondering if his visit had done more harm than good.

Clearly, Callahan would discount any information Devlin brought to light.

As he pushed through the heavy precinct stationhouse door, Devlin felt those disturbing thoughts about Freddie's innocence nag his mind once again. They were growing stronger.

"This ginger cake is absolutely delectable," Jonathan said before popping another forkful into his mouth.

"It's quite delicious," Amanda said. "Especially the frosting."

Devlin savored his last bite of cake and frosting. "Mary Jane has outdone herself. This is wonderful."

"Thank you, I'll be sure to tell her. Mary Jane prides herself on her cakes and pastries." Winnie made a slight gesture to the butler. "Jameson, we'll have brandy and sherry in the library, please." Jameson nodded and held back her chair as Winnie rose.

"Extend my compliments to Mary Jane for the entire dinner, Winnie. The ribbed roast was most succulent," Devlin said as he dropped his napery on the table and assisted Amanda with her chair.

"We're so glad you could join us for dinner, Amanda," Jonathan said as he beckoned them down the hall. "It isn't often Winnie and I get to enjoy a simple private dinner with friends. We do hope you will join us again."

"We'll make sure of it," Winnie said, encircling Amanda's arm with hers.

"You're too kind," Amanda said with a smile. "I'd be delighted to return. I cannot recall when I've enjoyed such delightful company. I realize I've denied myself the pleasure of good friends too long. Thank you for encouraging me to re-appear, so to speak." Amanda patted Winnie's hand.

Both women's silken skirts rustled softly as they walked down the hallway, Devlin noticed. The rustle of silk. Unmistakable. One of Devlin's favorite sounds.

Amanda settled into one of the four armchairs clustered near the parlor's fireplace, which was cold now because of the early warm spring weather.

Devlin chose the armchair directly across from her. Jameson appeared then with a silver tray bearing an aged cognac and an equally fine sherry.

"I'll have the Armagnac, Jameson," Jonathan said as he chose the armchair across from his wife. "I expect Devlin will have the cognac. Ladies?"

Devlin sank back into the royal blue velvet while Jameson served Amanda and Winnie their sherry's. It had been a thoroughly enjoyable evening. Amanda Duncan was a delightful dinner guest and looked radiant in rose pink silk. Winnie and Jonathan were clearly charmed. And Mrs. Duncan was enjoying herself, Devlin could tell. Amanda's cheeks were slightly flushed and her smile was ever present. She and Winnie got along famously. Devlin couldn't remember when his sister had taken such a shine to someone. Winnie and Amanda were about the same age and they had very similar tastes. Jonathan had entertained them all with more tales of the less-than-esteemed members of the Senate. Laughter at the men's antics floated above the Carrington dinner table. Devlin had willingly kept his own comments subdued so as not to detract from Jonathan's stories.

Despite all the good cheer surrounding him, Devlin had been unable to shake the feelings of anxiety that had been with him ever since he left Chief Inspector Callahan's office earlier today. He had hoped to convince the inspector to expand Chester's murder investigation and look at both Miller and Wray. Instead, Devlin feared he had made the entire situation worse. He'd angered Callahan, and only inflamed his desire to charge Freddie with the crime.

"Devlin, you are quieter than usual this evening," Winnie observed. "Did your meeting with Chief Inspector Callahan not go well?"

Devlin accepted his cognac and swirled it beneath his nose, inhaling the rich, powerful aroma. "I'm afraid that is an understatement, dear Winnie. The inspector not only discounted the information I shared with him, but he became positively furious when I suggested he question both Miller and Wray as aggressively as he questioned Freddie. He did not take kindly to my suggestions, to put it mildly." Devlin took a deep sip of the smooth, yet potent brandy.

"Oh, my, that is distressing," Winnie said. "That means he's still focusing on Freddie as the guilty one."

"I'm afraid so, even though I practically accused his detectives of bias." He took another large sip.

"What did Inspector Callahan say when you told him about the stranger trying to locate Francie?" Amanda asked, her concern evident. "Surely he took that seriously."

"Yes, he did. In fact, I could tell he had heard nothing about it. Seeing that, I made sure he knew how concerned the priest and nuns were at the convent, especially now that Francie's father knows her whereabouts. Unfortunately, Callahan didn't appreciate my obtaining information before he did. And that made him even madder. In fact, he escorted me out of his office after that." Devlin took another sip.

"Oh, dear," Winnie face puckered in a slight frown.

"I can attest that Inspector Callahan does not accept information he has not gleaned himself or through his detectives," Amanda said. "He refused to take my warnings about the murder seriously. I believe he called them, 'hysterical imaginings.'" Amanda gave Devlin a sympathetic look.

"Don't be too hard on yourself, Devlin," Jonathan said from behind his glass. "I'm sure Inspector Callahan is considering your theories, even though he didn't want to let on."

"I'm afraid I may have caused more harm than good," Devlin said disconsolately. "Callahan seems more fixated on Freddie now than ever. I practically demanded that his detectives investigate Miller's and Wray's whereabouts more thoroughly." Devlin let out a discouraged sigh. "That's when I reminded him that Senator Remington had said he spent the evening with Freddie. But Callahan simply sneered at me and said Freddie's alibi was only good until eleven o'clock that night. Remington had sworn that he'd taken Freddie to the Willard by eleven, then returned to his own home around midnight. Then, Callahan reminded me that Freddie had ample time to go to Murder Bay and commit the crime."

"Humph! Remington must have some very slow horses," Winnie said before draining her sherry. "Doesn't he live down the avenue from us, Jonathan?"

"Yes, he does, my dear, and we may be seeing even more of him. He announced he would be having a fairly large party in a week, so expect the invitation. A lawn party, I believe."

"Celebrating his ascension to senior senator, I imagine," Winnie said.

Jonathan signaled for Jameson to refill his glass. "You know, Devlin. I think you need to expand your search as well. You've been looking at the most obvious suspects, so to speak. The men who had a visceral hatred of Chester. But I can attest that there are several more in the Senate who simmered with a low level rage at Chester's past dealings with them."

Devlin pondered Jonathan's suggestion. "That's a good idea, Jonathan. I've run through all the obvious suspects. But I can't shake the feeling that the killer has concealed himself in more ways than by wearing a uniform." He held out his glass for Jameson. "Do you have any suggestions where or with whom I might start?"

"Actually, I have an even better suggestion. I think you should speak to the elderly senior Senator from Virginia, George Smythe. He's well respected in the Senate and has done much to heal divisions since the War. He's become something of a sage in the Senate, and junior senators come to him regularly for advice." He sipped his cognac. "Senator Smythe also seems to know everything that goes on in that chamber. I'm sure he will know of anyone who's harbored a lingering grudge against Chester."

Devlin brightened. "That's an excellent idea, Jonathan. Could you arrange a meeting with the Senator for me?"

"Of course, I'll speak with him."

"Winifred, you must tell that cook of yours to use less ginger in the spice cake," Grandmother Carrington announced from the library doorway. "I fear it will wreck havoc with my digestion."

"I'm so sorry, Grandmother," Winnie said sympathetically. "I'll speak to her tomorrow. Would you care for an aperitif? A bit of mint liquor, perhaps?"

Jonathan sprang from his chair. "Let me fetch it for you, Grandmother." He crossed the room to an ornate mahogany cabinet where Jameson had placed the brandy and sherry decanters.

"Perhaps a bit of mint," Grandmother Carrington said,

"Grandmother, let me introduce our dinner guest, Amanda Duncan. You may have glimpsed her at the soiree last week," Winnie said, gesturing to Amanda. "Her family has been in Washington since before the Great War, isn't that correct?"

"Yes. My grandfather settled in Georgetown first and established the Washington Bank of Commerce."

Grandmother Carrington peered down her long nose at Amanda. "Ah, yes, I've heard of you. Aren't you the widow who prefers to spend her time in the filthy tenements with the lower classes than with genteel society?"

Devlin closed his eyes and counted to ten. After putting up with Inspector Callahan's pig-headedness, he didn't have much patience left for Grandmother Carrington's boorish behavior.

Winnie flushed scarlet. "Grandmother Carrington! Amanda is our guest."

"I am merely repeating what was whispered amongst your guests, Winifred."

Jonathan approached her, glass of clear liqueur in his outstretched hand. "Nonetheless, Grandmother, your comments could be taken as rudeness. Amanda's family is established in Washington society."

That was an understatement, Devlin thought, watching Amanda's reaction. Strangely enough, Mrs. Duncan didn't seem the least bit flustered. Instead, she smiled back at Grandmother Carrington.

"Do not concern yourselves, Winnie and Jonathan," Amanda said with a pleasant smile. "I was well aware that my decision to spend less time with societal obligations and more helping our city's less fortunate would draw unwelcome attention and misunderstanding. Grandmother Carrington's opinions are shared by many of my peers, I am sure."

"You are more than charitable, Mrs. Duncan," Devlin couldn't help adding. *Damn the old harridan.* She could lay into him over breakfast.

Grandmother Carrington sipped the mint liqueur. "Weren't you a member of Saint John's Episcopal? Why then, do you spend all your time with the Papists at Saint Anne's?"

This time, Devlin bit his tongue while he counted to one hundred. Jonathan tucked his head, clearly embarrassed. While Winnie rolled her eyes then spouted, "Grandmother! I am shocked that you would say such a thing! Whatever has come over you?"

"I'm simply repeating what is whispered about, Winifred," Grandmother said, nonplussed.

Again, Devlin noticed that Amanda Duncan was the only person seemingly unperturbed by Grandmother Carrington's comments. This time, her smile turned playful. "I admit I spend a fair amount of time with the good Sisters and priest of Saint Anne's parish because they seem to be the only ones in the city who try to improve the daily lives of some of the city's most wretched poor. As for parish attendance, personally, I've never believed the Almighty cares which pew one sits in," she said with an amused smile.

"Hmmph!" was all Grandmother Carrington said before tossing down the liqueur. "I will bid you all a good night." She then turned with a mighty rustle and left the library.

Winnie rolled her eyes. "Jonathan, you simply must speak with her. We cannot have her insulting our guests like that. Amanda, can you forgive that unbelievable display. She has always been opinionated, but now she's become positively rude."

"Please excuse her, Amanda," Jonathan interceded. "She's becoming a bit senile, I believe."

Devlin leaned forward in his chair. "Winnie is absolutely right, Mrs. Duncan. Please do not take Grandmother Carrington's insults seriously. She insults me on a daily basis. Thrice during breakfast alone."

At that, Amanda laughed softly. "I assure you, I took no offense at Grandmother Carrington's comments. In fact, I rather enjoyed her forthrightness. She's far more honest than most of society's denizens, who will smile sweetly then whisper snide comments behind one's back. I rather prefer Mrs. Carrington's honesty."

Devlin shook his head. "Your charitability rivals the good Sisters, Mrs. Duncan."

Winnie reached across and grasped Amanda's hand. "Promise me Grandmother's antics will not discourage you from visiting. I shall be devastated if it does."

Amanda patted Winnie's hand. "I assure you, I would not miss an opportunity to enjoy your company. You, Jonathan and Mr. Burke have provided me an expeditious way to gradually re-introduce myself into the arena once again. But right now, I should be going. It is late."

Devlin sprang from his chair as Amanda started to rise. "I'll accompany you home, Mrs. Duncan. Jonathan, could you have Jameson check on Mrs. Duncan's coachman, please?"

"Yes, of course." Jonathan approached and took Amanda's hand in both of his. "Promise me that you meant what you said, Amanda, about returning. I can't remember when I've had a more relaxing and enjoyable dinner. Such a pleasant change from the political affairs Winnie and I must attend."

"Definitely," Winnie said, approaching. "We'll walk you out. I'm glad you're accompanying her, Devlin. After Grandmother's tirade, you'll need to convince Amanda that our family is not composed of dolts."

"I assure you that I will be fine, Winnie," Amanda said as Winnie encircled her arm and escorted her down the hallway.

Jameson appeared with Amanda's cloak and Devlin's cane.

"I insist, Mrs. Duncan. I can regale you with other stories of Grandmother Carrington's excesses along the way."

"Now, Devlin," Winnie chided as Jameson helped Amanda with her cloak. "Let me check our calendar, but perhaps dinner again next week."

Amanda paused in the open doorway. "That would be lovely, Winnie. Thank you again for an...enchanting evening," she said with a twinkle in her eye.

"Charity again, Mrs. Duncan. The good sisters have indoctrinated you, to be sure." Devlin said, then leaned over and gave his sister a quick kiss upon the cheek. Jonathan approached then and stood by the door while Devlin escorted Amanda to her coach. Mathias stood ready and waiting, door open.

"I am taking your mistress home, Mathias," Devlin announced as he climbed in after Amanda. "She's had a stressful evening."

"Really, Mr. Burke, you make too much of this," Amanda protested lightly. "As I said, I rather enjoyed the thrust and parry of the exchange. Which tells me I've missed the arena more than I thought."

The carriage lurched into motion and proceeded down Connecticut Avenue, the newly-installed electric arc lights illuminating the street.

"This is the second time you've referred to these societal encounters as 'the arena', Mrs. Duncan," Devlin said, watching the arc lights flicker, casting shadows and light across Amanda's face.

"Oh, but they are, Mr. Burke. Reputations can be made and lost in an evening. I may have been out of society's view for a few years, but I have an excellent memory. And gossip travels everywhere. Family connections can protect you only so much. Repeated blunders are not forgiven."

Devlin laughed as he watched the coaches pass along Connecticut Avenue. "I couldn't have put it better, Mrs. Duncan. I've seen many a well-born country gentleman eviscerated for sport in the salons. And, I've seen a pretty face and quick mind carry others to the heights of society."

Not hearing a reply from Amanda, Devlin glanced at her. There was no trace of a smile on Amanda Duncan's face. She stared wide-eyed into the carriage instead. Devlin had seen that look on her face once before.

He quickly leaned over towards her. "Mrs. Duncan? Are you having another vision?"

The pale arc lights flickered across Amanda's face as the horse clip-clopped along the avenue. She continued to stare unseeing for a few seconds more, then visibly shivered, and she stared into Devlin's face.

"Mrs. Duncan, you've seen something, haven't you? What was it? Was it Francie?" Devlin reached over to touch her arm.

"Yes. . .I saw a shadowed figure hovering over Francie, clearly intent on harm." Her hand at her breast, Amanda gazed into his eyes. "We must go there immediately. Francie's in grave danger. I feel it!"

Devlin rapped on the side of the coach and called out the window. "Mathias, take us to Saint Anne's convent on the double!"

CHAPTER EIGHTEEN

Amanda and Devlin raced from the carriage to the convent front entry. Seeing that the heavy wooden door was already ajar, Amanda's heart sank. "This should never be open," she said to Devlin as he pushed through the door.

Farther down the gas lit hallway, an elderly nun was trying to rise from the floor.

"Sister, let me help you up," Devlin said, rushing to the older woman's side. "What happened? Did you fall? Are you hurt?"

"I went to answer the door. . ." She put her hand to her head. "And. . .and this man barged inside and. . .and knocked me down. I must have hit my head." She glanced around fearfully. "Is he still here?"

"Stay here, Sister, while I find out," Devlin said, advancing down the hallway. "You, too, Amanda."

"No, I'm going with you. That's Francie's room up ahead," Amanda said, pointing toward the light coming from a room at the far end of the hallway. Fear clawed at her inside, afraid of what they would find.

"Stay behind me, Mrs. Duncan. We do not know if this villain is still here," Devlin warned before rounding the corner. Once in the room, Devlin came to an abrupt stop—so sudden Amanda nearly ran into him. Francie lay in bed, one arm draped over the side, not moving.

"Ahhhh, I fear we are too late," Devlin said softly.

Amanda hurried over to the bed. Francie's large blue eyes stared lifelessly out into the dimly lit room. The bandages around her throat were ripped and dangled over the bedcovers. Bruises were already visible on her slender wounded throat. Amanda gave a little gasp. Her worst fears were confirmed. Francie was dead. Killed by the shadowy assailant.

Devlin stepped beside her and felt for Francie's pulse. He held Francie's slender arm for a full minute before placing it gently on the bed. "I'm afraid she's gone, Mrs. Duncan. It appears she's been strangled, and a short while ago because her body is still warm. Whomever you saw in your vision got here before us."

Amanda clasped her hands over her heart and closed her eyes as grief for the poor murdered girl swept over her. And rage. What manner of man could be evil enough to squeeze the life from this poor defenseless girl? Francie had escaped his attack, only to be tracked down like a wounded deer and devoured by this monster.

The elderly nun suddenly appeared in the doorway. "Oh, no! Please God, no!" she cried out as she hurried to the bed. Burrowing her face in her hands, she began to cry. "Who would do such a thing?"

Devlin attempted to comfort the elderly woman, but she sank to her knees beside the bed and began to pray, fingering the beads of the rosary that hung around her neck.

Amanda knelt beside the praying nun and patted her on the shoulder, offering what small comfort she could. Amanda had no comforting words. She'd learned years ago that prayers often went unanswered. And there was no comfort for the grieving.

Father Tom's voice echoed down the hall then. Amanda recognized the urgency. "Sister Ruth? Are you here?"

Sister Ruth stirred from her prayers and Amanda helped her to her feet as Father Tom rounded the corner of the bedroom, Sister Beatrice right behind him.

"Oh, Holy Mother, no," the priest said as he raced over to Francie's bed and felt for her pulse.

Sister Beatrice hastened over beside him. "Oh, dear God! How did this happen?"

Devlin stepped up to them. "Mrs. Duncan and I arrived only minutes before you. We found Sister Ruth on the hallway floor. Apparently, some man forced his way into the convent and knocked her unconscious." His face hardened as he looked at the dead girl. "And then he came to do his vile handiwork."

Sister Beatrice clasped both hands to her face. "It was a trick! A ruse to get us away from the convent," she cried.

Father Tom turned to them, his face paled. "We must call the police inspector. This dastardly villain lured us out of the convent so he could come in while Francie slept."

"Did you speak with the man?" Devlin asked.

"No, no," Father Tom said, beginning to pace. "I received a message at the Rectory earlier tonight. It said a family had been injured in Snow's Court. They needed help. Naturally, I went over right away. Sister Beatrice came with me. We went to the family's home, the Batson's, but they were fine. There was no injury. We knocked on several different houses and asked if they knew of a family being injured, but they said they didn't. That's when Sister and I returned. We met the other sisters on the way back."

Amanda glanced to the doorway and saw Sister Teresa and several other nuns, hands clasped in prayer.

Sister Ruth spoke up in a voice choked with grief. "Father Tom and Sister were only gone a few minutes when a young boy came knocking on the door to say that Father had been hurt and needed help. Of course, several of the sisters rushed right over to assist. They left me here with Francie. And ailing Sister Florence."

Sister Beatrice picked up her rosary and turned towards Francie. "We should never have left Sister Ruth alone."

"Do not berate yourself," Amanda consoled her. "Whoever did this obviously planned the best way to accomplish his foul crime. You had no way to know you were being tricked."

"Did you see any of the man's face, Sister Ruth? Could you describe his features at all?" Devlin asked gently.

Sister Ruth turned her tear-streaked face toward them. "No, no. . .his face was hidden by the hood of his cloak. He was tall; that's all I remember. It happened so quickly."

Father Tom put his hand on his forehead. "I am forgetting myself. This poor child has to receive the Last Rites. Let me get my things from the parish."

Just then, a small figure hovered in the doorway. Daisy. She looked over toward the bed where her sister lay and let out an anguished wail. "Francie! Noooooooo! Noooooo!" Daisy ran over to the bed and threw herself sobbing onto Francie's lifeless body Sister Beatrice gently tried to pry a hysterical Daisy from her sister with Father Tom's help. "Come, Daisy, we'll take care of you, now," Sister soothed.

"Francie's gone, sweetheart," Father Tom tried to console as he took Francie into his arms.

The child's grief sliced through Amanda like a heated blade. Why had she not listened to her sensing when she'd been warned about the danger to Francie? *Why?* Listening to Daisy's anguished cries pierced her heart. She balled her fist at her mouth to keep her own despair at bay.

"Mrs. Duncan, do you want me to take you home?" Devlin asked quietly, his eyes searching her face. "This must be beyond painful for you to witness."

"If only I had heeded my inner sensing," Amanda whispered to him. "This tragedy could have been averted. If I had brought Francie into my home for safekeeping when I first felt the danger around her, she would be alive now."

Devlin placed his hand on her arm. "Mrs. Duncan, do not berate yourself. Nothing would have stopped this vicious killer. Bill Kelly would have found out from Daisy where Francie was, and the killer would have shown up at your home. And you and Bridget would both be lying dead now as well as Francie."

Amanda stared back into Devlin's dark blue eyes, darker now with concern. He was right. The killer would have found them. "You're probably right, Mr. Burke, but I still feel that I've failed Francie somehow."

"We've *all* failed Francie, Mrs. Duncan," he said, dark eyes flashing. "None of us knew the depth of evil we were dealing with. Not the police and certainly not these good people of Saint Anne's. But I promise you I will not rest until I've found the heinous killer who took the life of this poor, wretched girl," he said in a tight voice, his grip tightened on her arm.

"Go to Sister now, Daisy," Father Tom said, handing the crying child to Sister Beatrice. "I have to get ready to bless your sister. She's already safe in the Almighty's care. No one can hurt her now."

Devlin headed toward the hallway. "Father Tom, do not concern yourself with the authorities. I will go outside and alert them. I promise they will be here promptly." With that, the crowd of nuns in the hallway parted to allow Devlin to pass.

Devlin sped up the steps to the Willard Hotel. He must apprise Freddie of what happened. Hopefully, Freddie had continued his newly-reformed habits of the past two weeks of staying in the hotel and conversing with acquaintances. Devlin had ordered Freddie to remain in the Willard's public areas like the dining room and parlors, where everyone could see him. He could meet with associates.

Striding to the hotel's front desk, Devlin inquired, "Would you happen to know if my nephew, Freddie Livermore, has retired for the evening or is he in the bar, perhaps?"

The uniformed clerk shook his head. "I don't think he's returned from his walk yet, sir. He mentioned he would be back late."

Devlin's heart skipped a beat. Out for a *walk*? Was Freddie insane? Why had he gone for a walk on tonight of all nights? Somehow, Devlin managed a polite smile. "Thank you. I'll wait for him in the parlor. Could you tell the server that I'd appreciate an Armagnac?"

"Very good, sir," the young man said, then pointed over Devlin's shoulder. "There's your nephew now."

Devlin whirled about and saw a smiling Freddie walk across the lobby towards him. "Why, hello, Uncle. What brings you out so late?"

Devlin intercepted him mid lobby. "I came with some shocking news, Freddie. Imagine my surprise when I found that you'd disobeyed my direct order to remain here at the Willard."

Freddie frowned. "I know, Devlin, but I was so bloody bored. I've been caged here for nearly two weeks. I simply had to get out, so I took a walk. Nothing more."

"Did you take anyone with you?"

"No, I went alone. I needed to clear my head. I was only gone for an hour or so. What's the harm in that?"

Devlin took Freddie by the arm and escorted him toward the parlor. The lights were dimmed because of the lateness of the hour, and the room was emptied, much to Devlin's relief. He didn't want eavesdroppers on this conversation.

"There is more harm than you know, Freddie." Devlin directed him to an armchair in a back corner of the parlor, where a flickering gas wall sconce illuminated the spot near a window. Devlin chose the armchair opposite. "Tonight, the young girl who survived the killer's attack the evening Chester was killed was murdered. Strangled in her bed at the convent where she was recuperating. Approximately an hour ago. Precisely the same time you felt the need to clear your head, Freddie." Devlin glared at his nephew, furious at Freddie's heedless disregard of his situation.

Freddie paled, visible even in the low light. "Oh, no," he whispered.

Devlin let his voice drop to the floor. "Oh, no, is right. You're already Chief Inspector Callahan's prime suspect in Chester's murder, primarily because you have no alibi. And now, this poor girl is killed while you are wandering about the city alone. You realize that the inspector will leap upon this as yet more evidence of your guilt."

Freddie blanched even more, if that was possible. He tried to speak, but all that came out was a stutter. "B-but I. . .I didn't d-do it. . ."

"Ahhhhh, but it looks like you could have," Devlin pinned him. "You have no one to vouchsafe for your whereabouts for either crime."

"But. . .but I would have no reason to k-kill the girl!" he protested is an urgent whisper.

"The press has reported that the girl survived the attack, and the police know that she heard the Senator call out the killer's name. Alas, she cannot remember. But the killer doesn't know that. Therefore, eliminating the girl would eliminate any threat to the killer's identity being revealed."

This time, Freddie just stared back bleakly at Devlin but didn't answer.

"Callahan will learn of this murder tonight. I alerted a patrolman on the street near the convent before I came here. And you can expect that Inspector Donnelly will fairly fly over here to the Willard to question you tomorrow morning. And I cannot imagine the mustachioed inspector being able to restrain his glee when he learns that, once again you have no alibi for the time of this murder. Even our family's influential connections cannot protect you from Callahan much longer. I fully expect he will bring charges in a matter of days."

Devlin wasn't sure, but he thought he spotted Freddie start trembling. He also noticed the server approach with his cognac. "Thank you. And could you bring my nephew a glass of water, please?"

"Could. . .couldn't I have a brandy? I. . .I need it," Freddie rasped as the server walked away.

"No, I want your head and your tongue clear," Devlin said, a little less harshly. He decided he'd best try to calm Freddie before he fell apart. "What I want you to do now is to take a deep breath then go back in your memory. I want you to remember everything that happened the day and the evening of Chester's murder. Start with your altercation at the Capitol."

Freddie stared at Devlin, swallowed twice, then did as he was told. He took a deep breath and began to recite the events of that fateful day. Devlin sat, sipping the aged cognac, and listened. Listened for something, anything that leapt out at him, knowing that the act of recitation itself would bring the events more sharply into Freddie's mind. And they needed to be. Devlin had no doubt that Freddie would be questioned by Callahan's detective's tomorrow morning.

"And I showed up at five o'clock that evening, the time Remington arranged for my meeting with Chester. But when I arrived at Chester's office, he acted as if I was intruding. He said he didn't recall a meeting with me. So of course, everything went from bad to worse after that. I refused to leave and accused him of deliberately cheating me." Freddie's face darkened again as it had the first time Devlin watched him recount the tale. "That's when he laughed. Chester laughed at me and said he had no intention of returning the money." Freddie closed his eyes. "Then he walked out. That's when I chased him down the corridor and gave him the thrashing he deserved."

Devlin watched Freddie, watched the emotions flash hot across his face. Those nagging doubts about his nephew's innocence rose to nag at him again. The waiter reappeared with the water, which allowed Freddie to regain his calm as he quenched his thirst. Afterwards, Devlin asked, "After the other Senators pulled you off Chester, what happened then?"

Freddie released a breath. "Chester threatened me with the police but the others calmed him down and took him away. Then Senator Remington came over to me and offered to take me to his club so I could collect myself. We caught a carriage and went to his club on New Hampshire Avenue where he had dinner."

"That was extremely kind of Remington to do that," Devlin commented.

"Yes, I thought so, too, especially since Remington had never paid any attention to me before. I was quite surprised, actually, but appreciative. It allowed me time to collect myself."

Devlin looked out into the Willard's parlor, pondering what Freddie just said. At the Carrington soiree, Senator Remington told Devlin that he'd "taken a liking to Freddie" and had tried to "warn him away from Chester." Yet, according to Freddie, Remington had never paid attention to him before. Interesting.

"Had Senator Remington ever spoken to you about Chester and his investment schemes?" Devlin asked.

Freddie looked surprised. "Never. As I said, I'd only met the man once before in some large banquet months ago. I'd been introduced to him once and we chatted briefly. That was all."

Intrigued, Devlin continued to probe. "What did you talk about during dinner? Do you recall?"

Freddie nodded. "Of course. Remington regaled me with stories of other men that Chester had defrauded and cheated. In fact, the list was endless. We talked well past dinner and over drinks."

"How long did you stay with Remington at his club that evening?"

"I can't remember exactly, but probably a little after ten o'clock. We were talking and then I began to feel unusually sleepy. Remington kindly offered to escort me to the Willard so that I could retire."

Devlin's inner sense started to tingle. "Really? That's rather early for you, isn't it, Freddie?"

Freddie gave a self-deprecating laugh. "Yes, it is. I remember telling Remington when he left me at the Willard that it was the first time in memory that I'd gone to bed before midnight."

"And what time did you arrive at the Willard?"

"Eleven o'clock. I remember because Remington pointed to the large clock mounted on the wall behind the hotel's front desk and remarked at the time."

Following his instincts, Devlin continued to probe. "Tell me, Freddie, do you recall what you and Remington were drinking after dinner? Wine? Spirits?"

Freddie pondered for a second. "I believe we both enjoyed an aged Kentucky bourbon, the club's private stock. Quite good, as I recall."

"Anything else? Any other brandies or liqueurs?"

Freddie closed his eyes and thought. "Oh, yes, I also had some special aged brandy which Remington kept in his flask. That was quite good. And obviously quite potent because I began feeling sleepy a short while afterwards."

Devlin's pulse began to race. Suddenly several bits and pieces and assorted items of disjointed information began to fit together. He stared off into the Willard's darkened parlor.

Did Remington drug the brandy to make sure that Freddie stayed asleep at the Willard and have no alibi for that night? Was Remington solicitous to Freddie only so that he could ensure that Freddie was implicated in Chester's murder? Why would Remington do that? What reason would he have, Devlin wondered?

Clearly, Devlin needed to learn more about the new senior Senator from New Jersey. Perhaps Jonathan could arrange a meeting with that elderly Southern Senator he'd mentioned earlier this evening.

Devlin pulled out his pocket watch. Nearly midnight. The relaxed and enjoyable dinner he and Mrs. Duncan had shared at the Carrington's this evening seemed days ago instead of hours. He glanced over at Freddie. It would be morning soon, and Inspector Donnolly would come calling for Freddie. The best thing that Devlin could do right now was to provide Freddie with the last shred of family protection available.

He tossed down the last of the smooth cognac and rose from the chair, beckoning Freddie to do the same. "Come along, Freddie. You and I are returning to the Carrington's. Since it's past midnight now, they're no doubt sound asleep, so we'll endeavor to move quietly. Go up to your room and pack your things as quickly as possible. I'll have the doorman flag a carriage." He dropped a large bill on the end table.

A bewildered Freddie followed Devlin from the parlor. "But. . .but why do I have to leave here? I'm quite comfortable, and I can meet with my friends."

"Your friends can find you at Winnie and Jonathan's," Devlin replied, eying his nephew. "Meanwhile, I don't want you cowering at the Willard alone when Inspector Donnolly swoops in like a hawk, ready to grab you like an unsuspecting field mouse."

Freddie flushed and protested. "I say, Uncle, that's a rather demeaning description."

"I can only judge from the last interview I witnessed," Devlin replied in a cool tone. "Donnolly was restrained then. I suspect he'll be swooping in, talons bared this time. So, I want to throw him off. Make him come to us. He'll have to question you in our presence, which should take away some of his ferocity. It's the only protection we can offer you right now, Freddie."

Freddie's eyes widened, positively mouse-like in fear. "I appreciate it, Uncle. Thank you."

"You're welcome, Freddie. Now be a good lad and go up and pack your things. We need to be off."

CHAPTER NINETEEN

"I will seek out Senator Smythe this morning, Devlin. Hopefully, I'll have an answer from him before this afternoon," Jonathan said as he donned his hat.

"Thank you, Jonathan. I need to hear what this sage of the Senate knows about Edmund Remington." Devlin stood in the open doorway.

"I agree, Devlin. Your account of Remington's conflicting comments and his behavior with Freddie at his club make me curious as well. We must get to the bottom of this. Till this evening." Jonathan nodded then sped down the front steps to his carriage where the Carrington's coachman, Bartholomew, waited.

Winnie stepped beside Devlin and waved to her husband before closing the door. "I do hope Jonathan returns home earlier this evening. We have a dinner engagement at the Californians."

"Well, I shall volunteer to stay in with Freddie and keep him company this evening," Devlin said as they walked down the hallway together. "I rather think he'll need some company. I fully expect Chief Inspector Callahan to send his detectives to question Freddie sometime today."

"That was clever of you to bring him home from the Willard last night. Jameson told me you two came in well after midnight. I agree Freddie shouldn't be alone when he's interviewed by the authorities."

Devlin entered the sunny breakfast room again and went to pour himself another cup of tea. "Has Freddie stirred yet?"

"Not yet. Jameson said he looked awfully tired and forlorn last night. Poor thing." Winnie said sympathetically.

"Poor thing, nothing. Freddie's behavior throughout this investigation has been responsible for putting him squarely in Inspector Callahan's sites." Devlin gave a derisive snort. "Taking a walk all alone on the very night that poor girl was murdered. Stupid! If Freddie wasn't my nephew, I swear I would throw him to the wolves."

"That poor, poor girl," Winnie said, her expression concerned. "What manner of monster could sneak into a convent and strangle a sleeping girl in her bed?"

"A vile monster, indeed. And I intend to speak with Father Tom today to see what the police are doing to search for this killer. I dare not visit Inspector Callahan again. I fear I wore out my welcome with the last visit."

"How did Amanda stand up to the shock of Francie's death?" Winnie asked with a concerned expression. "She'd been visiting Francie ever since she came to the convent."

"Amanda took it very hard," Devlin said to his sister. "She blamed herself for not doing more to help protect Francie. She'd even thought of taking the girl into her own home. I told her that would have resulted in even more tragedy. The killer would have learned of Francie's whereabouts and both Mrs. Duncan and her maid, Bridget, would have been killed, too."

Winnie drew in her breath in a gasp. "Oh, Devlin, please tell Amanda I agree. She should never take such a risk. Amanda is too brave for her own good."

Devlin declined to tell his sister about some of Amanda Duncan's riskier adventures. "I will make sure I tell her of your concern, Winnie."

Winnie reached into the pocket of her stylish dress and withdrew a small envelope. "Could you give her my note, and tell Amanda to please drop by any morning? I'll be happy to have an excuse to cancel those tedious morning calls."

"I shall, dear Winnie," Devlin smiled and kissed her cheek. "Let's see...if this is Tuesday, then it must be..."

"Senate wives. And I have several that I owe a return visit. Still, it will be more interesting than staying at home on Friday and receiving those dreary Congressional wives." Winnie rolled her eyes. "Some of them have clearly never been out of the provinces before. One woman even had the gall to venture upstairs, can you believe? Jameson had to escort her back to the parlor with the rest of them."

Devlin laughed softly as he took his hat and cane from Jameson. "I bid you a less adventurous morning then. I am off to the investment house offices first, then I'll walk over to Saint Anne's parish and see what I can learn. Please send Bartholomew after me if Detective Donnolly shows up." He donned his hat and headed out the door.

"Exactly who is Detective Donnolly?" Winnie asked from the threshold.

"He's Inspector Callahan's right hand man and a veritable bull terrier. I want to be here when he questions Freddie."

Amanda looked across the convent inner courtyard at Daisy. The child sat beside Sister Teresa's flower gardens, idly picking at the petals of the blooming plants—tulips, daffodils, daisies. No longer joyfully picking flowers for her sister, Daisy sat disconsolately now.

"How is she doing?" Devlin asked quietly as he stood beside Amanda.

"She spent all morning following after either Sister Beatrice or Sister Teresa. She stayed with me while the Sisters said their prayers. Thankfully, I was able to distract her while the undertaker came."

Devlin shook his head. "Poor child. She's truly bereft without her sister."

Amanda felt a little sting of grief. "I know. I offered to take Daisy home to stay with Bridget and me, but Daisy seems petrified to leave the convent. I believe she sees the convent as a safe haven, a sanctuary. And the sisters are the guardian angels, I suppose. Even though they weren't able to keep Francie safe." She looked intently at Devlin. "And that's my fear, Mr. Burke. That the killer may learn of Daisy and come back for her, thinking she knows something."

"I don't think you have to worry on that account, Mrs. Duncan. The press doesn't know of Daisy's existence."

"Well, let us hope it stays that way."

"Tell me, Mrs. Duncan, which detective came last night to investigate this crime? Was it a somewhat taciturn, mustachioed gentleman with an ill-fitting suit by the name of Donnolly?"

"Why, yes, Mr. Burke," she replied, surprised by his question. "It sounds like you've met him before."

"Yes, I have, and I found him to be quite thorough. Can you tell me how he proceeded with this investigation? What was his demeanor? Did he seem shocked at finding poor Francie strangled in her bed?"

Amanda nodded. "Indeed he was. He continued to express his condolences to Father Tom and the Sisters on not being able to protect the girl from this horror. He appeared to be really upset that the killer had found her and planned out such a stealthy attack."

"Did he make mention, perchance, that this culprit is the same man who killed Senator Chester?"

Amanda gave him a small smile. "No, he didn't, Mr. Burke, but I mentioned it to the detective. He looked rather startled at my suggestion. Then he appeared to remember seeing me before at the station house and asked if I was the 'woman who sees things'. I affirmed that I was, indeed. And that you and I had walked in only minutes after the killer had been here. And we were the ones who found Sister Ruth on the floor and discovered Francie."

"I daresay that information didn't sit too well with Inspector Donnolly," Devlin said wryly.

"Actually, he took it in stride. He did ask how the two of us happened to visit the convent at that hour of night." Amanda couldn't resist smiling wider. "Then I told him about the vision I had in the carriage."

Devlin laughed softly. "I imagine that shut off the good inspector's questions rather quickly."

"Actually, Inspector Donnolly seemed more interested than Inspector Callahan in the details. He asked me to describe each one of the visions I'd had concerning these murders. He took copious notes, so who knows if Inspector Callahan will pay heed or not."

Sister Beatrice entered the courtyard and approached Daisy, leaning down to give her a hug. Daisy scrambled to her feet beside the diminutive nun. "Daisy, would you like to pick a bouquet of flowers for me? I'd love to put it in my alcove."

Daisy nodded solemnly and bent over the flower beds once again, choosing flowers this time. Sister Beatrice swiftly approached Amanda and Devlin. "I wanted to distract the child while I spoke with you two. Father Tom just informed me that Bill Kelly has come to the Rectory again this morning, asking about Daisy. Father told him about Francie and the man barely blinked an eye, apparently." The nun wagged her head. "I'm afraid Bill Kelly doesn't care for Daisy either. He simply wants her to cook and clean for him."

"Father Tom isn't seriously considering returning Daisy to that brute, is he?" Amanda asked, incredulous.

"Where do your local authorities stand on this matter, Sister?" Devlin asked.

Sister Beatrice gave a little shrug. "We've been able to shelter some women from their brutal husbands for a day or two, but then the men demand their wives return or they'll go to the police and lodge a complaint. So, we have to allow the women to return to their homes, even though we often come back months later when it's too late to save them. They've passed away."

Amanda felt a chill settle over her. That would not happen to Daisy. Not while there was breath left in her body. "Sister, we cannot allow Daisy to return to her father, especially not in her fragile mental state. The poor child is still grieving her sister."

"I agree, Sister," Devlin added. "Perhaps we can threaten Kelly to keep him away. Tell him we'll report him to the authorities."

"I'm afraid Bill Kelly would merely laugh at us, Mr. Burke," Sister said. "But don't worry. Father Tom is holding firm. I believe he's threatened Kelly with the authorities for his beatings to Daisy."

Another nun hastened into the courtyard and drew Sister Beatrice aside, whispered to her, then left as quickly and quietly as she came.

"Is there a problem, Sister?" Amanda inquired.

"Not for us, but I sense there may be for Mr. Burke and his family. Sister Sarah informed me that there is a coachman outside waiting for Mr. Burke. Apparently he is needed at his home immediately."

"Ah, I believe a visitor has arrived at my sister and brother-in-laws' home, so I must return." Devlin touched the brim of his hat. "Sister, Mrs. Duncan, please forgive my abrupt departure. Rest assured that I will keep you both apprised of whatever I learn concerning this sordid business. Good afternoon, ladies."

Amanda followed Devlin. "I hope your afternoon visitor brings good news, Mr. Burke," sensing that Devlin was saying less than he would have if they were alone.

Devlin met her gaze. "Indeed, I hope the visit turns out well. Inspector Donnolly has no doubt arrived to question our nephew. If you will be at home tomorrow afternoon, I shall stop by and apprise you of the information I have recently learned." Then he reached into his vest pocket. "I almost forgot. My sister sent this note and hopes you will visit with her again soon. Until tomorrow, Mrs. Duncan." He said and hastened form the courtyard into the convent.

Amanda took the note and slid it into the pocket of her crepe de chine gown. Indeed, there was more going on at the Carrington household than Devlin Burke let on.

"Mr. and Mrs. Carrington are in the library with your nephew and Inspector Donnolly," Jameson said as he took Devlin's hat and cane.

"Thank you, Jameson. How does Freddie look?

"Anxious, sir."

Devlin sped down the hallway into the parlor. Winnie and Freddie sat stiffly on the settee, while Jonathan stood by the fireplace. Inspector Donnolly sat in an armchair, notepad and pencil at the ready, Devlin noticed. "My apologies to you all for the delay. And especially to you, Inspector. I appreciate your waiting until I arrived to begin your interview with my nephew. But, I'm sure you understand that we all want to be present." Devlin chose a chair opposite Donnolly but across from Freddie so he could monitor Freddie's reactions.

Donnolly turned to Devlin with that same air of imperturbability that was apparent the first time Devlin watched him interview Freddie.

Nothing seemed to fluster Inspector Donnolly. "Nothing to worry about, sir. I totally understand. Families have to stick together, they do." He glanced around at the tense little group. "Well, shall we begin?"

"Please do, Inspector," Jonathan said as he rested his arm on the mantel, observing.

Donnolly leafed through some pages of notes and read, then spoke in that calm, matter-of-fact tone of voice that Devlin remembered. "Tell me, Mister Livermore. You're still residing at the Willard Hotel I believe, are you not?"

Freddie started to speak, then paused to clear his throat. His voice was still raspy soft. "Yes, I was, Inspector. Until last night, that is, when I returned to my aunt and uncle's home."

"And did you meet with various business colleagues while at the Willard?" Donnolly scribbled while he spoke.

"Y-yes, sir."

"Have you had an occasion to visit the Capitol building since the evening of your altercation with the late Senator Chester?"

Freddie looked properly appalled, much to Devlin's relief. "Good heavens, no!" he said forcefully.

Donnolly nodded solemnly and scribbled. "I would imagine not, sir. Have you had occasion to dine out with friends in the evening lately? At various restaurants around the city, perhaps?"

"No. . .no I haven't. I usually meet friends and colleagues at the Willard for dinner."

Devlin recognized Donnolly's roundabout style of questioning. All designed, no doubt, to lull the person being interviewed into a comfortable sense that they were simply having a conversation, so they would drop their guard. That's what Donnolly was waiting for; Devlin could feel it. That's when Donnolly would pounce.

"I see." Donnolly wrote down his reply then looked at Freddie. "Tell me, Mister Livermore, did you dine with friends last evening?"

"Yes, I did," Freddie said, straightening a bit.

"Could you give me their names, please?"

Devlin listened while Freddie rattled off the names of the two men he'd dined with last night. Meanwhile, Devlin glanced to Winnie who sat stiff as a rod beside Freddie, hands in her lap. His sister's face was composed, but Devlin recognized the signs of tension and worry around her eyes and mouth. He tried to catch her eye, but Winnie had been fixated on Donnolly since the questions began. However, Devlin did exchange a glance with Jonathan. Clearly, he was as worried as Devlin.

"When did you gentlemen finish your dinner, sir?"

Freddie cleared his throat again. "Approximately eight o'clock."

"Did you enjoy an evening libation afterwards, sir?" Donnolly continued taking notes, without looking up.

Devlin sent Freddie a warning look when he glanced his way, as if to say: "Do <u>not</u> lie."

Freddie stared at his uncle, eyes wide. "Yes. . .yes we had brandies in the bar."

"And what time did your friends finally leave yesterday evening?"

"It was a-after nine o'clock," Freddie said, glancing to Devlin again. "I-I can't be sure of the exact time."

Donnolly looked over at Freddie. "And what did you do then, sir? Did you retire for the evening?"

Freddie glanced to Donnolly briefly, then stared down at his trouser leg. "No. . .I went for a walk."

Donnolly eyed him. "A walk, sir? Why was that? Are you in the habit of taking walks late in the evening?"

Devlin held his breath, hoping that Freddie would hold up. Donnolly was circling Freddie, dropping lower and lower, keeping the unsuspecting field mouse in view. And Freddie was turning more mouse-like by the minute.

"I-I-I wanted to get a breath of fresh air, that's all," Freddie said softly.

"And where did you walk, sir, if I may ask?"

Freddie started rubbing one finger against the other. He seemed to sink back into the settee, as if he were trying to get away from these distressing questions. Then, he spoke in a quiet voice. "Uhhh, along Pennsylvania Avenue, then I walked toward Lafayette Square, then up to Washington Circle."

Devlin wanted to reach over and shake him. Tell him to sit up straight, look Donnolly in the eye, and don't waver—instead of this pathetic posture.

"And what time did you return, sir? To the Willard, that is?" Donnolly's notepad was resting on his knee. Devlin sensed he already knew the answer. No need to write it down.

Freddie shrugged, then brushed invisible lint from his trouser leg. "I'm. . .I'm not sure. Perhaps ten o'clock or so."

Donnolly picked up his notepad and read from a page that he'd already turned to. "According to the Willard desk clerk who was on duty that evening, you returned from your walk well past eleven o'clock that evening." He fixed Freddie with a sharp eye. "That's a long walk, if I do say so, Mr. Livermore."

Freddie finally looked up and was caught in Donnolly's gaze. He paled. "I. . .I. . .lost track of time. . ."

"Indeed, so, sir. That's a two hour walk or more."

Freddie hastily looked away. "I. . .I suppose so. . ."

"Tell me, Mister Livermore, were you aware that the young girl who was with Senator Chester at the time of the murder survived the brutal attack upon her?"

Freddie examined his trousers again. "I may have read about it. . ."

"I'm sure you did. It was in all the newspapers," Donnolly said in a matter-of-fact voice. "She's been recuperating at the Convent of Saint Anne's not far from Washington Circle. Someone entered the convent by stealth last night and strangled the poor girl in her bed. The Chief Inspector believes that killer was the same man who murdered Senator Chester. He came back to remove the only person who could identify him, apparently."

Freddie looked over at Donnolly, eyes wide, clearly mesmerized. Devlin watched helplessly as Donnolly swooped down over Freddie, talons out. He couldn't save Freddie now.

"Tell me, sir, did you meet anyone on your walk last night? Speak with anyone who could verify your whereabouts?"

Freddie shook his head, his voice but a whisper. "No, no I didn't."

"That's a shame, sir. Because that means that you have no alibi for your whereabouts for the murder of this poor girl. Just as you had no alibi after eleven o'clock for the night Senator Chester was murdered." Donnolly hovered, ready to scoop him up. "Is there anything you'd like to tell me, Mr. Livermore?"

Devlin jumped at that opening. "I believe our nephew has answered enough questions for tonight, Inspector Donnolly," Devlin said forcefully. "The next time you need to question him, it will be in the presence of our family attorney. I'm sure you understand."

Donnolly shot Devlin a look, then his air of calm implacability returned. "Of course. I understand completely, sir. As I said earlier, families need to stick together." He flipped his notepad closed and rose. "In that case, I will bid you fine folks a good evening."

Jonathan strode over to the hallway. "Jameson will see you out, Inspector. Thank you again for waiting."

"You're quite welcome, Senator Carrington." Then, as Devlin sensed he would, Donnolly paused, then turned, eying Freddie. "Oh, and please make sure you stay in the city for the next few days, Mister Livermore. Our investigation is continuing, you understand."

Freddie nodded, mute.

"Good evening, Mrs. Carrington, Senator, Mister Burke." Donnolly gave a polite little bow their way and walked out.

Winnie began to console a clearly desperate Freddie, while Jonathan drew near Devlin. "I will speak with our attorney first thing in the morning."

"Yes, it's time. Excuse me for a moment, Jonathan. I want to ask Donnolly another question."

Jonathan nodded, then added. "Oh, yes, I almost forgot. I spoke with Senator Smythe today and he'll meet with you tomorrow morning at ten."

"Thank you," Devlin said as he hurried down the hallway and out the front door. Glancing up the street, he spotted Donnolly on the sidewalk. "Inspector, may I have a word with you?"

Donnolly turned and waited for Devlin to reach him. "What can I help you with, Mr. Burke?"

"I wanted to ask you if you'd had a chance to question a Mr. Broderick Wray as to his whereabouts on the night of Chester's murder. I learned that he bears a strong hatred toward Horace Chester, having been cheated out of his family's railroad. And, Mr. Wray also is residing alone at the Willard." Devlin looked Donnolly directly in the eyes. "Inspector Callahan told me that Wray would be investigated. I wondered what you have learned."

"I interviewed Broderick Wray myself, Mr. Burke, and I can report that, like your nephew, he claims that he was asleep at the Willard Hotel the night of Chester's murder and had no witnesses to vouch for him."

"Indeed," Devlin said encouraged. But it was short-lived.

"However, I spoke with Mr. Wray this morning and he was with four other business associates last evening. They dined at the Ebbitt Grill and then stayed in the tavern for drinks until after eleven o'clock." Donnolly fixed Devlin with a knowing gaze. "And if my notes are correct, that is well-past time that you and Mrs. Amanda Duncan arrived at Saint Anne's Convent and found young Francie dead. Am I right?"

There was no tricking Donnolly, Devlin knew, and didn't try. "That is correct, Inspector. Mrs. Duncan dined here with my sister, brother-in-law, and me last evening. I took her home by carriage and while riding, Mrs. Duncan had another of her visions. She saw a shadowed figure hovering over Francie, intent on harm. Naturally, we headed to the convent right away. We found elderly Sister Ruth regaining consciousness after being knocked down by the villain. And poor Francie was already dead in her bed—her body still warm."

Donnolly observed Devlin for a long moment before speaking. "Yes, that is the same account I obtained from Mrs. Duncan and Sister Ruth late last night. You, however, were no longer there, Mr. Burke. Did you return home?"

Devlin didn't bat an eyelash. "No, Inspector. I went to the Willard to speak with my nephew, as I'm sure you're aware from questioning the desk clerk. Needless to say, I was quite distressed to discover that Freddie had just returned from a long walk, alone."

"Yes, indeed. I can imagine you were perturbed to hear that," Donnolly said in a wry tone. "Tell me, Mr. Burke, how is it that you became acquainted with Mrs. Duncan?"

Devlin allowed himself a smile. "Actually, it was Chief Inspector Callahan who informed me of Mrs. Duncan's existence and of her psychic visions of the Chester murder. He suggested that I seek her out. I rather suspect the good inspector thought we were two birds of a feather, so to speak."

A hint of a smile flirted with Donnolly's mouth. It was hard to tell with the bushy mustache. "You have a good evening, Mr. Burke," he said before continuing down Connecticut Avenue.

CHAPTER TWENTY

"Thank you for meeting with me, Senator Smythe. I know how busy you must be with the Senate still in session." Devlin settled into a captain's chair across from the Senator's maple rocker. Glancing about Senator Smythe's office, Devlin saw every inch of the walnut paneled walls was covered with memorabilia, most from the Great War. The War Between the States as some Southerners referred to it, while others simply called that bloody confrontation a Civil War. Devlin knew there was nothing civil about war, especially one that pit brothers against brothers.

Senator Smythe lowered himself into his rocker slowly. Devlin guessed him to be nearly seventy years old, judging from the medals that hung proudly on his wall next to the crossed swords. Senator Smythe had to be in his forties when he rode off to fight for the Confederacy. An age when a man of his family's stature should have enjoyed restful later years with grandchildren on his knee, not slogging through marshy battlefields.

"Would you care for some of our fine bourbon, Mr. Burke?" Senator Smythe asked as he reached to the mahogany table beside his chair, where glasses and a decanter sat. "It's from my own family's recipe, so I can attest to its quality."

"I'd be delighted, Senator. And please, call me Devlin."

"Let me know how you like it, Devlin," Smythe said with a smile, handing a glass half-filled with the tawny liquor. "We're quite proud of our efforts. And I imagine you've sampled a fair share of fine liquors in your time."

"Indeed, I have, Senator," Devlin said, returning the Senator's warm smile. He swirled the bourbon, closed his eyes and inhaled its aroma. Rich and smoky and mysterious. There was something else there which he couldn't quite decipher. Devlin savored the bourbon, letting it roll on his tongue, leaving its pleasurable burn. "Excellent, Senator. Truly supurb. My compliments to your family."

"Thank you, Devlin. I'm glad you enjoy it. Our family's been making bourbon since before we won our freedom from England. My great grandfather had one of the first stills in southwestern Virginia in the 1680's." He took a sip, closing his eyes. The sunlight streaming in through the tall windows illuminated his white hair.

"Is that how you first became friends with Jonathan? His mother's family is from Kentucky. If I recall your geography correctly, those two Southern states are close to each other."

Smythe nodded, his silvered hair creating a halo-like effect around his face. "Yes, our families became acquainted after the War. We were all trying to keep our farms and properties going during those difficult years." Then he smiled, as if he'd closed the door on those old, painful memories. "We bootleggers had to stick together. Our whiskies were the only source of income that kept our families from starvation. People will pay for good whiskey whether it was Union or Rebel made."

Devlin laughed softly. "You're right about that, Senator. It's interesting to know that your family and Jonathan's were connected."

"I think we even had a marriage or two back a ways." Smythe savored the bourbon again. "Now, Devlin, Jonathan said you had some questions about the late departed, but not regarded, Senator Chester. I'll be glad to recollect whatever I can. I've been in this chamber for years. And Chester has been here as long."

Devlin enjoyed another sip. "I'm curious about some of the enemies that Horace Chester made while in the Senate."

Smythe gave a soft snort. "I'm afraid a recitation of that list would take us all day, Devlin."

"I have already heard some of the ones whose passions were inflamed by hatred for the man, but I wondered if you could recall anyone who might have had a heated exchange with Chester recently. Or, had a long-simmering feud with him."

"Hmmmmmm, Chester had several feuds going. He seemed to enjoy them. The longest running and the most vitriolic, of course, was the one with Sherwood Steele. They'd been at each other's throats for years. Ever since Chester became head of the Commerce Committee, Steele lusted for that position, and now he has it."

"Yes, I've spoken with Senator Steele. A thoroughly unpleasant man. Tried to bribe me before I'd finished my lunch." Devlin savored the bourbon and chased Steele's memory away.

Edgar Smythe chuckled. "Steele certainly doesn't try to obfuscate his goals. There's that to be said for him. Straightforward."

He sipped his bourbon and rocked for a couple of minutes. Devlin waited patiently.

"As for recent altercations, the one that comes to mind is the argument Chester had with Senator Buchanan a month ago. Chester refused to cooperate with Buchanan's plan to gather support on a vote. Buchanan was livid, as I recall. But, of course, he always seems to be angry about something. Now, *there* is someone who holds a grudge. Buchanan still begrudges Jonathan being chosen for the Appropriations committee instead of him. He's not someone who inspires cordiality, shall we say."

"I have met the gentleman and I have to agree that he can be quite unpleasant. And he seemed to take quite a dislike to me. Now, I understand why. I'm related to Jonathan. I wondered why he always made it a point to say something cutting. And I sensed his resentment of Jonathan."

"I've told Jonathan to be wary of Buchanan. He's a secretive man and he can be quite vindictive. If he thought he could wound Jonathan in any way, he would."

Devlin pondered that. "Perhaps that's why he took such a cruel delight in our nephew's predicament. He knows that any scandal attached to Freddie will stick to Jonathan as well."

"Exactly."

Devlin sipped his bourbon. "Can you recall any arguments you may have witnessed between Chester and others?"

Smythe laughed. "Chester was always arguing with someone." He closed his eyes and rocked again, sipping the savory bourbon. "Well, yes, as a matter of fact, I do recall a surprising row between Chester and his junior counterpart, Edmund Remington."

That captured Devlin's interest immediately. "Really? Was it a heated argument or a simple disagreement?"

"Ohhhh, it was a row, all right. And a heated one, too. I was surprised, because Remington has always appeared to be a mild mannered man, who seemingly didn't want to be too outspoken for fear of offending a powerful interest or ally."

Devlin sipped the bourbon while his instinct tingled. "Any idea of what their argument was about?"

"Unfortunately, I was privy to the whole thing, unbeknownst to them. They were standing beside a hearing room where I was perusing some documents. Obviously, they thought the room was empty." He took a deep drink. "As I recall, Chester was forcing Remington to resign from his Senate appointment so the New Jersey Governor could choose someone else, another confidante of Chester's. Remington balked. Chester told him either resign and retire wealthy or refuse and be ruined. Remington sounded distraught after that. He protested that he couldn't bear to lose his position of prestige. He'd worked diligently for Chester all these years. He felt he earned it. Remington said in a choked voice that his wife dearly loved Washington's social life. He begged Chester to reconsider. He knew the Governor would appoint whomever Chester recommended. Chester ignored Remington's emotional protests and told him he had no choice. He wanted Remington's resignation in a month."

Devlin's pulse began to race. "Did you have a chance to speak with Senator Remington after that?"

"No, I didn't want to embarrass the poor man by admitting that I knew what happened. But Remington was in a black mood for several days after that, as I recall."

"Do you recall how long ago this argument took place?"

"Ohhhh, perhaps three or four weeks ago."

Devlin's mind began to race as thoughts started to dart about, ideas popping out, demanding his attention. He needed to sort through all of this. He drained the last of the savory whiskey. "Senator, you have been more than kind to put up with my questions. I will not take any more of your time." Devlin rose from his chair.

Senator Smythe slowly rose. "It's been a pleasure, I assure you, Devlin. It's always nice to share a good whiskey with another connoisseur." He said with a twinkle in his eye.

"But you're right. I must return to that dreary hearing that is about to begin. I trust your morning's activities will be more interesting."

"Trust me, Senator, this visit has proved more than interesting," Devlin said as he took his hat and cane from the stand near the door.

"Yes, I could tell," Smythe said with a twinkle in his eye. "Keep me posted, will you?"

Devlin promised that he would, then hastened from Senator Smythe's office. He tipped his hat briefly to the women clerks who worked in the Senator's outer office, then sped through the senate corridors toward the outside doors. Devlin's brain was about to burst with the theories that filled it now.

Devlin strode down Pennsylvania Avenue, the maple and oak trees leafing out in pale green. He was oblivious to the vendors. Neither did he see the pedestrians on the sidewalk, the shops he passed, not even the noisy carts and wagons and carriages in the street. All that noise was the perfect backdrop for thought.

Now, Edmund Remington's behavior with Freddie made sense. Remington couldn't bear to lose his position of power in Washington and had obviously come up with a way to prevent that from happening. Remington could not confront Chester and refuse him. Not at all. Chester had all the power as well as the ear of the Governor. But if Chester was eliminated, then Edmund Remington wouldn't have to leave this life of privilege and power he'd become so accustomed to.

The problem was how to eliminate Horace Chester. The man was healthy as a horse. He had plenty of vices but no discernible weaknesses. . .except one. His lust. Chester needed to frequent the brothels regularly to slake his desires. That would be the only time he was vulnerable. When his back was literally turned.

Devlin crossed over Fifteenth Street, beside the newly constructed Treasury. The sun beamed down strongly, and at any other time, Devlin would notice that it was past midday. Any other time he might be hungry, but not today. He kept up his rhythmic fast walk, his mind still spinning scenarios.

Clearly, as his junior colleague who had worked for Chester for years, Remington knew Chester's habits as well as anyone. He surely knew where Chester's key ring was kept and which one was the key for Joey Quinn's brothel. Remington knew Chester's schedule. Knew when he left for his Murder Bay haunts and how long he would stay.

If Edmund Remington had made the decision to eliminate Chester and his oppressive control over Remington's own career, then he would know exactly where and when to find Chester at his most vulnerable for an attack. Clearly, Remington had no desire to be discovered. So a disguise was necessary. And what better disguise than a Union officer's uniform. One of thousands in the city of Washington. He would not even cause attention as he moved throughout the streets that night, his face darkened with soot, perhaps. No one would pay him any heed. Washington was used to soldiers, old and young, striding about.

Devlin turned the corner onto Pennsylvania Avenue again and walked past the President's House. A man as methodical and clerk-like as Edmund Remington would also be looking for a likely suspect. Someone he could implicate in Chester's murder. An unwilling and unaware person who could be manipulated.

That's when Freddie stumbled right into Remington's sites. The perfect dupe. Remington must have rejoiced when Freddie had his very public altercation with Chester— showing up at his office and shouting. Remington must have realized he had his target. That's why he suggested to Freddie that he would set up a meeting. Remington, however, had no intention of arranging a meeting. Thus, guaranteeing Freddie's angry response. He sensed Freddie would become incensed when Chester ignored him. So enraged, he would assault Chester in the Senate hallway.

That would also give Remington time to set his plan in motion. He would drug the brandy, obtain a uniform, and have a copy of the brothel key made. He'd set the trap well. Chester was defenseless against his savage attack. And Freddie unwittingly was already in a drugged sleep at the Willard, blissfully unaware that he was being carefully set up for murder.

Devlin hastened across Pennsylvania Avenue and angled toward Lafayette Square. He needed to bounce these theories against someone else who was vested in finding the truth in this crime. Amanda Duncan immediately came to mind. She would certainly tell him if there was a flaw in his reasoning.

"Good afternoon, Mr. Burke," Amanda greeted Devlin as he entered her parlor. "Please have a seat. Bridget, please tell Matilda we'll have tea."

"I'm glad I found you at home, Mrs. Duncan, I have much to share with you." Devlin walked to his favorite velvet armchair, directly across from Amanda's. "Much has happened since we were last together."

"Yes, I sensed you had something to tell me, but Sister Beatrice's appearance prevented it. First, tell me if all is well at the Carrington home. You were called away for a meeting there."

Devlin let out a sigh. "Yes, all is as well as can be expected. Inspector Donnolly arrived to question our nephew, Freddie. Today, Jonathan conferred with his attorney to represent Freddie. We expect Chief Inspector Callahan will file charges in a few days for Chester's murder. And Francie's." Noticing Amanda's shocked expression, Devlin leaned forward in his chair and implored, hand over his heart. "Mrs. Duncan, I cannot believe Freddie killed Senator Chester. And I would swear on my sister's life that Freddie could never kill that innocent girl." He implored Amanda, who still had a wary look in her eyes.

"Why, then, is Inspector Callahan filing charges?" Amanda asked her expression skeptical. "He may be boorish, but Callahan is not a careless man. He must believe there's enough evidence to convict your nephew."

Devlin sank back in his chair. "Alas, all the evidence is circumstantial. But because of Freddie's intemperate behavior with Chester, attacking him in the Senate hallway in front of witnesses, Freddie seems the likeliest suspect. Freddie is the only one who has no explanation for his whereabouts at the time of both murders. He was asleep at the Willard while Chester was killed."

"And where was he the night of Francie's murder?"

Devlin looked into her wary gaze and let her see his anxiety. "I left the convent that night and went straight to the Willard to check on Freddie and found that he had taken a walk about the city. . .alone."

"I see," Amanda said, her eyes revealing a concern that Devlin had not seen since he first spoke with Amanda Duncan in her carriage outside the precinct station house.

"I understand your suspicion, Mrs. Duncan. And if I didn't know Freddie so well, I would believe him guilty, too. But, he is simply not that calculating. It's somewhat plausible that Freddie might have followed Chester to the brothel still enraged. But Freddie had no way of knowing where to find Chester's private key for the back entrance. Only someone who was a familiar figure at the Capitol could have gained access to that key in his office. And the killer wore a Union officer's uniform. Freddie would never have even thought of that, let alone be able to procure one."

Devlin stopped as Matilda brought the tea tray. He spied two slices of cake beside the teacups, and his stomach growled. Devlin had completely forgotten about the time, now his hunger demanded attention. He watched Amanda pour a double serving of cream into his tea. He accepted the cup eagerly and tried not to down it in one gulp.

"I see your point about Chester's murder, Mr. Burke. But what of Francie's?" Amanda questioned. "You must admit your nephew's long walk alone that night leads one to make the assumption that he did indeed kill her."

Devlin drained his cup. "I agree it looks very bad, but Freddie simply could not have killed Francie. Whoever did kill that poor girl thought through the crime carefully and deliberately planned how to lure the priest and sisters away from the convent so that he could do his dark deed. But the truth is, Mrs. Duncan, Freddie is simply not that smart," Devlin declared. "I swear he is not. To be perfectly blunt, Freddie is just shy of being stupid." Devlin sank back in the chair, dejected. Listening to himself try to convince Amanda of Freddie's innocence made Devlin realize how unbelievable it sounded.

Amanda handed him a dessert plate. "You have that lean and hungry look, Mr. Burke. Here, have some of Matilda's Louisiana rum cake. It's quite good. I'll pour you another cup of tea."

Devlin accepted the plate and scented the enticing aromas of rum and sugar wafting to his nostrils. His stomach growled so loudly, he was afraid Mrs. Duncan might hear it. "Thank you," was all he managed before he took a bite. *Heavenly*. Devlin closed his eyes and savored. "Delicious does not do this justice," he said after taking another large bite.

"Yes, it is delicious," Amanda said, placing another cup of tea at his elbow. "Now, let us assume for the moment that your belief about your nephew is true, and Freddie did not commit the murder. How can you convince Inspector Callahan of his innocence? Have you learned anything new from your meetings? I believe you were going to meet with another Senator, correct? Someone Jonathan suggested, I believe."

Devlin polished off the last bite of cake and licked his lips. "Yes, I met with Senator George Smythe this morning, and I learned something which has aroused my interest considerably."

Amanda sipped her tea. "Senator Smythe is an honorable man. I've met him and his family. What did he say that caught your interest?"

"He told me that Senator Chester and the junior Senator from New Jersey, Edmund Remington, had a heated argument only a month ago. Smythe accidentally overheard the entire exchange. Chester wanted Remington to step aside so the Governor could appoint someone else to the Senate. Someone Chester favored more. Remington refused and became quite emotional, pleading with Chester not to push him aside. But Chester told him to retire and be wealthy, or refuse and be ruined." Devlin took a deep drink of tea, and glanced toward the second slice of cake. "Smythe added that Remington was in a foul mood for days afterwards."

Amanda eyed him. "Are you suggesting that Edmund Remington killed Chester?"

Devlin released a long breath. "I believe it is a strong possibility. And, there's more that leads me to that conclusion." He glanced toward the cake again.

"Please have another piece, Mr. Burke," Amanda said, smiling as she gestured to the tray. "I'll have Matilda bring more."

Devlin hesitated. "Wouldn't you like it?"

"I've had Matilda's cake for a lifetime," she said with a wry smile. "Go ahead. Enjoy yourself. Matilda's a fine cook."

Devlin accepted her offer and tried not to gobble down another delectable bite, but the brown sugar and buttery taste tempted him to forget his manners. "This is delectable," he said after swallowing.

"Yes, isn't it?" Amanda said from behind her teacup. "Bridget, would you ask Matilda to bring the rest of the cake, please?"

"The entire cake?" Bridget asked, in surprise. Glancing to Devlin, she wagged her head before leaving.

Chagrined, Devlin had to smile. "Leave it to Bridget to make me remember my good manners. Forgive me for acting like a ravenous beast."

"You were clearly hungry, Mr. Burke. I rather enjoy watching someone savor Matilda's fine cooking. Now, you were about to tell me something else that roused your suspicions about Edmund Remington."

Devlin licked brown sugar from his upper lip. "After I found Freddie at the hotel the night before last, I sat him down and made him recite everything he remembered about that evening. I listened for anything I had not heard before. Like you, I was losing faith in the possibility of proving Freddie's innocence. Then he told me how solicitous Senator Remington had been to him after his altercation with Chester in the Senate hallway. He said that Remington had never paid any attention to him before. Yet Remington had told me personally that he had taken a liking to Freddie and tried to warn him about Chester."

"Perhaps Remington was merely telling you that because you're Freddie's uncle."

"I realize that. But, Freddie went on to say that he and Remington had drinks after dinner at Remington's club. And Remington offered Freddie some brandy from his own flask. After that, Freddie said he immediately became sleepy, so much so that he asked Remington to take him back to the Willard." Devlin lifted the last morsel of cake to his mouth.

"So you think Remington's brandy was drugged."

"Yes, I do. Why else would Freddie still be asleep when I knocked on his door at nine o'clock the next morning? I know my nephew's habits, and he's never been one to retire early."

Amanda gazed toward the window that looked out on Lafayette Square. "So, your theory is that Edmund Remington plotted to kill Horace Chester because he was being forced out of the Senate?"

"Remington had the motive and the opportunity. You see, he would know Chester's habits and his vices. He would also know where to find Chester's key ring with the key to the brothel's private back entrance. He would also be able to move about the Senator's office without arousing suspicion. Something Freddie could never do."

"Hmmmmm, that's plausible." She nodded.

Encouraged by her response, Devlin leaned forward. "I sense Remington had the crime planned out and was looking for someone that he could implicate in the murder. Someone who would be gullible enough for Remington to manipulate. Enter Freddie." Devlin sank back and drained his teacup. "And Freddie played right into Remington's hands with his emotional outbursts and public tirades against Chester. In the halls of the Senate, no less. In fact, I think Remington helped provide the stimulus for Freddie's attack on Chester. Freddie said Remington had promised to set up a meeting with Chester, which he did not do, of course. Freddie arrived at the office only to be shunted aside by Chester. Insult added to the injury of being cheated out of every dime. Freddie flew into a rage and attacked Chester in front of witnesses. I daresay Remington was fairly rubbing his hands in glee. Freddie had done more than enough to incriminate himself. All Remington had to do was to attack Chester when his back was turned."

"And Francie," Amanda reminded.

"And Francie. Remington had to have heard Chester call out his name. That's why he attacked her. And when he learned from the newspapers that she survived, that's when he began to plot a way to eliminate her as well. Francie was the only one who might be able to recognize him."

Amanda stared off through the windows for a long minute. Devlin replaced the dessert plate and waited for her response. Finally, she turned to him. "You've created a logical if complex theory, Mr. Burke. Your reasoning makes sense."

"Thank you, Mrs. Duncan. I wanted to hear your response," Devlin said, pleased that she agreed with his theories.

"However," Amanda continued. "You have absolutely no proof that Edmund Remington is the murderer. Yes, Remington seems to have had the motive to kill Chester and could easily gain the opportunity to do so. And I understand why he would hunt out and kill Francie. He had to eliminate all possible witnesses. But alas, you have no proof. Edmund Remington never exhibited any overt animosity toward Chester. But your nephew, Freddie, did so on many occasions and in front of many witnesses. Even violently attacking Chester in the Senate hallway." She shook her head sympathetically. "I understand that all the evidence against Freddie is circumstantial, but that is also true of Edmund Remington. And, I hate to say it, Mr. Burke, but Remington would never arouse Inspector Callahan's suspicions, even if he learned of Senator Smythe's overheard conversation, whereas, Freddie's own actions have caused him to look guilty."

What slight elation Devlin might have felt at Mrs. Duncan's initial praise, disappeared as quickly as air from a child's broken rubber balloon. Deflated, he distracted himself with Matilda's entrance carrying another full tea tray. Half a Louisiana cake sat temptingly with two slices already on the plates.

"Alas, I'm forced to admit you are right, Mrs. Duncan," Devlin said, dejectedly. "Smythe's overheard conversation between Remington and Chester had bolstered my belief that Remington is the killer. But, alas, we have no way to prove it. And I agree, Remington would never be suspected as long as Freddie is such an attractive target." He glanced toward the tea tray again.

"Matilda's cake is a wonderful balm for many sorrows, Mr. Burke," Amanda suggested with a warm smile. "I'm sorry if I was blunt. May I suggest another piece?"

Devlin glanced toward the tempting cake again. He could swear he smelled the brown sugar and butter. "I really shouldn't. Three pieces would be entirely too much."

"It doesn't sound as if you had time for lunch, Mr. Burke. Why don't you make Matilda's cake your midday meal?"

Devlin chuckled as he retrieved another luscious slice of cake. "You would have made an excellent barrister, Mrs. Duncan. You're quite persuasive."

"Why, thank you, Mr. Burke. I find that talent is rather useful." She smiled as she poured another cup of tea.

Devlin let the luscious flavors of brown sugar, butter, and rum dissolve on his tongue. *Divine.*

"I had the strangest dream last night, Mr. Burke," Amanda said, staring out into the parlor. "I was in an unfamiliar house, and there was a large grandfather clock standing against the wall. The glass case was open, and the hands of the clock were moving backward. I do not know what to make of it."

Devlin set his fork on the plate and took a sip of tea, picturing the image Amanda has described. "Perhaps it means that time is running out for Freddie," he said grimly.

CHAPTER TWENTY-ONE

"Amanda, how delightful to see you," Winnie said as Amanda entered the Carrington parlor. "Come in and sit down."

"Forgive me for intruding during the morning hours, Winnie. I realize you've got several morning calls to attend to, but I wanted to speak with you."

"It's no bother at all, Amanda," Winnie said, gesturing to a chair. "I love having an excuse to skip those calls occasionally. They can be tedious. Please, tell me what's on your mind. You haven't forgotten that you're dining with us this evening."

"I know, and I hope my suggestion doesn't interrupt your schedule terribly." Amanda chose a velvet armchair.

"What suggestion? I'm all ears, Amanda," Winnie said as she sat across from her.

Amanda clasped her gloved hands in her lap. "I gather Mr. Burke has informed you of his visit with Senator Smythe yesterday? He stopped by and apprised me of what he'd learned and his suspicions about Senator Remington."

Winne's expression turned solemn. "Yes, he did, and Jonathan and I agree that Edmund Remington's actions are more than suspicious. Unfortunately, his actions have always been above board, while Freddie's. . ." She sighed. "Freddie's actions have been damning."

Amanda leaned over and placed her hand on Winnie's arm. "I am so very sorry that your nephew and your family have become involved in this horrible crime. He told me your nephew may be charged any day now."

"I'm afraid so. Jonathan took Freddie to the solicitor's office again this morning. I fear for the worst."

Amanda watched a pained expression cross Winnie's face. "Mr. Burke's theories about Edmund Remington made sense to me, Winnie. Alas, all we have are suspicions. This morning I had an unusual idea of how you and I might possibly help Freddie."

Winnie's eyes lit up. "What is it, Amanda? I desperately want to help Freddie. He's bumbling and stupid, but he is certainly not a vicious killer."

Amanda paused before offering her unorthodox proposal. "I propose we obtain more information about Edmund Remington, and I thought the best place to find it would be to question his wife, Betsy Remington."

"Ohhhhh, that is a wonderful idea," Winnie said, her eyes wide. "When should we go?"

Amanda checked the locket watch pinned to the breast pocket of her stylish rose-pink suit dress. "I assumed Mrs. Remington would be out with morning calls, so I suggest we visit her in the early afternoon. Hopefully, she'll be in."

"Excellent idea, Amanda," Winnie said with a bright smile. "And I suggest that we use our time between to dine at the Ebbitt Grill. They have a lovely Ladies Luncheon. We can plot out our questions for Mrs. Remington."

"I can see you've inherited a fair share of the detection sense that your brother has," Amanda said with a smile, delighted that Winnie hadn't appeared shocked or shied away from what Amanda realized would be a rather unorthodox afternoon social call.

"Indeed," Winnie said, springing from her chair. "Why should Devlin do all the work? Jameson, please tell Bartholomew we'll be needing the carriage right away."

Bartholomew helped Amanda from the Carrington carriage and she stepped onto the sidewalk outside the Remington's trim, red brick rowhouse on Connecticut Avenue.

"Please wait for us, Bartholomew. I'm not sure how long we will be," Winnie said as she stepped from the carriage. "Mrs. Remington may throw us out after a few minutes; am I right, Amanda?"

"She very well may." Amanda had to smile. Winnie Carrington was as flushed as a schoolgirl at her first evening outing. She was clearly excited by the thought of "sleuthing" like her brother. Bartholomew looked from Winnie to Amanda then back to his mistress. His face, the color of melted chocolate, registered a trace of surprise. "Yes'm. I'll be here."

Winnie stared up at the rowhouse. "Are we ready, Amanda?"

"I think we are. Lead on, McDuff." Amanda gestured forward. Winnie climbed the cement steps quickly, Amanda following behind. Giving the brass knocker a solid two thumps. A maidservant opened the door and peered out at them.

"Please excuse our tardiness, but we've come to pay a call on your mistress if she is in." Winnie handed the maid her card as did Amanda. "I am Mrs. Jonathan Carrington, and my friend is Mrs. Jonathan Duncan."

"Yes, ma'am, won't you come inside while you wait?" She stepped back to allow them to enter.

The Remington front hallway resembled most of the similar brick rowhouses built in the last twenty years. A long hallway ran through the center of the building with rooms jutting off to each side. A walnut entry table stood against the wall as well as a tall vase of ostrich plumes. A perfectly ordinary hallway, Amanda thought as she watched the maid walk away.

Then Amanda's glance fell upon the clock. A tall grandfather clock that stood near a large archway leading into what looked like a sitting room or parlor. Amanda stared at the clock. It looked exactly like the clock in her dream. A chilling feeling rippled over her skin. What did that mean?

A middle-aged woman appeared from a room farther down the hall and approached. She was dressed in a more modest dress than normally used for visiting as she hastened towards them.

"Mrs. Carrington, how good of you to visit," she gushed as she took Amanda's hand. "My husband Edmund speaks so highly of your husband, Jonathan." She turned to Amanda and took her hand. "And Mrs. Duncan, it's a pleasure to meet you. I don't believe we've met before. Is your husband in the Congress?"

"No, my late husband was a banker here in Washington. My family's been in the city for decades. Thank you for receiving us at this late hour."

"Yes, indeed," Winnie said brightly. "Amanda and I met for lunch and we thought it was such a lovely day we'd continue calling on friends. I do hope we haven't disturbed you."

"Oh, not at all, not at all," Mrs. Remington said, gesturing to the sitting room. "Please come in and have a seat. We'll have tea and pastries. I've just discovered that quaint little bakery on Twelfth Street. They have excellent cakes and pies."

Amanda removed her lacy gloves as she walked into the sitting room, still feeling a bit chilled. The feeling was still with her.

Winnie took the chair beside her. "Thank you so much, Mrs. Remington, and please call me Winnie."

Mrs. Remington flushed with pleasure, which told Amanda that Winnie's visit outside of morning calls would be considered a social coup for the wife of the now-senior senator from New Jersey.

"Thank you, and please do call me Louisa," she said, hand to her breast.

"You have a lovely home," Winnie said as she glanced about the respectable-if-not-lavishly-furnished sitting room.

Bookshelves lined the walls, and pictures along with framed embroidery and various stitched biblical sayings hung on all four walls.

"Is that your needlework, Mrs. Remington?" Amanda asked sociably.

"Why, yes it is," Louisa beamed. "I've worked crewel as well as needlepoint. Those are my favorite."

"And the most challenging," Amanda added. "My grandmother used to work in crewel as well. Looking at these brings back memories. I'm afraid I have no talent for it."

Louisa flushed again with pleasure at Amanda's praise. "Thank you, Mrs. Duncan, I do enjoy it." She beckoned the maid forward with her tea tray.

"I imagine you haven't had much time for stitchery lately," Winnie said, accepting a cup of tea from the maidservant's tray. "Your social obligations have surely increased since. . .well, since Senator Chester's recent demise."

"Why, yes. . .yes, they have," Louisa said, coloring again, not with pleasure Amanda imagined this time. "Will you and your husband be able to come to our reception next week?"

Winnie smiled warmly at her. "Of course, we will. Jonathan and I wouldn't miss it for the world."

Oh, that's wonderful," Louisa gushed again. "It's our very first large function, and I confess I'm a bit nervous."

Winnie leaned over her teacup. "I'll be happy to help you in way that I can, Louisa. Please let me know. It's the very least I can do after your husband's many kindnesses to our nephew Freddie."

Louisa's smile disappeared and she looked a bit embarrassed. "Yes. . . yes. . .I've heard about all that."

Amanda gave a loud sigh and shook her head. "Such a distressing situation."

"Yes, yes, dreadful, simply dreadful," Winnie echoed her sigh. "Jonathan and I want to thank your husband, Edmund, for taking it upon himself to remove Freddie from that unseemly altercation he had at the Capitol with Senator Chester." She gave a dramatic shudder. "And to take Freddie to his club afterwards and calm him down was more than kind, Louisa."

"Why. . .thank you," Louisa said, slightly surprised at Winnie's declaration.

"Freddie even said Edmund took him back to the Willard where he was staying and made sure he was all right." Winnie placed her hand on her breast. "That was more than kind. Be sure to convey our thanks to him." Winnie sipped her tea.

Louisa glanced down to her lap, clearly embarrassed at Winnie's praise. "I will. Edmund is a very kind gentleman."

"I do hope your sleep wasn't disturbed too much, Louisa. Freddie said they didn't return to the Willard until eleven o'clock at night." Winnie looked at her solicitously.

"Oh, do not concern yourself," Louisa said with a dismissive wave of her hand. "Jonathan had already told me he would be in late that night and not to wait up for him."

Amanda's heart skipped a beat. She waited until Louisa reached for her teacup to send a look Winnie's way. Their glances met. Remington wouldn't know he'd be returning late unless he'd already planned out the evening's events ahead of time.

"I'm so glad," Winnie said from behind her cup. "Because I'm sure it was much later than that by the time he arrived. I'm constantly amazed how long it takes Jonathan to travel all the way up here to Connecticut from the Capitol."

"Yes, it was late. I remember hearing the clock downstairs chiming midnight." She wagged her head with a smile. "I remember because Edmund roused me awake so he could tell me he was home. He didn't want me to worry. Silly man."

Amanda's pulse raced now. Did Remington wake his wife that night to make sure she heard the clock strike twelve? Did he turn the clock back to conceal the extra hours he'd needed to commit the murder and escape? Was *that* the meaning of her dream?

Louisa offered Winnie a pink and white teacake. "Please, do try these. They're delectable." She handed one to Amanda as well.

Amanda tasted the delicate pastry. "This is quite good, Mrs. Remington. You'll have to tell me where that bakery is. I must patronize it."

Louisa beamed again. "I'll be happy to, Mrs. Duncan."

"Please, call me Amanda," Amanda said with a warm smile. "My family has lived in Washington for decades, yet somehow you have shown me something new in our city. I am impressed."

Louisa sat up taller. "The bakery is situated on Twelfth between E Street and F Street. I confess those are such funny names for streets. Letters of the alphabet. I get them mixed up."

"Has your family been in New Jersey for many generations, Louisa?" Amanda continued, hoping to work around to another question that danced at the back of Amanda's mind.

"Oh, yes. My grandfather settled near Trenton after the War of Independence. And Edmund's family has been in Passaic for longer than that."

"I always find it strange to hear people speak of the War of Independence," Winnie joked. "Then I recall that we were the enemy in that war."

Amanda waited until the soft laughter and jesting subsided then circled in on the subject she was seeking. "I imagine both your father and your husband's father fought in the great conflict to preserve our union."

"Edmund's father did. My father, unfortunately, died when I was a small child. But Jonathan's father had a distinguished career in the Union Army."

"Do you recall what regiment Jonathan's father served in? My father is ill and his only joy in life is writing his memoirs of that great conflict. And he loves nothing more than to learn of other soldiers who fought." Amanda catches Winnie watching her carefully.

Louisa glances into the room, musing, "Oh, my, I'm afraid I cannot remember. I'll have to ask Jonathan."

"I wonder if he was in the same division as my father," Amanda said. "There was a distinctive ribbon on the uniform. Does Jonathan still have his father's uniform, perchance?"

"Why, yes. It's upstairs in a storage closet," Louisa replied.

Amanda decided to push past the point of politeness. She and Winnie had gotten this close. They had to find out if that uniform still hung in Remington's closet. If so, then all their suspicions about him came to naught.

She looked at Louisa sadly. "Oh, Louisa, could you be a dear and have your maid check the uniform, please" she pleaded. "My father is so ill, near death. It would mean a lot to him to learn of another comrade."

Amanda glanced away, her hand to her mouth. Winnie stared at the teacup in her lap.

Louisa leaned over and patted Amanda's arm sympathetically. "Of course, I will." She signaled her maidservant. "Please go to the upstairs closet in the guest room and search for a Union officer's uniform. It should be in a cloth cover. And bring it down here to show Mrs. Duncan, please."

The maid nodded and scurried from the room. Meanwhile, Amanda caught Winnie's gaze and saw her amusement. She drained her cup. "My goodness, I believe I would like another cup of tea."

"Why, of course, Amanda."

Louisa poured a cup for Amanda and Winnie, then herself. Amanda then asked for another delicious pastry while awaiting the maid's return. Another few minutes passed, and Winnie asked for another pastry, just as the maidservant returned.

"It's not there, madam," she said anxiously. "I looked in all the closets, and could not find a uniform of any kind.'

Louisa looked perplexed. "Are you sure? I saw the uniform only two months ago when I organized the storage closet. I know it's there."

"I couldn't find it anywhere, ma'am."

Louisa clucked her tongue. "Let me show you. If you ladies will excuse me, I'll be back in a minute. I know exactly where to look." Louisa left swiftly.

Winnie leaned over toward Amanda and whispered. "I vow the uniform's missing because it was left in the rubbish bin behind the Willard."

"That's why I asked. I had a vision about a grandfather clock the other night, and the hands were moving backwards."

Winnie's eyes widened. "Oh, my word. Do you think Remington moved the clock hands backward to conceal the real hour he returned?"

"Yes, I do. And I think he woke his wife so she would hear the clock chime midnight to conceal his absence."

Hurrying feet sounded and Louisa walked back into the sitting room. Her face was flushed, not with pleasure this time but with embarrassment. "I. . .I don't know what to make of it, ladies. I saw that uniform only two months ago, and now it's gone. Disappeared. I cannot explain it."

Amanda rose from her chair and Winnie did so as well. "Do not trouble yourself further, Louisa. My father is resting peacefully. I'll not mention it to him. I'll simply ask him if he recalls a Remington."

She took Louisa's hand. "You were very sweet to look. I shouldn't have presumed."

"No, no, it was fine." Louisa gestured to them both. "You ladies don't have to leave, do you?"

"Yes, I'm afraid we do. Duties at home beckon. I have no idea if Jonathan will be late this evening or not, but I still must have dinner arranged." Winnie shook her head. "I swear, it can be quite stressful working around our husbands' senate schedules, isn't it, Louisa."

"Yes, it can be," Louisa said, brushing a lock of hair behind her ear.

"For instance, Jonathan didn't get home until midnight two nights ago. He said there was a debate in committee. Did Edmund have to stay late?

Clearly flustered, Louisa mused out loud. "Two nights ago? Yes, yes Edmund stayed late, but he told me not to wait up."

"The senate is such a strain on family life, wouldn't you agree, Louisa?" Winnie laughed lightly as she headed for the hallway.

"Yes, yes, I suppose so. . ." Louisa said, following both women down the hall.

Devlin looked around the dinner table, first at his sister, then Amanda, then Jonathan. He raised his wineglass, filled with a fine Burgundy. "I say a toast is in order. To my dear sister, Winnie, and our dear friend, Mrs. Duncan. You both are to be congratulated on your investigatory efforts this afternoon. Most impressive. Jonathan and I salute you." He raised his glass higher, and then drank.

"Here, here," Jonathan added. "What a clever idea to visit Mrs. Remington. And it yielded much useful information."

Winnie fairly glowed with satisfaction, Devlin noticed. His sister had finally found an outlet for her naturally inquisitive nature. He only hoped Mrs. Duncan wouldn't suggest the more daring adventures to Winnie.

"Thank you, gentlemen," Winnie gave a gracious nod, "but the idea was Mrs. Duncan's."

"But it was Winnie who was able to glean the most information from Mrs. Remington."

"I almost feel sorry for Mrs. Remington," Jonathan teased. "Winnie can be a veritable terrier when she's after information."

"I can attest to that. I still bear the scars from childhood," Devlin added.

"Oh, bosh," Winnie said with a wave of her hand. "But you really should have seen Amanda's performance that got Mrs. Remington to go look for the uniform." Her hand went to her heart. "She even feigned tears. It was truly worthy of Mrs. Bernhardt."

"You exaggerate, Winnie. Amanda protested, sipping her wine.

Devlin gave Amanda a sly look. "An actress, eh? I had no idea you had dramatic talents, Mrs. Duncan."

Amanda caught his teasing look and replied in all innocence. "Yes, I've helped the Sisters with their Passion play several times. Perhaps that helped."

"Ah, yes, the good sisters," Devlin smiled into his wineglass. "They're responsible for your thespian tendencies."

"Everything you two learned today only confirms our suspicions that Edmund Remington killed Chester," Jonathan mused while he swirled the wine in his glass. "But we have no *proof*! Nothing definitive that can be attributed or attached to him. It's damnably frustrating!" Jonathan drained the glass.

"It's more than frustrating," Winnie protested. "It's a miscarriage of justice. Remington is the guilty one, not Freddie! Amanda and I confirmed it with our discoveries. Don't you think Inspector Donnolly or Callahan would pay attention to what we learned?"

Devlin gave his sister a sympathetic look. "I highly doubt it, Winnie. All we have are assorted suspicious events, bits and pieces. A missing uniform, a dream about clock hands turning backward, a flask of brandy, Remington telling his wife ahead of time that he'll be late. Bits and pieces. It's all conjecture. We see the picture clearly, because we *want* to see it. We want to prove that Freddie is innocent."

"It's so unfair," Winnie complained softly.

"Since I have yet to contribute to these sleuthing efforts, I will make it a point to find out if Edmund Remington actually was working late that night. His office staff would know." Jonathan reached for the bottle of Burgundy and poured some into his wife's empty glass. "Still, that's simply circumstantial. Just like everything else."

A dejected silence fell upon the table now, Devlin noticed. And after several minutes, Devlin decided to dispel it. "I say, these two ladies have inspired me to see the theatre. Is anyone performing in Washington at the moment?"

"I don't think so. I'll check, but I think the theatre season is drawing to a close," Winnie said.

Devlin frowned. "I rather had my mind set on a fine performance, since Jonathan and I missed Mrs. Duncan's. It's a long time until next year's Passion Play."

His jest worked, and light laughter rippled around the Carrington dinner table once more.

CHAPTER TWENTY-TWO

Devlin headed down Twelfth Street, passing the shuttered taverns. Only morning people were out on the streets this early. Laundries, lawyers' offices, barbershops, and grocers. Twelfth Street was a street filled with businesses. Small shops. The larger stores such as Garfinckel's, and Woodward and Lothrup had carved out choice corners of Eleventh and F Streets and G Street in far nicer neighborhoods.

Angling down Twelfth Street toward the less savory streets of Murder Bay, Devlin glimpsed the green trees of the National Mall farther ahead. Turning onto D Street at last, Devlin edged into the perimeter of Murder Bay. Here, one or two taverns were stirring, preparing, no doubt, for the workingmen's lunches they offered before noon. These streets weren't populated with office girls shopping in their trim long-sleeve white blouses and dark blue cotton skirts. Some with flat-brimmed white straw hats edged with dark ribbon. Here, the people were dressed for a harder sort of labor. The backbreaking work of the laundress and the heavy lifting of carpenters, cement mixers, hod carriers.

Devlin nodded to a laundry woman who caught his eye. The woman flashed him a broad smile and greeted, "A good day to you, sir."

Devlin replied with a nod and a smile absently, then suddenly recalled that the woman's face was familiar. She was the laundress that had provided information on Joey Quinn's location when Bridget, Amanda, and he last visited. Devlin turned and called out to the woman. "Madam, do you have a moment, please?"

The middle-aged woman spun about quickly and raced over to him. "Yes, sir. Do you need some more help, sir?"

Devlin smiled, remembering the woman's elation at the sight of the large denomination he had handed her that day. No doubt, it helped her family immensely. "If I recall correctly, you are the same kind woman who helped me two weeks ago when I was searching for Joey Quinn."

The woman beamed. "Yessir, it was me, all right."

Devlin reached for his billfold. "Well, it seems I need your help again, madam. Would you happen to know where Quinn is right now? I thought I might find him sound asleep at his establishment, considering the earliness of the hour."

"Ohhh, he ain't asleep," the woman said with a short laugh. "Joey don't sleep so sound since word got out that little Francie was done in by that maniac."

Devlin looked properly surprised. "Oh, really?"

She nodded sagely. "Yessir. Seems like the little thing was healin' up over with the Sisters of Saint Anne's, when that maniac snuck in and killed 'er!"

"Good lord!"

She leaned forward and rasped. "Slit her throat, he did."

"The villain! The police are hot on his trail, I trust."

She snorted. "Not likely. Nobody knows who he is." She leaned forward again, glancing over her shoulder, re-balancing the empty laundry basket on her hip. "That's why Joey is so scared. Word is, Joey tipped off the guy where to find her. Now, Joey's lying low, afraid the cops will be picking him up to question him."

"Ahhh, I see," Devlin said with a smile. "I gather Quinn doesn't have a very good relationship with your local constabulary."

The woman chuckled, low. "Ya might say that, mister."

"Would you happen to know where he is right now?" Devlin asked, slipping a large bill from his wallet.

The woman gazed at the money with a look of hunger that sent a twinge through Devlin. "Yessir, he's eatin' some eggs over at the Devil's Fork right now." She glanced around to see if anyone was looking.

Devlin took the initiative and reached for her basket. "Here, let me help you with that." He surreptitiously dropped the bill inside the basket.

"I don't need no help with that, mister—" she protested until she saw the crumpled bill. She looked up at Devlin with a look of gratitude that reached inside him. "Thank you, sir," she whispered.

"You're quite welcome, madam," Devlin said, stepping away from her. "Have a good day."

"Same to you, sir," she said, as she returned to her path down the sidewalk.

Devlin crossed D Street and headed straight for the Devil's Fork Tavern ahead. As he passed the dingy windows, he noticed the "Open" sign. Devlin pushed through the scarred wooden door and stepped inside. The tavern was practically empty, except for the bartender wiping off the bottles behind the bar and two men seated at a round wooden table eating. One of the men was Joey Quinn.

Quinn stared up at Devlin, eyes popped wide. A look of fear crossed his face.

Devlin grinned at him as he walked towards the bar. "Ahh, Mr. Quinn, the very man I've been looking for. I have some questions for—"

Devlin didn't get a chance to finish the sentence. Quinn leaped from his chair, knocking it over, and raced towards the back of the tavern, disappearing thru two swinging doors.

"He didn't like the eggs?" Devlin asked with a wry smile, pointing toward the swinging doors.

The bartender eyed him. "Better save your questions, mister. Joey's long gone by now. You'll never find him."

Devlin surmised that already. "Have the police been around asking questions? Is that why he's so skittish?"

The bartender snorted. "Skittish? Yeah, you might say that. The cops have come around twice trying to find Joey. Seems they think he saw the bastard that killed Francie."

Devlin was amazed that the Murder Bay gossip network was better than the *Washington POST*. He'd learned more this morning than he had from the daily press.

"I see. Did anyone else spy this villain or was it only Quinn who spoke with him?"

He shrugged. "Don't know, mister. All I know is, I've never seen Joey so scared in all the years I've known him. And with good reason. That killer found Francie and she was with the nuns. Joey figures that guy could find him if he wants to. And Joey don't want to have his throat cut in the middle of the night."

Amanda fairly leaped from her carriage before Mathias could even set the stepping stool in place. "Please wait here, Mathias." She hastened toward the large wide front doors of Saint Anne's convent and banged the knocker loudly.

Sister Teresa opened the door after recognizing Amanda. "Welcome, Mrs. Duncan," the young nun said, allowing Amanda inside.

"Is Daisy all right?" Amanda asked anxiously. "I had a dream about her last night which frightened me."

"Why, yes, Daisy's right here. She's safe, Mrs. Duncan. Do not be concerned." Sister Teresa said, walking Amanda down the hallway. "I believe she's with Sister Anne doing her lessons right now. Ahhh, here's Sister Beatrice." Sister Teresa ushered Amanda into the small library. The elder nun sat at a writing desk.

"Amanda, how are you this morning?" Sister Beatrice rose from her desk, which was covered with paper and envelopes.

Amanda rushed over to her. "I'm terribly worried, Sister. I had a frightening dream about Daisy last night. I saw her being abducted by a man in a black cloak and. . .and he took her away. . .in a carriage, I think!"

Sister Beatrice's face clouded with worry. "Oh, dear. That is concerning. These visions of yours are most always prescient."

"Always, sister. But it wasn't a vision this time. It was a dream. But my sensing seems to come in dreams now, too. The other night I dreamt I saw a grandfather clock in a house. . . and. . .and the hands were going backwards. . .and the next day I visited a senator's wife with Mrs. Carrington and I saw that same clock!" Amanda spoke so fast, her words fell out one upon the other.

Sister Beatrice blinked. "I see. . .ah, well, perhaps these dreams are not like your visions. They are simply dreams. Which means they're not the same. They won't come true."

Amanda realized what she said probably made no sense, but the fearful feeling of urgency was still with her. She sensed danger around Daisy. Just like she had sensed danger around Francie.

This time she took a deep breath before answering. "I understand how strange this sounds, Sister, but I have this feeling of dread inside about Daisy. I've had it ever since I awoke this morning. I had the very same feeling about Francie. This. . .this sense that something awful would happen to her. And Francie is now dead."

Sister Beatrice's face pinched with worry. "Oh, my dear, let us pray that. . .that these dreams are just that. Nighttime frights. Nightmares meant to scare us."

"I wish I could believe that, Sister, but my other dream proved true, and I—"

Sister Anne popped her head in and beckoned. "Sister, it's time to help Father with Midday Mass."

"Excuse me, Amanda, I have to assist." She took Amanda's hand in hers. "Do not worry, my dear. Daisy is safe with us. She's learning her lessons well. Meanwhile, I will pray that these horrible night frights of yours will cease." With that, Sister Beatrice hastened from the library, her voluminous habits swishing about her feet.

Amanda stared after her for a moment. She wished prayers could help. But they never had before, why should they now? The Almighty was completely disengaged from the lives of His simple folk it seemed to her. All Amanda had to depend on was her own intuition and her sensing. And her inner sensing was warning her. Daisy was in danger.

She glanced down at the writing desk. She needed to let Mr. Burke and the Carrington's know about this new revelation. They were the only others who would listen and not consider her mad.

Amanda sat at Sister Beatrice's writing desk and picked up pen and paper. Writing quickly she filled up two sheets of stationery, then folded them, and sealed them in an envelope. She addressed it to Winifred Carrington.

Hastening down the convent hallway, Amanda let herself out, then hurried toward her carriage. A thoroughly surprised Mathias jumped from his driver's seat to assist her.

"Please take this letter to the Carrington's first, Mathias. Then, you can take me home."

"Senator and Mrs. Carrington are in the parlor. They said for you to come in as soon as you arrived," Jameson said as he took Devlin's hat and cane.

"Where's Freddie?" Devlin asked as he started down the hallway.

"He's in the library conferring with the solicitor," Jameson said. "Shall I bring you a wine or a brandy, sir?"

"Make that a cognac, Jameson. It sounds like I'll need it," Devlin said as he rounded the archway into the parlor.

Winnie and Jonathan were sitting in their companion chairs beside the cold fireplace. It appeared that each had a wineglass in hand. Neither one was smiling. They both looked anxious.

"How long has the solicitor been here with Freddie? And why aren't you two readying for the evening? Don't you have a dinner engagement?"

"I sent a note to the hostess telling her we wouldn't be coming," Winnie said, despondent. "And in answer to your first question, the solicitor has been here for over two hours."

"Hopefully, he's coaching Freddie on how to answer questions," Devlin said as he chose his favorite blue velvet armchair across from them both. Jameson appeared then with his cognac, which Devlin lost no time in tasting.

"I'll have some as well, Jameson," Jonathan said. "This evening will be a long one, I'm afraid. I had word from the Police Commissioner himself that he would be stopping by later tonight after his dinner engagement."

"That doesn't sound good," Devlin said. "Have you told the solicitor and Freddie, yet?'

"We haven't had the chance," Winnie answered. "Jonathan arrived home only minutes before you. And the solicitor and Freddie have been cloistered in there ever since he arrived."

"What did the commissioner say, Jonathan?" Devlin asked.

"I didn't speak with him. He simply sent a note. I daresay it will be an awkward visit where he will inform us that Inspector Callahan will be charging Freddie with the murder of Horace Chester. I have no idea if there will be an additional charge of murdering that young girl or not." He accepted the glass from Jameson and donned half the cognac in one gulp.

"This is dreadful, simply dreadful," Winnie said, fidgeting with her wineglass. "Freddie is innocent. We know he is! Jonathan, tell Devlin what you learned today, and what Remington told you." She gestured impatiently to her husband.

"I went to Senator Remington's office this morning, early, hoping that only his staff and aides would be there. And I asked if any of them remembered if he had worked late three nights ago. I blamed a faulty memory on my part for asking, saying I had to find out some information from a committee session that was supposedly held that night." Jonathan took a deep sip of the amber liquid. "And Remington's staff told me there was no meeting that night. No late sessions of any kind."

"You see!" Winnie gestured again. "That proves Remington lied to his wife."

"If that were a punishable offense, dear Winnie, then every man on the face of the earth would be brought up on charges," Devlin quipped with a sly smile.

Winnie gave him a dismissive wave. "Nonsense, Devlin. Listen to what happened next. Tell him, Jonathan."

Jonathan sipped his cognac. "Only a short while later, Remington came up to me in the Senate hallway and pulled me aside. I've never seen the man look the way he did. He was livid. He said that Winnie and Amanda's visit to his wife yesterday upset her terribly. He could understand our family's grave concern about Freddie, but that did not give us the right to go about upsetting others with our intrusive questions. That was the word he used. 'Intrusive.'" Jonathan shook his head. "Remington was so angry, he was almost shaking. His voice certainly was."

Devlin swirled the rich cognac in his glass. "That sounds like the reaction of a man who has something to hide."

"It's a travesty," Winnie protested softly. Then she reached into her pocket and withdrew an envelope. "And if that isn't bad enough, this note arrived from Amanda this morning when I was out making calls. Read it aloud, Devlin. I haven't had a chance to tell Jonathan. It gave me chills when I read it."

Devlin took the envelope and recognized Amanda Duncan's flourishing hand. He opened the note and began to read.

"Dear Winnie, Please share this with your brother and Jonathan. I'm presently at the convent to check on Daisy. Fortunately, she is safe and well. But I had a frightening dream about Daisy last night which has left me with a feeling of dread. I saw Daisy being abducted by a man in a black cloak and being dragged into a carriage that drives off. That is all I saw. Needless to say, I am scared for Daisy's safety. I had this same feeling of danger about Francie before she was murdered. And now, I sense the same fate may be in store for Daisy. I am at a loss as to how to protect the child.

I am sorry to share this emotional news with you, but I know of no one else save the Sisters and Father Thomas who understand what we have all experienced. And I do not mean to add to your considerable concerns about your own nephew.

Thank you so much for your friendship. Sincerely, Amanda Duncan."

Devlin held the two pages and stared at them. He too felt a chill reading Amanda Duncan's account of her dream. Like her previous startling visions, her last dreams, while not as vivid as her visions, still proved true, if somewhat mysterious. Unlike the visions, the dreams seemed to be puzzles almost, something to solve or figure out. The grandfather clock and the hands moving backwards actually lead Amanda to visit the Remington house and learn even more. Could it be this latest dream was a puzzle? Or was it a warning? Daisy was still safe in the convent. But would she stay safe?

"That is more than unsettling," Jonathan said, looking over at his wife and Devlin. "Amanda's visions have proved most prescient. I, too, feel a sense of dread about that child."

"Is there something we can do to protect her?" Winnie asked. "Surely we can't sit idly by and let something happen to her?"

"May I keep this?" Devlin asked, slipping Amanda's note into his vest pocket.

"Of course, dear. I know she meant it mostly for you," Winnie said. "I simply cannot—"

Jameson appeared at the edge of the parlor then, his face graver than usual. "Madam, Senator. Commissioner Bailey is here to see you."

"Send him in, Jameson," Jonathan said rising from his chair. Glancing around at his wife and Devlin, he added, "Let's get the inevitable over with."

CHAPTER TWENTY-THREE

Sunlight reflected off the bright white dome of the Capitol building as Devlin strode down Independence Avenue and across Capitol Street. Private carriages and hired hansom cabs were lined up along the streets surrounding the Capitol. Congressmen, senators, lobbyists, aides, assistants, petitioners, all streamed out of the carriages or on foot to climb the stately white marble steps to the entrance doors above.

Devlin merged with the flow of people who climbed the steps. Most of them were seeking answers or money or positions or patronage or simply to have someone hear their pleas. Their elected representatives dwelt within these white marble walls. Surely, they would pay heed. Devlin had no favors to ask, no position to seek. His trip into the halls of Washington power was not to seek gain of any kind, nor to plead a cause. Devlin was here on a gamble. A very risky gamble at that.

He pushed through the heavy ornate metal doors into the central Rotunda of the Capitol. Since he'd accompanied Jonathan to the Capitol on several occasions and joined Winnie in the gallery several times, Devlin knew his way around the cavernous hallways. Others stood confused, glancing up and down the long corridors until finally seeking help.

Devlin walked down the hallway leading to Edmund Remington's office. He'd been practicing what he wanted to say countless times, rehearsing, if you would. He'd been awake most of the night, worrying. Worrying about Daisy. Worrying about Freddie. Worrying that Amanda Duncan's latest dream might prove true.

Mostly, Devlin was up half the night, pacing, racking his brain trying to find a way to prove Edmund Remington's guilt. It was unconscionable that Remington would get away with murder. Poor, stupid Freddie could easily be convicted of the crime based on the damning circumstantial evidence of his reckless behavior. But Remington would be free. Free, after murdering two people. Winnie was correct. It was a miscarriage of justice. But what could he do?

Devlin prided himself on solving puzzles and problems. No matter how intricate, he always found a clue, a way into the puzzle, a way to solve the problem. But this problem felt totally insoluble. He and Amanda had solved the puzzle of the murders, but that seemed to count for naught.

Remington had cleverly built up such a plausible case for Freddie's guilt that no one would believe the family's claims that Remington was the killer. If Devlin dared suggest it, everyone would laugh in his face. Edmund Remington's façade as a respectable upstanding Senator was unassailable.

Near dawn, however, Devlin had had an inspiration. Either that or a fitful dream as he drifted off to sleep near the fireplace. There was only one way to prove Remington's guilt in these murders. Remington would have to implicate himself. And the only way that could happen would be if he was tricked. Tricked into implicating himself. Devlin would have to create a ruse so believable that Remington would be drawn in, unsuspecting, and trap himself.

The problem was *how*? How to trap Remington? What manner of ruse would entice him enough to draw Remington far enough in to spring the trap. Like the mouse, Remington would be wary of any obvious situation. Only very tempting bait would draw Remington into a trap. And there was only one bait that came to Devlin's mind that would be sufficiently tempting to lure Edmund Remington out into the open. Daisy.

It was Amanda Duncan's dream that spurred Devlin's heated imagination near dawn. The frightening image of Daisy being dragged into a carriage by a man in a dark cloak started Devlin's mind racing.

Remington was unaware that Francie had a sister who was asleep at the convent the night he slipped in and killed Francie. What if he learned that Daisy was there, but had awakened in the midst of the attack and had watched horror-struck at her sister's killer? Remington would be stunned. And scared. Scared that Daisy might be able to describe him to police in a way that would cause them to doubt Freddie's involvement. Then, the entire house of cards that Remington had so carefully constructed to conceal his guilt would come tumbling down. Remington could not risk that. And would be willing to go to great lengths to eliminate that risk.

That's what Devlin was counting on. If he could give Remington enough reason for worry, then Devlin could bait the trap and pray that Remington reached for it.

Devlin pushed inside the polished wooden door bearing Senator Remington's name. Several men were clustered inside the Senator's outer office, conferring when Devlin entered. One of the men was Edmund Remington. He looked surprised, Devlin noticed.

"Senator Remington, I beg pardon for walking in without an appointment, but I was hoping to be able to speak with you for a few moments. On a private family matter. I'm sure you understand."

Remington appraised Devlin for a second, then spoke to the men around him. "Please excuse me, gentlemen, I'll return shortly." He gestured to an open doorway. "Please, come into my office, Mr. Burke."

"You're very kind to take the time, Senator," Devlin said as he entered Remington's wood paneled office. Selecting a captain's chair on the other side of Remington's huge walnut desk, he continued. "I promise to stay but a few moments. First, let me apologize for my family's intrusion yesterday. I'm sure my sister Winnie never meant to upset your wife. She's simply distressed over what has happened with our nephew. I'm sure you understand."

Remington settled behind the desk, his expression considerably more relaxed, Devlin noticed. "I understand completely, Mr. Burke. How is Freddie holding up?"

"He's understandably anxious, as we all are." Devlin gave a dramatic sigh. "Fortunately, though, this whole ordeal may soon be resolved."

"Resolved?" Remington looked surprised again. "Has the Chief Inspector filed charges?"

"Not yet," Devlin paused before spinning the web. "There may be a delay because authorities have learned that there was a witness to

Francie's murder. Apparently, her young sister was asleep on some blankets on the floor beside the bed and woke up to witness the attack. She was petrified in fear, understandably. Surely, she will be able to identify the killer. Inspector Callahan has promised to question her after he's finished with Freddie. Maybe as soon as tomorrow afternoon."

Devlin sat and watched the effect of his lie cross Edmund Remington's face. At first, Remington just stared at him. Then, Devlin glimpsed the mask drop for a second as disbelief and fear flash through Remington's eyes. Then, a brief second of doubt, then the mask was back in place again.

"Indeed," Remington said quietly. "That *is* interesting."

Devlin's pulse raced, watching Remington's reaction. He deliberately took a calming breath before continuing his ruse. "Yes, I spoke with Father Tom at Saint Anne's. He and the Sisters are taking care of the young girl at the convent. Daisy is her name, I believe. And the good priest said that the Sister's plan to take Daisy to a sister convent in Virginia after Callahan's questioning. They want to keep her safe. Apparently, the girl's drunken father, Bill Kelly, keeps showing up at the convent demanding to see his daughter. Father Tom and the Sisters do not trust this man. I agree. Young Daisy must be protected."

Remington studied Devlin. "I imagine you're quite relieved, Mr. Burke."

Devlin gave an exaggerated sigh and smiled. "Unbelievably so, Senator. This whole ordeal has been excruciating." He rose from the chair. "Well, I will not take up any more of your time, senator. I simply wanted to apologize for any discomfort your wife might have felt with my sister's visit yesterday."

"Your apology is appreciated, Mr. Burke," Remington said, walking Devlin to the door.

"And thank you again for your many kindnesses to Freddie," Devlin said, extending his hand, which Remington took. "Thank you again. Let us hope this whole ordeal will soon be behind us."

"Yes, let us hope," Edmund Remington said as he opened his office door.

Devlin strode out of the office without another word.

"Why, Mr. Burke, how did you know I was here?" Amanda asked as Devlin was ushered into the convent library.

"Bridget was good enough to tell me, Mrs. Duncan," Devlin said, doffing his hat. "Sister Beatrice directed me to the library."

Amanda turned back to the glass doorway leading into the interior garden where Daisy played hopscotch. "I confess I've spent most of yesterday and today here, watching over Daisy. The anxious feeling still haunts me."

Devlin approached, choosing his words. "I can understand, Mrs. Duncan. In fact, that's why I'm here. Your note last evening kept me awake most of the night. I wracked my brain all night trying to find a way to lure this killer into the open where the authorities can see his guilt. Only then will he no longer be a threat to Daisy or anyone else."

Amanda studied Devlin. "I agree, Mr. Burke. But the problem remains how to lure the killer into the open. As we've said before, the Senator has concealed his guilt well."

"I believe I have come up with a way, a ruse, if you may, that can lure Remington out of hiding. I've asked Father Tom to join us, for he will need to play a part in this ruse, as will I."

Voices sounded down the hallway then, and Father Tom appeared in the doorway, Sister Beatrice right behind him. "Mr. Burke, you asked to see me?"

Devlin beckoned them into the library. "Come in, Father. You too, sister. I was about to tell Mrs. Duncan my plan to lure Senator Remington out into the open and reveal himself as Francie's killer. And Horace Chester's."

"You certainly have our attention, Mr. Burke. Please, go on," she said.

Devlin looked around at them. "The only way we can trick Remington into revealing himself is to bait our trap with something he can't resist. Only that will bring him out into the open."

Amanda eyed him. "What sort of bait do you propose using?"

Devlin paused. "I went to Remington's office this morning on the excuse of thanking him for his kindness to Freddie. Then I mentioned that everything would soon be resolved because the police had learned that Francie's younger sister was asleep on the floor during the attack and witnessed it. Surely, she would be able to identify the killer. And the police would be questioning her tomorrow most prob—"

"Have you gone *mad?*" Amanda cried, clearly appalled.

Taken aback by her swift reaction, Devlin tried again. "Please let me explain—"

"How could you jeopardize Daisy's safety like that? Remington wasn't even aware of her existence, and now you've exposed her to him! How <u>could</u> you?"

Stunned by her angry reaction, Devlin said, *"Please* trust me, Mrs. Duncan, it was your very dream which gave me the idea of a way to trap Remington. If he comes after Daisy—"

Amanda looked horrified for a moment, then pounced again, not letting Devlin speak. "That was a <u>nightmare</u>, Mr. Burke!" she protested, advancing toward him. "Are you seriously proposing to dangle Daisy out there so Edmund Remington can drive up in his carriage and snatch her? That is madness. How could you be so callous?"

Devlin drew back, stung by her criticism. He had never seen Mrs. Duncan express anything close to annoyance let alone this blaze of anger that she directed at him. Devlin felt singed by the flames. "Mrs. Duncan, please let me finish," he pleaded. "I swear that nothing will happen to Daisy. That is where Father Tom and I come in. We will be close by to protect Daisy."

"You cannot protect her if she is no longer with you," Amanda countered.

"Your plan, while ingenious, does pose a serious threat to Daisy, Mr. Burke," Father Tom ventured.

He turned to Father Tom who had been standing, like Sister Beatrice, quietly observing this debate. "Father, I believe Remington will want to move quickly because he thinks the police will question

Daisy tomorrow afternoon. I believe he'll contact Bill Kelly today. He's already in Kelly's good graces because of the money he gave for Francie, which Kelly undoubtedly drank away. Remington will probably suggest that Kelly take Daisy to some less populated area of the city, where he could ostensibly meet her. Kelly won't be a problem. All Remington has to do is wave money under his nose. Any plausible explanation will ensure Kelly's cooperation."

"And what then? What if Remington grabs Daisy and rides off in the carriage? It will be my nightmare come true!" Amanda accused.

Wincing inwardly, Devlin continued. "Father, I propose you and I disguise ourselves and follow after Kelly. We will follow Daisy closely. We won't let her out of our sight. We'll be close enough to pounce when necessary."

Father Tom looked at Sister Beatrice then glanced to a still-fuming Amanda before replying. "How can you be sure the Senator will take your bait, Mr. Burke?"

"I cannot. Although I endeavored to be as guileless as possible, Remington may be so leery of exposure that he will not step into our trap. In that case, my nephew will most certainly be wrongly convicted of two murders and be executed. While Edmund Remington will get away with murder. Two murders, to be honest. And no one will be the wiser, save us."

"But Daisy will be safe," Amanda declared.

Father Tom looked from Amanda to Devlin and back again. "If you don't mind, Mr. Burke, Amanda. Sister and I need a moment," he said, beckoning the elderly nun towards the doorway.

"Of course," Devlin said, watching them leave. Then, he tentatively peered at Amanda. She was still glaring at him. Devlin decided to hold his tongue and allow Mrs. Duncan to fully vent her wrath, however painful that would prove to be. Devlin was surprised at how much her earlier criticism had stung. Mrs. Duncan's opinion had become quite important to him lately.

Amanda started pacing the worn oriental carpet. "I cannot believe you would suggest such a dangerous gamble, Mr. Burke. You are gambling with Daisy's life. How could you? Is this scheme designed to prove your nephew's innocence at all costs?"

Devlin winced. "My fervent wish is to rescue both Daisy and Freddie."

Amanda pounced on that. "Daisy didn't need rescuing, Mr. Burke. Had you forgotten that? Not until today when you placed her squarely in the midst of Remington's sites."

"I swear to you, Mrs. Duncan, my intentions were solely on trapping Remington."

"At what price, Mr. Burke?" she accused. "If you miscalculate, Daisy will pay with her life. That is too risky a gamble." She stared at him. "And you accused me of taking reckless risk. The difference is that I only risked myself. Not the safety of an innocent child."

Devlin flinched inwardly at that. He had no reply. Fortunately, Father Tom and Sister Beatrice re-entered the library.

"Sister and I have discussed your plan, Mr. Burke, and I have decided to help you. I, too, believe that you and I can protect Daisy. Meanwhile, this murderer's evil must be exposed."

A small muscle inside Devlin's chest relaxed. "Thank you, Father, Sister Beatrice. I swear that we will not let Daisy out of our sights." He cautiously glanced to Amanda and saw her staring wide-eyed in amazement.

"There are some workman's clothes downstairs that you could both use," Sister Beatrice said in a helpful voice. "Our gardener died this past winter."

Dead man's clothes, Devlin thought wryly. That was fitting. "Thank you, Sister. They should be fine."

Amanda gathered her purse and gloves. "You must excuse me. I cannot listen to more of this madness. Father Tom, Sister, I will be here first thing in the morning." She hastened to the doorway, then glanced over her shoulder to a chastened Devlin. "Good day to you, Mr. Burke," she said with a curt nod.

"Amanda has grown quite fond of Daisy, Mr. Burke," Father Tom interceded. "Ever since her family was taken away, she's become quite protective of the helpless ones. Please don't take her comments to heart. She's like a mother lion protecting her cubs."

Devlin believed that with no trouble. He'd already felt Amanda Duncan's claws.

CHAPTER TWENTY-FOUR

Devlin strode into Saint Anne's convent library and saw Amanda dressed in pale blue silk as if she were about to go on morning calls on this sunny April day. He observed her demeanor and saw none of the fury he'd witnessed and been flogged with yesterday. He gave a quick sigh of relief and sent her a warm smile.

"Ah, Mrs. Duncan, I saw Benjamin outside with your coach and realized that you had arrived. Obviously, you arose earlier than I. It is but eight o'clock in the morning."

"I wanted to be here to break bread with the nuns and Daisy," Amanda said in a quiet voice. "I wanted to spend some time with her."

The awesome sense of responsibility that had weighed Devlin down all yesterday evening was still pressing. What Amanda Duncan had begun that afternoon, his sister Winnie had continued last evening. Even Jonathan had warned that the risk to Daisy was too great. Remington was a cold-blooded killer. "What if he slits Daisy's throat in the brief moment he has with her?" Jonathan had warned.

That was all Winnie had needed to harangue Devlin for an hour more. Another protective lioness. Devlin felt positively mauled between two great cats.

Devlin cleared his throat. "Mrs. Duncan, first let me apologize for not discussing my plan with you before I went to see Edmund Remington yesterday. I realize now that I was too presumptuous in assuming everyone would agree to my plan. You have been intimately involved in protecting Daisy as well as Francie, whereas I have not. I clearly intruded and overstepped. For that, I sincerely apologize."

Amanda studied him for a moment. "I sense your sister and brother-in-law had their own opinions about your plan."

Devlin cautiously sat on the chair across from her. "Indeed, Mrs. Duncan. You'll be pleased to learn that my sister must have harangued me for hours. Jonathan would take over long enough for Winnie to draw wind. They did not cease until I was properly chastised."

"I have no sympathy for you, Mr. Burke. You deserved their ire."

She may not have sympathy, but Devlin thought he spied a faint hint of amusement in her eyes, which he took as an encouraging sign. Deciding that continued self-flagellation would be the safest way back into Mrs. Duncan's good graces, he continued, contrite. "Rest assured, Winnie pointed that out repeatedly. My self esteem has been flattened to the point of invisibility."

"Somehow, I sense you'll recover, Mr. Burke."

Devlin was about to find yet another way to apologize or prostrate himself when Sister Beatrice rushed into the library, a bundle of grey clothes in her hands. "Mr. Burke, you were correct. Bill Kelly has just walked into the rectory. Sister Teresa's been watching. He's over there now with Father. Sister said he demanded that Daisy come home with him now or he'll call the police." Her eyes were wide.

Devlin glanced to Amanda then back to the concerned nun. "It has begun, then. Are those the work clothes, Sister?"

"Yes, Mr. Burke. Please come with me and I'll show you where to change." She beckoned down the hall.

"Say a prayer, Mrs. Duncan," Devlin said to her before he followed after the nun.

"Where is Father Tom?" Amanda asked, peering through the window, which overlooked the entrance to the rectory. Bill Kelly was pacing back and forth on the sidewalk. An elderly nun stood on the sidewalk near him.

"He's just gone into his study to change clothes," Sister Beatrice said. "There's Sister Florence. I asked her to talk to Kelly until Father and Mr. Burke were ready."

"Sister Florence is nearly deaf. How on earth can she talk with that man?"

"That is precisely why I sent her, Amanda. I wanted to distract Kelly long enough until Father and Mr. Burke were ready. Then, I'll bring Daisy down. I won't hand her over to Bill Kelly one minute before I have to."

Amanda had to give the little nun credit. She and Devlin Burke weren't the only ones who could create a ruse.

Devlin Burke walked down the hallway then, attired in baggy gray work pants and grey work jacket. A black wool cap pulled down over his eyes, Mr. Burke was barely recognizable. "Does my disguise meet your standards, Mrs. Duncan?"

Amanda looked him up and down. Gone was the dapper English gentleman, replaced by a man who looked like hundreds of other men working in the city of Washington and walking the streets. "Indeed, it does, Mr. Burke."

Sister Teresa scurried over to the window. "Father has changed and is slipping through the courtyard. He'll be here in two shakes of a lamb's tail."

Devlin peered through the window beside Amanda. "Who's out there with Kelly?"

"Sister Florence, who's deaf as a post. Sister Beatrice wanted to distract him," Amanda replied, watching Kelly pace, then turn and say something to Sister Florence.

Devlin smiled. "Quite clever of Sister Beatrice. Kelly's conversation is bound to be laced with profanity."

"Ah, Mr. Burke, I see you're ready as well," Father Tom said on entering.

The grey work clothes hung a bit on his shorter frame, but with the black cap, they concealed the priest's identity. Amanda noticed.

"We are ready, then," Devlin said, glancing from Father Tom to Sister Beatrice to Amanda.

"Sister, you should take Daisy now," Father said, his face revealing his concern.

"Yes, Father," Sister said, then hastened from the entry foyer.

Father Tom folded his hands and closed his eyes, his lips moving in silent prayer, Amanda noticed. Then he crossed himself. "May God bless our plan. Amanda, this would be a good time to say a prayer. Daisy will need all the heavenly protection available."

Devlin peered through the side window again. "There's Sister Beatrice with Daisy."

Amanda and Father Tom approached the window beside Devlin. Bill Kelly was gesturing broadly to Sister Beatrice, then grabbed Daisy's hand, and yanked her away from the nun. Amanda felt her heart wrench. She could see Daisy crying, turning back toward Sister Beatrice as her father pulled her down the sidewalk against her will.

Amanda had to turn from the window. "I cannot watch," she whispered. "The poor child is distraught and petrified."

Devlin opened the convent entry door and beckoned to the priest. "Come, Father. We must go now while Kelly is preoccupied."

Amanda watched as both men raced out the front steps and headed down the sidewalk after Bill Kelly and Daisy. Then, Amanda hastened down the steps and ran to her carriage.

Devlin watched Bill Kelly walking up ahead. Daisy was obviously trying to keep up with her father. Whenever the child slowed down, Kelly gave Daisy's arm a yank and jerked her forward again. Devlin could hardly wait until he got his hands on Kelly. *Villainous wretch.* He'd give Kelly some of the treatment he'd inflicted on his daughters.

Kelly crossed over Fifteenth Street and turned, heading south. Was he aiming for Murder Bay, Devlin wondered? But, instead of turning onto the street which held so many of the taverns and brothels, Kelly continued south, down to the area of warehouses closer to the tree-filled mall. After another block, Kelly turned onto B St.

Devlin and Father Tom followed from half a block away. "Father, I've noticed that the number of people on the street has diminished considerably. Perhaps, we should lag back a bit more so we don't draw Kelly's attention should he glance back."

"Perhaps, so, Mr. Burke, but not too far. . .look!" Father pointed ahead.

Bill Kelly had stopped in the midst of B Street beside a lamppost. Devlin quickly stepped into an alley beside a warehouse and beckoned the priest to join him.

"Quick, Father. Before Kelly sees us."

Devlin peered around the edge of the frame warehouse building. Kelly was looking behind him now and all around, clearly searching for something. Or someone.

"He must be waiting for the Senator," Devlin said, as he scanned the sidewalk and street ahead. Unfortunately, there were no more obvious places for Devlin or the priest to conceal themselves. Not even an alley. And they were more than half a block away from where Daisy and Kelly stood.

The sound of horses' hooves caught Devlin's attention and he noticed a carriage rolling past on the far side of the street, beside the trees of the mall. The coachman was slouched over and the carriage shades were drawn. Could that be Remington, he wondered? His pulse speeded up. However, the coach continued down the street, finally turning up Fourteenth Street and disappearing.

"Do you see anyone, Mr. Burke? I don't," Father Tom said, glancing around at the deserted street.

"Nor do I, Father. I had thought that carriage belonged to Remington, but it drove away. I wish we could get closer to Kelly, but alas, I see no alleys or hiding places along this stretch of city block."

Once again, the sound of horses' hooves clopping on pavement caught his attention, and Devlin watched as a hansom cab turned the corner from Fifteenth Street onto the street where they were. Kelly had turned and begun waving at the hansom cab, Devlin noticed, his pulse racing.

"Ah, he's slowing down," Father Tom whispered. "That must be him."

"I think so, Father. And we should take this moment when Kelly's attention is distracted to creep closer. As stealthily as we can." Devlin slowly edged around the corner of the alley and flattened himself against the warehouse building, inching along its length. Father Tom did the same, holding himself against the frame building as he followed.

Watching the hansom cab slow down and pull to a stop at the lamppost, Devlin saw Bill Kelly approach the carriage. The carriage door opened, and a well-dressed man dressed in black clothes and tall black top hat stepped out. A chill ran through Devlin's veins. Amanda Duncan's dream was coming true. He had set it in motion. Now, Devlin had to stop it.

The man started speaking to Kelly, and Kelly was gesturing. Meanwhile, Devlin started moving faster along the side of the building. He and Father Tom were still at least a quarter of a block away from the carriage. But they couldn't risk moving faster and drawing attention to themselves. They needed to catch Remington in the act of abducting Daisy. If he spotted them, Remington would cease his actions and ride off in the hansom.

Getting closer, Devlin could almost catch some of the words. Kelly had raised his voice. Then, the man handed Kelly a packet from inside his coat. Kelly stopped talking and opened the packet, clearly counting money.

Suddenly, the man grabbed hold of Daisy and, despite her struggling, lifted her into the carriage. Then, he jumped in after her.

Caught by the suddenness of the action, Devlin hesitated but a second, then broke into a run, Father Tom right behind him. The cabbie snapped his whip, and the hansom swiftly pulled away from the curb and down the street away from them. Devlin picked up his pace, racing faster, easily outdistancing the priest.

He had to overtake the hansom cab! Once the cab reached a main avenue, it would be lost in the traffic of many carriages and cabs. And Daisy would be lost. It had all happened so fast. Daisy was grabbed and gone. His heart in his throat, Devlin pushed harder, his long legs striding over the pavement, trying to catch the coach. If only he could have crept closer without being seen. Now, Amanda Duncan's nightmare was coming true. Daisy was grabbed and gone, and Devlin couldn't rescue her. No, matter how fast he ran, the coach was moving faster, pulling farther ahead, almost to the main thoroughfare of Fourteenth Street. The hansom picked up speed. His heart pounding, Devlin raced desperately behind, terrified that Remington would escape.

Suddenly, out of nowhere, a laundry basket full of clothes flew through the air right at the horse's face. Clearly startled, the horse reared up in surprise, causing the hansom cab to careen from side to side, nearly toppling over. The cabbie driver fought for control but wound up falling into the street.

Devlin couldn't believe his good fortune and felt a second wind send a burst of speed to his feet. He raced up to the tottering carriage, Father Tom lumbering behind him. Devlin yanked open the carriage door.

Edmund Remington had Daisy gripped tight. He stared at Devlin, clearly not recognizing him. "What do you think you're doing?" he bellowed at Devlin and Father Tom.

"We're stopping your murderous plot, senator," Devlin shot back as he yanked Remington's arm away. "Come, Daisy. Father Tom is right here."

Father Tom removed his hat and reached out for the child. "Come, Daisy. I'll take you back to the convent with Sister Beatrice." Daisy gave a little choked cry and leaped into the priest's arms, burying her face in his shoulder while she sobbed.

Devlin spied the cabbie climbing back into his seat and took action. "Cabbie, this man is a wanted criminal. There's a handsome reward in it for you if you bring the police quickly."

The cabbie's eyes flew wide, and he leaped from the seat down to the cobblestones again. "Aye, sir. I'll be back on the double."

Glancing at Remington, Devlin leaned into the coach and looked him in the eye. "Don't even think about trying to escape, senator. We'll catch you."

Remington's defiant pose held for another moment, then crumbled as he sank in the seat and put his head in his hands. "Oh, God, what have I done? What have I done?" Remorseful too late.

From the corner of his eye, Devlin noticed Bill Kelly start to slink away down the street in the opposite direction. Devlin spotted the cabbie running on the other side of the street and yelled at him. "Cabbie! That man is a criminal, too. Grab him and bring him over here, and I'll double the reward!"

The cabbie stopped in his tracks, spied Kelly, and took off after him in a run. Kelly picked up speed, but years of carousing had clearly taken his wind. He was no match for the younger lithe cabbie, who grabbed him by the collar and yanked Kelly back toward Devlin and the others.

"The only place you're going, Kelly, is the police station house," Devlin declared when the cabbie pushed a sputtering Kelly to the ground.

"Ow, be careful," Kelly complained.

Devlin leaned over into his face. "Another word from you, Kelly, and I swear I will beat you far worse than you beat your wife and daughters." Looking over at the cabbie, he said, "Bring your whip and tie him up to the carriage wheel, will you? That way this filth won't try to run."

"Yes sir," the cabbie said, climbing up to the driver's seat and returning with the carriage whip. He proceeded to secure Bill Kelly to the wheel.

Devlin glared at the stricken Remington inside the coach and threatened. "Don't make a move, Remington, or we'll tie you to the carriage wheel as well."

"I'll keep an eye on him, Mr. Burke," Father Tom said, holding a snuggling Daisy.

"Cabbie, if you bring back a patrolman within ten minutes, I'll treble the reward," Devlin promised.

The cabbie's face flushed. "I promise, sir." He took off in a run heading toward Fifteenth Street.

Glancing around, Devlin noticed a washerwoman picking up clothes that were scattered about the street. He quickly approached to thank her. Without her tumbled basket, Remington would have escaped with Daisy.

"Madam, let me help you retrieve these scattered items," Devlin offered, picking up a cotton shirt. "I have to thank you. Your tumbled laundry basket allowed us to apprehend a true villain. Without your intervention, he would have escaped and the young child inside the carriage would have been killed. I want to reward you for your assistance and for the inconvenience with your laundry."

The washerwoman bent over and scooped up the remaining cotton shirt from the ground, dropping it into her basket. Then she stood and looked over at Devlin with what looked to be a smile.

That was curious, he thought. "Please, let me offer you a reward, madam," Devlin offered again.

The woman didn't answer. Instead, she slipped off the white cotton scarf she had wrapped around her head. Down tumbled the wealth of lustrous chestnut curls that Devlin had so often admired. Amanda.

Devlin stared at her, astounded, "Mrs. Duncan! What. . .? How. . .?" He was at a loss for words.

Amanda Duncan smiled, her eyes alight. "What am I doing here? I came to help rescue Daisy. As to how did I get here, I came by coach." She turned to wave at the coachmen who was parked around the corner, barely visible.

The coachman steered the carriage around the corner and approached. Devlin remembered the first coach that drove down the street when father Tom and he were concealing themselves in the alley. "That was your coach that passed earlier, wasn't it? I see now that even Benjamin disguised himself. And the window shades were drawn. I congratulate you on your stealthy approach, Mrs. Duncan." Amanda looked rather pleased, he noticed.

"Thank you, Mr. Burke. I followed you and Father Tom right after you left the rectory. I told Benjamin to stay well enough behind you so as not to draw attention. Once we saw where Bill Kelly stopped on B Street, apparently waiting for someone, I instructed Benjamin to pull around the corner onto Fourteenth." She eyed Devlin. "You see, I gambled, too, Mr. Burke. I gambled that Remington would take off in his carriage and head in this direction toward Fourteenth Street. It's a main thoroughfare and would be easier to disappear into the sea of other hansom cabs just like it."

Impressed by her intuitive strategy as well as her daring, Devlin decided praise was due. "Brilliant, Mrs. Duncan, if I do say so."

Amanda colored a bit, with obvious pleasure. "A bit exaggerated, but flattering, nonetheless."

Observing her drab clothes—faded cotton skirt and white blouse rolled up at the sleeves—Devlin had to tease her about her apparel. "A clever disguise, Mrs. Duncan, and quite accurate, too. But I must admit I am curious. When we left you at the convent, you were dressed in fashionable silks. Wherever did you change clothes?"

"Why, in the carriage, Mr. Burke," Amanda said with a sly smile. "With the shades drawn, of course."

Devlin had to laugh out loud. "But, of course, Mrs. Duncan." For some reason, the image of Amanda Duncan disrobing inside a carriage proved quite disturbing.

CHAPTER TWENTY-FIVE

"Do not hesitate, Freddie," Jonathan Carrington said to his nephew as he stood in the hallway outside the dining room. "You've been closeted here with us for over a week now. We realize how anxious you are to spend an evening with your friends. Go, enjoy yourself."

"Are you sure?" Freddie hesitated, looking anxious. "I don't want to be rude, especially after everything you have done for me."

"Absolutely, dear, go and celebrate," Winnie added, giving Freddie a quick kiss on the cheek. "Thanks to Devlin and Mrs. Duncan, you have a new lease on life."

Freddie looked back into the dining room where Devlin and Amanda stood beside the table, which was already set for dinner. "I-I-I still don't know what to say," he stumbled. "It's not all sunk in, yet. I cannot believe Edmund Remington was behind all of this. . .this madness. I cannot grasp it."

"Don't worry, Freddie. Chief Inspector Callahan has grasped it with both hands from what I've heard from Commissioner Bailey," Devlin said, before sipping his cognac.

"Go on, Freddie," Jonathan said, beaming. "Go to your friends and stay out all night if you want."

"Oh, Jonathan, I'm not sure that's a good idea. Jameson will let you in, Freddie."

Freddie's boyish grin returned, Devlin noticed. "All right, Aunt and Uncle. Have a good evening, everyone. And thank you again, Uncle

Devlin. And you, too, Mrs. Duncan. I can never thank you enough. I will spend the rest of my life thanking you."

"That is not necessary, Freddie," Amanda said as she stood beside Devlin. "We were searching for the truth. And justice."

"Well said." Devlin raised his glass. "To truth and justice."

Winnie and Jonathan both raised their glasses and joined Devlin and Amanda in the toast. Freddie slipped out the front door, Devlin noticed. Winnie and Jonathan returned to the dining room as Devlin held Amanda's chair while she sat.

"If I have anything to say about it, Freddie will spend the rest of his life in some mindless task back in Devonshire. Bertie will get him married off to a plump country girl, and Freddie will be up to his neck in children and hunting hounds before he knows it."

"Oh, Dev, you can be too wicked at times," Winnie said as laughter floated above the Carrington dinner table once more.

THE END

MEET THE AUTHOR

Maggie Sefton is the *New York Times* Bestselling author of the Berkley Prime Crime Knitting Mysteries. **UNRAVELED**, 9th in the series, made the *New York Times* Bestselling Hardcover Fiction List after its June 2011 release. All of the mysteries in the successful series have been Barnes & Noble Top Ten Bestselling Mysteries. The 12th in the series will be released June 2014, **YARN OVER MURDER**.

Maggie was first published in historical fiction in 1995 with **ABILENE GAMBLE**, Berkley Jove, under the pen name Margaret Conlan. She had written over a million words of historical romance fiction before she ever wrote the first mystery. **DYING TO SELL**, with real estate agent sleuth Kate Doyle, was published by Five Star Mysteries in 2005.

Maggie Sefton was born and raised in Virginia, and she received her bachelor's degree in English literature and journalism from The George Washington University in Washington, DC. Maggie has been a CPA and a real estate agent in the Rocky Mountain West, but finds nothing can match creating worlds on paper. Mother of four grown daughters, Maggie resides in the Rocky Mountains of Colorado with a bossy Border collie and a playful Blue Tick Hound.

Website & Blogs:

www.maggiesefton.com, www.cozychicksblog.com, www.facebook.com/MaggieSeftonAuthor, maggie@maggiesefton.com

Made in the USA
San Bernardino, CA
19 June 2019